NEW
P
PRESENTS

Unfaithful
to the game

Man-Man & Suave

www.newvisionpubliction.com

ISBN: (13) 978-0-9826772-8-5
Cover design: www.mariondesigns.com
Inside layout: www.mariondesigns.com
Editor: Dolly Lopez and Linda Williams
Typeset/Inside Layout: Linda Williams

Unfaithful to the Game a novel/Man-Man & Suave.

P.O. Box 2815
Stockbridge, GA 30281
www.newvisionpublication.com

First Printing May 2011
Printed in Canada

10   9   8   7   6   5   4   3   2   1

Dedication

This book is dedicated to all the true hustlers who have adhered to the code of the streets.

And to all those hustlers who haven't forgotten, the integrity of the game.

Please, God,
Give me the strength to cross this River,
The streets of North Carolina.
Please, God,
give me the strength and the tools —
Big ass guns —
To lay these niggas down right where they stand.
Please, God,
give me the strength, the tools and the Intelligence
To cross this river,
Survive the Unfaithful Niggas to the game,
When they cross my path.

Amen.

Prologue

"What the fuck is you doing?" For a second I thought my eyes were playing tricks on me when I saw Mike pointing his gun at my chest. I give this bitch ass nigga a blank stare and waited on his response.

"What do you think?"

"What, you fin' to kill me?"

"I ain't got no other choice. I ain't fin' to keep hustling all my life, and I ain't gon' be no do-boy for no one else. I ain't got millions like y'all niggas, and I ain't got enough money to move away and live some fairytale life like you."

"So that's what this is all about, huh? Is this shit about money, Mike?" I barked angrily. I couldn't believe Mike was actually standing in front of me waving a gun in my face. Some muthafuckas are just unfaithful to the game.

"Nigga, like I said, I'm not gon' to keep hustling all my life. Plus, whatever I take from you, I earned!"

"Mike, you can keep the money you owe me, and you can take this punk ass two million and go. Leave the state or the country. I don't give a fuck what you do, just don't take my life!"

"Oh, you can take a life, but you don't want yours taken? Nigga, don't bitch up now! Every dog got his day, and yours has arrived," Mike said with a serious smile.

I knew my life was now in danger. I never been a bitch and I wasn't about to bitch up now. "Y'all know y'all ain't going to get away with this."

"We already have."

"Mike, no matter what you do to me; no matter what you take from me; no matter how hard you try to stop hustling, you will *never* be me. Nigga, I made you! I kept you in the game! Y'all right. Y'all have no choice but to kill me, 'cause if I live, I will kill you, your family and anybody associated to you. So, do what the fuck you got to do."

"Who the fuck you think you are?" Mike snapped with hostility in his voice.

"A jealous nigga never makes it in this game," I said as I pulled my dick out and added, "You and your punk ass partner can both suck my dick! Nigga, every life I took deserved it. Just consider yourself lucky!" With that said, I looked Mike in the eyes, letting him know I was not gonna beg for my life.

"And who the fuck is you to say who lives or dies? Is you God, motherfucka? Huh?"

Chapter One
"I Ain't Mad At Y'all"

My name is Amir, and I wanna give y'all a glimpse of how real thoroughbred niggas can get lost in the game, lose focus and begin breaking and violating all the rules that determine if a nigga or bitch is cut out for the streets. I'm a product of the streets of North Carolina, and I make no excuses for some of the dumb shit I've done in life, even if I was *Unfaithful To The Game.*

The year was 1989, and I was thirteen years old. Even at an early age, I had the hustler mentality. I wasn't your typical thirteen-year-old. I clearly understood that my family was poor as shit. Ma Duke was single, struggling to raise me and my trifling ass sister, Sharon, but somehow she always managed to make ends meet. Sometimes I wondered if she was selling ass on the down low, because although we were poor, we always kept food in the fridge, clean clothes and a clean house.

We lived in a small town called Clayton, just outside of Raleigh. Some of y'all call it the "Dirty South". Me, I call it home, the place that raised me to be a heartless nigga, hungry for what the world had to offer me.

Ma Duke owned a beat up white '74 Nova. This piece of a car was the ugliest to ever cruise the streets. The kids in the neighborhood called it "The One Eyed Bucket". It had a beige door with rust spots all over it. The windshield was cracked, and it had one headlight that looked like it was winking at you when it was driven down the street. It was our only means of transportation, and the only thing she could afford on a waitress salary working at the Waffle House. Witnessing Ma Duke driving that car made me want to go out on the block and hustle. I'd rather walk than be caught dead in that car. Fuck that! I knew I had to make shit better for my sister and Ma Duke. Being a broke nigga in the 'hood wasn't cutting it.

I played football and was the star on my team. I wouldn't have it any other way. My coach always told me that I was going to be special one day, and that I had the potential of becoming an NFL running back, if I kept my mind on the game. What he failed to realize was that I already was special. Football or not, I was determined to shine regardless of what obstacles stood in my path.

After football practice, I usually had to walk to the projects to my Aunt Debra's house, where I stayed until my mother got off from work, which usually was about ten o'clock at night.

The projects were the place to be. All of my friends lived there: Reese, B.B., Tab, Dre, and a bunch of other knuckleheads who were just as hungry as I was to fatten their pockets with some cheddar. But Jarius was my best friend. He was my nigga for real, and my partner in crime. We've been tight since knee-high. Our mothers were like sisters. They used to live with us, but now they lived with Aunt Debra in the projects.

My aunt's three-bedroom apartment was always full of muthafuckas. If my mom had allowed it, I would have moved in there even if I had to sleep on the floor.

It was Tuesday evening, and my friends and I had just made it back to the projects from football practice. I gave the fellows dap and told them I would catch them later. I had to go change my gear.

"Aunt Debra, I'm home!" I shouted as I walked in the house.

"Boy, stop yelling in my goddamn house!" Aunt Debra replied. She emerged from the back room with a cigarette in one hand and the phone in the other.

"I ain't yelling. I was just letting you know that I was home," I said as I walked past her and headed straight for the refrigerator.

"Your momma called and said you better not leave this house. From the sound of her voice, she sounded like she was upset."

"Why? What did I do?" I asked, knowing damn well what she was referring to. I was busted.

"Boy, don't play stupid. Why did you sign your momma's name on your Progress Report? You could've brought that shit to me and I would've signed it for you."

"I don't know," I shrugged, knowing I was in deep shit with Ma Duke. I wasn't worried about the ass whipping; I was worried more about having to hear her damn mouth all week — maybe even a month — about this shit.

"Well, you better know, 'cause she said she's gonna beat that ass when she gets home. Now, make yourself something to eat while I handle my business," Aunt Debra said as she turned around and took her fat ass back into her bedroom.

Aunt Debra was built like a stripper. Everything about her was provocative, but she was cool. She really didn't care about what I did while in her care. I was her favorite nephew, and she always had my back.

After I changed my gear and got me something to eat from the kitchen, I went into the living room where my cousin Porsha was sitting on the couch reading a book. She was a lil' freak bitch who tried to play the innocent role when she was around family. "Where's Jarius at?" I asked her as I sat down next to her.

"Nigga, why is you asking me about Jarius? Do I look like his mother? You need to worry about that ass whipping your momma's about to put on you instead of worrying about another nigga. Plus, I ain't his baby-sitter," Porsha replied, and continued to read her book that was written by Iceberg Slim.

The lil' bitch had a vicious attitude. I wanted to slap the shit out of her. "I hate you!"

"Yeah, whatever! I hate you too! You and a whole bunch of other niggas!" she said, flashing me a phony smile.

I gave Porsha the middle finger, and she grabbed it and tried to bite it. We started wrestling, and I won't front, her lil' fat ass had my dick standing at attention. I could've easily pinned her ass down on the couch, but I let her get her shit off on me. I was loving the way her body felt against mine.

"Girl, get off my lil' nigga! Get off him before you hurt him!" Jarius shouted as he walked into the living room.

Being two years older than me, Jarius always felt like he had to protect me. *Fuck! This nigga's always got to be blocking!*

"I do what I want to do to him! Plus, he's my family!" Porsha responded, still holding onto my neck and pressing her soft body against mine.

"Come on, dog, let's roll," Jarius said, putting his arm around me, then looked at Porsha and smiled.

"That lil' knucklehead can't go anywhere. He has an appointment with an ass whipping!"

"Shut the fuck up and mind your business!" I said, rubbing my right hand across my injured finger. "You tried to hurt me." The fact was, I loved the way her lips felt against my finger even though she was really trying to hurt me.

"I'm gonna tell your momma!"

"Ask me if I care! You be telling anyway, snitch! Cm'on, Jarius, let's roll."

"Where we goin'?" Jarius asked as we exited the house.

"Let's walk to the store."

"A'ight."

"Yo, you got any money?" I asked, looking at him in his eyes. I hated looking up at him. Even though he was a tall muthafucka, in my eyes, size meant nothing to me. If he got out of line, I was determined to check him.

"Yeah, I got five dollars." Reaching inside his pocket, Jarius pulled out a single bill and said, "Yeah, that's what I got."

"Cool, my nig, 'cause I only got two dollars."

Suddenly, I spotted a black Benz 190E coming to a complete stop. The driver was Red, Jarius's brother on his father's side.

"Yo, ain't that your brother? Why don't you ask him for some money?" I suggested.

"Nah, I ain't asking that clown for shit! That nigga be acting just like my dad, all funny and shit. Plus, I don't fuck with him like that. You ask him."

"Jarius, you need to stop taking shit personal. Your punk ass brother got what we need; big money. We only have seven funky dollars combined. So, suck up your pride and go ask him for some money."

"Nah, he already gave me some."

"Fuck that! Get some more! Let's both ask him."

"A'ight, I don't have a problem with that," Jarius agreed after realizing that I spotted the bitch in him. At that moment, I came to the conclusion that he wasn't as hard as he wanted everyone to think he was. He was pure pussy—a scary nigga afraid to ask his own blood for cheddar.

"What's up, Red?" I asked as I walked towards his car.

"Ain't shit up, niggas. Just chillin'. Why, what's up?"

"Man, we need some money. We're trying to get something from the store."

"Yo, I just broke Jarius off with a lil' sumptin' a lil' while ago."

"Nigga, that shit's gone."

"I like you, Amir, but we ain't blood related. I don't have to give you shit. Now, both of you lil' niggas go on about y'all business."

"Damn, Red! If you ain't tryin' to give us a handout, then let us earn that shit," I said, making him feel as though doing him a favor was a big thing. *Nigga, your ass is lucky I ain't a lil' older. If I was, I'd be robbin' your cheap ass for all your cheese!*

"Now you're talking my language! Before I give y'all this cheddar, I want y'all to do me a favor." Red chuckled. "Fair exchange ain't a robbery."

"What we gotta do for that cheese, nigga?" I asked.

Red was acting all hard and fronting as if he was that boy, showing off in front of the chocolate chick who was sittin' in the front seat of his car, smiling. "Go to Ashley's house and tell

C-Low I said to bring his ass on the block."

"Cool!" I said as Red reached into his pocket and brought out a fat ass bankroll, peeled off two ten dollar bills and gave Jarius and me ten dollars apiece. I looked at him as if he was fucking crazy or something. *Ten dollars! What the fuck was I gonna do with ten dollars when I knew this nigga's pockets were fat as hell!* "Ten dollars! Man, I can't buy shit with this! Give us another twenty apiece!" I demanded, eyeing the knot of money in his hands.

"I shoulda known better, fuckin' with y'all two lil' niggas!" Red said. *That lil' nigga got more heart and balls than some of these clowns out here. If he was a lil' older, I'd definitely put him on my team*, he thought to himself as he peeled off two crisp twenty dollar bills and handed them both to me. He then added, "Go handle your business. Tell that nigga, C-Low that Big Daddy wants to see him out here, now!"

Ashley was C-Low's baby momma, and she was one gorgeous chick. Every young bull on the block wanted to stick some dick up in her.

On our way to her house, Tab caught up with us. "Yo, where y'all going?" he asked, trying to catch his breath and pulling his pants up. "Everybody's at the park."

"Yeah, we know, but we got to handle some business for Red first before we head over there."

"Well, can I roll with y'all?"

"You can, but I'm not breaking you off any cheddar."

"Neither am I," Jarius said.

"Nigga, get off that lil' nigga's dick!" Tab told him, mean-mugging us both.

"Tab, you're the one who asked to roll with us. We're cool with you, or without you. If anybody is riding anybody's dick, it's you!" I snapped back.

"Y'all muthafuckas are greedy as fuck, but that's cool. I just wanna roll with y'all for a little while," Tab said.

"Greedy? Nigga, find yourself a hustle so your ass won't have to be broke all the time," I responded, ice grilling him.

When we arrived at Ashley's house, I noticed all the lights

were out, but I knew someone was home because I could hear a girl groaning. Plus, C-Low's car was parked in front of the house. The front door was unlocked, so we decided to creep into the house. "Hiss! Let's see what's poppin' up in this bitch."

"It sounds like somebody's getting fucked," Jarius said.

"How the fuck do you know? You ain't never had no pussy, nigga!" Tad responded.

"Neither have you! Trust me, my mom moans the same way when she's fucking her man. That fishy smell is pussy. Somebody's fucking."

"Why don't y'all shut the fuck up so we can see some pussy?" I whispered as we stood in the living room. To our surprise, C-Low had Ashley on the kitchen table, fucking her brains out. We watched with hypnotic wonderment as he fucked her with long, slow strokes.

"O-o-o-o, C-Low! I love the way your dick feels inside me-e-e-e! Give it to me, C-Low! It feels so hot inside me!"

"Push that fat pussy back to Daddy, Ashley!"

Ashley pushed her pussy towards C-Low's dick, making it penetrate another inch. She gasped and wriggled with delight. She rotated her pussy in tight, hot circles.

"Baby, squeeze me with your pussy lips!" C-Low commanded as he kept massaging her clit with his fingers, keeping her crazed with passion. Ashley tightened her pussy lips around him. The feeling was incredible.

Jarius and Tab were drooling all over themselves, and so was I. I mean, why not? The truth of the matter is that none of us had seen a real pussy… until now. Shit, I jerked off plenty of times watching my mom's porno flicks, and to *Black Tail* magazine. But seeing Ashley lying on top of the table with her pussy wide open and getting fucked by C-Low was gangsta.

"Man, I hate that nigga, C-Low!" Tab said as he grabbed his dick.

"Nigga, don't hate, congratulate! One day we're gonna get a chance to fuck bitches too," Jarius responded.

"Do y'all think C-Low would let us fuck Ashley?" I asked Jarius and Tab. I was dead serious about this shit.

"Nigga, that's some wishful thinking, but I dare you to ask him," Jarius said, looking at me as if he was testing my gangsta.

I know this bitch ass nigga don't think I'm a pussy like him! I thought to myself. "A'ight, I got no problem with asking. If he says yes, I'm first."

Jarius and Tab both busted out laughing.

"Who the fuck is in my crib?" Who the fuck are you? C-Low shouted as he began to pull his dick out of Ashley.

Jarius stared at C-Low with wide eyes, all scared and shit. He had that "I want to run" look.

"Red wants to see you on the block now!" I blurted out.

"Yeah, a'ight. But y'all HP niggas better learn how to knock before y'all run up in here again like y'all crazy!"

"Yeah, whatever!" I stated, eyeing Ashley as she lay on the table with her pussy dripping.

"Fuck you, punk!" Jarius spat before he ran out of the house.

"Yo, C-Low, can I ask you something without you getting mad and shit?"

"Come on, young buck. You already fucked up my mood. What the fuck you want?"

"I want to fuck your bitch, Ashley."

"Young buck, you got a lot of heart to be spitting that dumb shit at me. I'll tell you what. If Ashley wants to break you in, I won't be mad. How old are you?"

"Old enough. I'm thirteen."

C-Low and Ashley both laughed as if I said something funny.

"You're too young for me, baby. I'm not trying to go to jail. When you get a little older, come see me and I'll give you all the pussy you can handle," Ashley said, grabbing my face with both of her hands. She then pressed her big nipples against my face.

Damn! That shit feels good! One day I will get my turn... my day will come! "Nah, ol' head. When I get older, I'ma have my own pussy. Fuck you, C-Low!" I said as I walked out of Ashley's house with a serious hard-on.

On our way to the store, we passed a group of little 'hood rats. The girls were cousins, but they acted like sisters. Fuck with one, you fuck with all. Kita, Irish, Christy and Deemi were hot in the pants. Christy was the most developed out of the group, but make no mistake, they all had fat asses, nice suckable tits, and they were down for whatever.

Kita had a crush on Jarius, and she let it be known that she was ready to drop her panties and do what she needed to do to lock a nigga down. "Jarius, what's up?" she asked, looking at him with lust in her eyes and sucking on a Blow-Pop.

"You and that Blow-Pop you're sucking on."

"You going to the game on Saturday?"

"Yeah. You know I got to go watch my nigga play. But what's up with you? I wish I was that Blow-Pop you're sucking on."

Kita smiled, and so did the rest of the girls. "Why don't you walk me back to my house so I can show you how nasty I can get with a real Blow-Pop?"

"Fuck these nasty bitches!" I said, looking at Jarius and Tab, who was trying to get his Mack on with Christy, and acting as if he didn't hear me. *These lil' bitches think they're too good to give a nigga like me the time of day. I'm tired of being turned down. I'm not putting up with rejection anymore. Whatever the fuck I want in this world, I'm just gonna take. One day, all these lil' bitches are gonna have to deal with me!* "Are y'all coming or what?" I asked again.

"Yo, I'ma chill with Kita for a lil' while," Jarius said.

"Yeah, me too," added Tab.

"Cool!"

"Amir, maybe Jarius will tell you how I work a Blow-Pop!" Kita said with a smile.

"I'm gone!" I said, and walked away. *Those two niggas chose a bitch over me! That's dirty! One day they gonna pay for that shit!*

Chapter Two
"Give Me the Loot"

A Month Later:

"Nigga, where'd you get all that gwop from?" I asked Jarius out of curiosity. Even though I was still fuming from the way he and Tab disrespected my gangsta in front of those 'hood rats, I played it cool. Right now, it was about that gwop.

"Shh! I'll tell you when you get out of the shower," Jarius replied, still counting his money.

"Fuck a shower!" I was anxious to hear what he had been up to and how the fuck he got that gwop.

"Yo, this is between you and me, dog. I trust you, so you better not say shit to anyone. Promise?"

"I promise," I responded, looking Jarius straight in his eyes.

"Come on," he said, and led me out of the house and around the building. "Yo, I've been hustling!" he told me, full of excitement.

"For who?"

"My brother."

"*Red?*"

"Yeah, nigga, for Red."

"How long you been hustling?"

"Since last month, the day after we did that favor for him."

This dirty ass nigga's been hustling on the down low based on my strength! I'm the one who came at Red's neck about some gwop, so in all fairness, I should be benefiting too. But nah, this greedy ass nigga was starting to create a pattern that told me he was unfaithful to the game. "So, all that gwop belongs to you?" I asked with an evil stare and bad intentions on my mind.

"Nah. I got to give Red seventy dollars off of every hundred I rake in."

"Yo, that nigga is using you! Why the fuck you got to hand over seventy dollars to him when you're the one out on the block hustling? I'm telling you, Red is fucking pimping you! He's treating you like a straight up hoe!"

"Yeah, I know, but the flip side is that I'm making more money than the average nigga out here. I'd rather have thirty dollars than be broke," Jarius responded as he leaned up against the building.

"Damn! I want in!" I said. Even though Red was putting his pimping game down, I decided this could be a chance for me to make some gwop of my own.

"A'ight, but we got to holla at Red first."

"Where the fuck is he at now?"

"I think he's at the park. Let's walk down there and see."

When we got to the park, it was jam-packed. A nigga named Corey had all the crack fiends running around like crazy. He even had Ashley's little sister sucking a pit bull's dick in front of everybody. Bitches were shaking what their mommas gave them to the music that was blasting out of the hustlers' cars. Everybody that was into the game in Clayton was out in the park trying to outshine one another. Every 'hood rat in the city was on their grind, looking for a quick come-up, sucking, fucking and smoking up a nigga's weed.

Red was sitting in his Corvette, watching his surroundings when Jarius and I strolled up on him. Jarius gave him a knot of bills—three hundred and fifty dollars to be exact. In the front seat, Ashley had her head buried in Red's lap, bobbing it up and down.

Damn! That whore gets around! One day I'll have her all for myself.

"You finished already?" Red asked Jarius.

"Yeah," he replied, watching Red as he split a Dutch Master down the middle.

"Here, take this," Red said, giving Jarius another package.

"Yo, Red, I want in. I'm trying to fatten my pockets too," I said, interrupting his whole flow.

"Bitch, keep sucking! I'll let you know when I'm ready to feed you some of this hot cum," Red said as he gripped Ashley's head and pumped his dick down her throat. When he got the feeling of her lips back, he looked at me and said, "In on what, nigga?" He seemed surprised by my request.

"Red, I'm trying to get it just like he is."

"You're too small to be hustling. I don't know, boy. If your momma found out, she'd kill us both."

"Man, don't worry about my mom. She ain't gonna know. She works too fucking much," I replied, giving Red a hungry stare.

"Lil' nigga, these streets respect no one. If you want to be out there, you're gonna have to live by the code of the streets." Talking with his hands, Red gave me the game from a real street nigga's prospective. "Take these three packages and bring me back two-hundred. That's a hundred for yourself. You cool with that?"

I nodded my head, indicating to him that I accepted his offer.

"And you didn't get that from me!"

"I know."

"Well, act like you want to get some gwop, nigga! Jarius will show you what to do next."

"Bet!"

Red put the Dutch Master in his mouth and pulled Ashley off of his dick and ordered her out of the car. Once outside, he bent her over the trunk of the car, pulled her panties to the side and fucked her brains out in front of everybody. When he was ready to bust his nut, he pulled out and came all over her ass cheeks. "Lil' nigga, this is what you do when your gwop is right!" he said to me and Jarius as Ashley took the Dutch Master out of his mouth and put it in hers.

Chapter Three
"When it All Falls Down"

Jarius and I were the two coolest muthafuckas in school. We always kept our pockets full of cheddar. On any given day, we would be sitting on three or four hundred dollars. Not to mention, our gear was tight as fuck: Polo, Hilfiger, Starter jackets, the new Jordan's, and all the Air Max's. There was no doubt in anybody's mind that he and I were the niggas every broke ass in the school hated. Although Jarius was in the tenth grade and I was in the ninth, the entire school was feeling our swagger.

It was Friday, and I won't front, my shit was looking too precious and clean. *In a few minutes I'll be on my way down to the block to get my hustle on,* I thought to myself as I tried to bounce out of the house before my mom showed up and began bitching.

Just as I stepped outside, Ma Duke showed up, tripping and acting as if she had her panties bunched up in the crack of her ass. "Boy, where do you think you're going?" she asked me as she got out of her car.

I didn't know if I was more embarrassed by her tripping on me, or by her pulling up on me in her car. "Nowhere," I responded, stopping dead in my tracks. *Damn! Fuck! She's gonna fuck up my hustle!*

"I know you ain't, 'cause your ass is gonna turn around and go back in the house!"

"You said I can stay here with Aunt Debra this weekend," I responded with a frown on my face.

"Boy, you better straighten your damn face up and go get your stuff so we can go!"

"But I don't want to go out to that boring trailer park! I wanna stay here!"

"I don't want to go to work every day, but I do. Now, hush your mouth and go get your shit, now!"

I mumbled as I headed back to Aunt Debra's house to retrieve my clothes and my stash. I wasn't about to leave that shit behind.

On our way home, I noticed Ma Duke looking at me strangely. *I wonder if she found out that I was hustling. I wouldn't be surprised if she did, because the streets of Clayton were blazing with mine and Jarius's names. Older cats were jealous that two young niggas were caking it the fuck up while they were struggling. The difference between me and Jarius and those other cats was that they got high, and we didn't. Some also tricked half of their cheddar on pussy. Jarius and I bought clothes and saved the rest.*

"Boy, where are you getting those new clothes from?" Ma Duke asked me. Her voice brought me out of my trenches.

"Red. He bought me and Jarius these clothes. "What's up? What's wrong?"

"Yeah, okay. Let me find out you're out there hustling and selling that shit! I'm gonna beat the black off your ass!"

Her words did nothing but make me laugh. She'd stay beating my ass, but that shit would just wanna make me hustle harder.

"I said something funny?" she asked with an attitude.

"Nah, you cool."

"Cool! Like I said, I better not find out you're out there hustling!" she said, giving me her last and final word.

The rest of the ride home, I sat quietly, just thinking of all the cheddar I was gonna miss tonight.

As we pulled into the trailer park, I noticed my mother's

best friend, Sally, who was pulling up behind us. From the look
on Sally's face, I knew she was gonna drop a dime on me, if she
hasn't already done so. As soon as my mom parked the car, I got
out and headed straight to our trailer. *I really don't give a fuck if
Mom finds out or not!*

Once inside, I noticed my cousin, Shabaca. I enjoyed
spending time around him because he was like a big kid. At
twenty-four, he had never had any pussy, and still played video
games and watched cartoons.

"Where's your mom?" Shabaca asked, then added, "I bet
I can spank your ass in this new 'Madden!'"

"Nigga, are you crazy? You big ass, ugly muthafucka! Set
the shit up!"

"Where's your mom at?" he asked again.

"She's outside gossiping with Sally. They're probably
getting their drink on."

"Boy, didn't I tell you I was gonna beat the black off you
if I found out you were out there hustling?" my mother yelled
when she entered our trailer.

Shabaca looked at me with a confused look on his face.
I shrugged my shoulders and kept a hold of the controller,
playing "Madden" as if I didn't hear anything she was saying.

"Boy, put that fucking controller down, now! As a matter
of fact, Shabaca, get the fuck out of my house!" Mom spat,
angrily eyeing the shit out of me.

"I ain't selling shit! Who told you that lie?" I already knew
that Sally told her, because she was standing beside my mother
with her arms folded across her chest and staring at me.

"I told her! My brother told me you served him a few days
ago," Sally said, feeling as if she was saving the fucking world.

"Mom, are you gonna take the word of a crack head over
your own flesh and blood? Her brother is a fucking crack head!
He's lying! He got the wrong muthafucka!" I denied the whole
thing.

Mom bitched and moaned all fucking night. When I got
tired of hearing her damn mouth, I went to take a cold shower.
But before taking my clothes off, I hid my drug packages and

gwop. I had six packages of crack and three hundred and eighty dollars. After my shower, I got into bed and slept like a baby, not worrying about the bullshit Mom was talking. I was determined to get gwop, and there was nothing she could do to stop me.

When I woke up the next morning, Mom was up and ready, running her mouth so loudly that I was to the point where I was getting ready to do the unthinkable; treat her like a street nigga in every sense of the word. I fixed myself a bowl of Cap'n Crunch and called Jarius.

"Hello," a female voice answered.

"Who's this?" I asked, trying to recognize the voice.

"Whose house did you call?"

"Oh, shit! What's up, Auntie?"

"Nothing. And what do you want this early in the morning? Where's your momma at?"

Shit! I know Aunt Debra ain't trying to get Ma Duke started! "She's asleep," I whispered into the phone, making sure that Ma Duke was nowhere around. Then I added, "Plus, I called Jarius. What are you doing answering his phone?"

"Boy, don't you try that shit on me! You know that boy and his momma live here! As a matter of fact, he's asleep on the couch."

"Wake him up."

"Hold on, boy, with your worrisome ass!" she said, putting down the phone. I could hear her trying to wake Jarius up.

"What's up?" Jarius asked, yawning over the phone.

"Ain't shit. Ma Duke was trippin' last night."

"Are you coming tonight? Nigga, guess what?" he asked, eager to tell me his good news.

"What?"

"Man, last night was off the chain! I made eleven-hundred for myself!" he boasted as if he was sitting on some Jay-Z money.

"That's what's up. I'm happy for you," I responded in a mellow tone of voice.

"Nigga, did you hear what I said? Eleven-hundred!"

"A'ight!"

"Yeah, you missed it."

"I ain't miss shit! As long as there's drugs to be sold, there's money to be made. Last night was nothing."

"I heard about how your momma made you go home. Nigga, the whole 'hood is talking about it. Why she be acting all funny?"

"Man, I don't know," I said, shaking my head furiously.

"You got your stuff put up?" Jarius asked as if he was trying to look out for me.

"What do you think?"

"Nigga, don't be mad at me. I'm just making sure everything is safe."

"Man, that bitch, Sally came over here last night, running her fucking mouth, telling Momma I was selling drugs."

"I feel your pain, nigga. I always knew she was a snitch."

"Yeah, but Momma just fussed. She really don't know shit." I almost choked on a piece of Cap'n Crunch when I saw my mother walk into the kitchen. I knew the ass whipping was unavoidable. There wasn't much I could say. I was cold busted.

"Come on, let's go!" Ma Duke shouted as she grabbed her coat.

"Where're we going?" I asked, still expecting an ass whipping.

"Boy, get your black ass out that door!"

I hung up with Jarius, and we left and headed to Aunt Debra's house. But we never made it because Ma Duke spotted Red in the park. She drove the one eyed bucket into the park like a bat out of hell, and jumped out of the car, cursing like a sailor. "Red, you muthafucka! You bastard! How the fuck are you gonna have my boy out here selling drugs for you? You are out of pocket, muthafucka! I should—"

This caught Red by surprise, because he had never seen Ma Duke act like this, especially not in public. He knew she was super protective of me. "Yvette, calm down! I don't know what the hell you're talking about!" He wasn't about to admit to anything Moms was accusing him of. He denied it all with a big smile.

"Red, you know how hard I work to keep my son away from going down the wrong road, and here you come, enticing him with money and drugs, destroying his life. Nigga, I will call the—"

"Yvette, I already told you, I don't have anything to do with that!"

"Red, you are lying. I was ear hustling on Jarius and Amir's phone conversation. Come here!" she yelled at me. Her eyes were bloodshot.

"Huh?" I responded, acting as if I didn't hear her.

"You heard me, boy! Get your ass out of the car! Don't make me beat the black off you in front of all these no good niggas!"

Ma Duke was on a mission. I got out of the car and slowly walked towards her.

"Who gave you this?" she asked, holding up my drug package and money.

"I-I-I found it," I managed to say.

"Found it my ass! Get your dumb ass back in the car!" my mother said, slapping me on the back of the head. All the niggas that were standing around started laughing. "Red, don't let me find out you're giving my son these drugs. I swear to God, I will shut you the fuck down!"

"Yvette, chill! I don't have anything to do with this!"

"Yeah, right! Nigga, I have no problem calling the police on your ass," Ma Duke said as she threw the money and drugs in Red's face.

She never saw it coming, nor did she get the chance to keep running her mouth, because Red sucker-punched the shit out of her, knocking her the fuck out cold. I got out of the car and ran towards Red, ready to assist my mother, who was lying face down on the concrete with blood running out of her mouth.

"Bitch, do you know who the fuck I am? I'm Big Red!" he yelled as he picked up the drug package and money off of the ground and started stuffing the money into Mom's bloody mouth. "Bitch, I will kill you and your punk ass son! Now, call the police if you want to!"

I ran towards Red and started punching him, but I was no match for his 6'3" 250 pounds. He bitch-slapped me so hard that I saw stars. I wanted to cry, but I didn't.

After Red got in his car and drove off, neighbors, Aunt Debra and Jarius came out to help Ma Duke. After ten minutes of lying on the ground, she started to come to. I was embarrassed. *How the fuck did this shit get so ugly, so fast?* I asked myself as Ma Duke and I got back into the car.

"That nigga is going to jail!" Moms said as she wiped her bloody mouth with her coat sleeve.

I looked at her and couldn't help but smile to myself. *Maybe now she'll learn to mind her own business and let me hustle. Damn! I never expected Red to punch her in the mouth, but the nigga bitch-slapped me too! One day that nigga is gonna get what he deserves!* However, I needed to find a way to escape the ass whipping Ma Duke was going to put on me, so as she drove, I asked her, "Mom, can you drop me off at my game?"

"Hell no! Your ass ain't going nowhere near the damn projects anymore!"

"So, where am I going?" I asked, knowing she wasn't going to let me out of her sight—at least not tonight.

"You're going to catch the bus down to your grandfather's house. That's where the fuck you're going."

I already had my mind made up, and going to grand pop's house was out of the question. Grand pop was old fashioned. All he wanted to do was talk a hole in a nigga's head and make me work for free, and I wasn't about to put up with that shit. Grand pop needed a slave, not me.

Being that I couldn't go to my game or hang out in the projects, I figured I didn't have anything to lose, so I jumped out of the car at a stoplight and ran. I ran all the way back uptown. Ms Duke acted as if she didn't care. Even if she did, she knew she couldn't catch me.

Once I made it back uptown, I went straight to the park where Jarius was hustling. I also spotted Red sitting in the front seat of his car, smoking a Dutch Master.

"Lil' nigga, I know you didn't come back out here wanting

to fuck with me!" Red said when he saw me standing in front of his car.

"Nah, Red. I came here to apologize for the dumb shit my moms pulled on you. I didn't know she was gonna trip like that," I said, looking at Red in his eyes.

"Yo, lil' nigga, I didn't mean to hit you. I like you, Amir, and I want you on my team," he said as he pulled out a knot of gwop and peeled off five-hundred and eighty dollars and handed it to me. "There's the three-hundred and eighty your moms threw at me, and two-hundred extra for all the drama. Now, do you think you're ready to hustle tonight?" he asked me as he inhaled the smoke of his Dutch Master into his lungs.

"Fuck yeah!"

I stayed at Aunt Debra's house the whole weekend, and Jarius and I hustled the entire time. That weekend, my cousin, Porsha let me finger-fuck her for a hundred dollars. To me, finger-fucking her was like having sex. I made sure I got my hundred-dollars worth.

By Monday morning, I was beginning to wonder why Ma Duke hadn't come for me. *I guess she got tired of my shit. Good! I'm on my own now. It's on and poppin'!* I thought to myself as I walked into school. I was living the life most lil' niggas wanted to live. Throughout the weekend I made twenty-five hundred dollars, plus the five-hundred and eighty that Red broke me off with.

I was enjoying my day when my math teacher told me to report to the principal's office. I knew that I didn't do any dumb shit, so I went to his office. To my surprise, there stood Ma Duke with a swollen lip, along with a white lady I've never seen before. I looked at Ma Duke and asked, "What's this about?"

"Andrew," the white lady said, catching my attention. I wasn't used to people calling me by my government name. Even the teachers called me Amir. "My name is Peggy Havick, and I'll be your case manager. I understand that your mother can't control you, so we'll be placing you in a group home for boys."

"A *what?* Bitch, I ain't going nowhere with your white ass!

Get the fuck outta my face with that bullshit!" I spat, looking at the lady as if she lost her fucking mind.

"A group home. It's not as bad as you think."

I glanced over at Ma Duke and saw tears in her eyes. I couldn't tell if they were tears of concern or tears of joy. I wasn't feeling this shit. "Momma, what's she talking about? So now you want to lock me away in some group home with these white people? I see what you're doing. With Sharon in the Army and me in a group home, you could do you, huh?" I was trying to figure out what the fuck was going on.

"Baby, I'm not gonna let you end up like those fools," she said, wiping the tears from her eyes. "I'm determined not to let my son become a product of his environment."

I begged Ma Duke not to turn me over to the custody of these white people. I even promised her that I would stop hustling and do the right thing, but there was no changing her mind. I jumped up from the chair and took off out of the door, but I was bum-rushed to the floor by two white ass officers who were waiting for me outside of the principal's office. Ma Duke must have told them that I had rabbit in my blood, because if I had made it outside, those fat white fucks would've never caught me.

I sat back down, and as the lady began to tell me about the group home, I looked over at Ma Duke in disbelief. I didn't hear shit that the white lady was saying, except that the group home was out in Smithfield.

Chapter Four
"Group Home"

I have been in the group home for the past six months and it wasn't as bad as I thought. There were only eight kids in the home, and each one of us had our own room. The home was good for a lot of the kids. It was a home away from home. The food was pretty decent and they had all types of things for the kids to do. They had Sega Genesis, Super Nintendo, cable TV, weights and a basketball court. Plus, they took us on outings every week, to places like the museum, the park, the gym, or to go see a movie. One summer they took us down to Disney World in Florida.

All of the kids attended public school, and they even gave us an allowance once a week. We could earn up to forty dollars depending upon our level. We also got to go home on the weekends, if we had a home to go to.

I attended Smithfield-Selma Middle School where I continued to play ball. I also broke the school's rushing record. I stood out amongst the rest of the middle school kids. I had a swagger like no other. I had all of the young females chasing behind me and calling the group home at different times of the night. I even got my first piece of pussy at the group home.

I stayed in the group home for three years. I still kept in

contact with Jarius, Reese and Dre even though Reese and Dre
had moved to Raleigh. Jarius was eighteen now and was getting
a little money. He had taken over his brother Red's operation
because Red was doing a Fed bid. Word on the streets was that
Red and his connect got popped in New York with fifteen kilos
and a little over a quarter mill

•   •   •   •   •   •

Three Years Later...

It was the summer of '93, and I had finally convinced my
mother to take me out of the group home. I wanted to attend
school back home so that I could play ball for Coach Smith,
being as though they just came off of a State Championship.
I was glad to be back home and practicing with the varsity
football team. I was the only junior on the varsity team and was
playing behind senior running back Julius Jones, but I would
later earn the starting position after Julius broke his collar bone.

Jarius made sure that I was laced the fuck up for school.
He bought me all the latest designer clothes, and without a
doubt I was by far the flyest nigga in school. You couldn't tell
me shit.

Midway through the season I was named "High school
Player of the Week". I had rushed for two-hundred and eighty-
six yards and four touchdowns.

With my birthday fast approaching, I was showing my ass
off. I couldn't wait until November 15th to show these clowns ass
niggas out here how a real nigga does it. Jarius had promised
me a party at the CEO Club after the game. This was my chance
to show all those who thought that I was riding Jarius's dick
that I could in fact stand on my own.

It was third period, and my man, Rocky and I were on
our way to class when we turned the corner of Barber Hall and
spotted a fly ass chick with ass for days. She stood 5'6" and a
hundred and thirty pounds. She was a red bone just like I liked
them. She had a nice chest and a nice apple bottom, which was

out of control. She kind of put me in the mind of Halle Berry. *Damn, I never seemed her before! Either way, I got to have her!*

"Yo, who's the new chick?" Rocky asked.

"I don't know, but I'm fin' to go find out!" I replied, putting on my game face. "Excuse me," I said as I approached her.

"Yes?" she replied.

"Let me help you with those books."

"No thank you. I'm fine."

"You're right about that!"

"Right about what?" she asked, looking at me like I was weird or something.

"You are fine!"

She just smiled, and at that moment I knew I had her.

"So, what's your name?" I asked with interest.

"Shanta."

"Nice to meet you, Shanta. I'm Andrew. Where are you from?"

"Atlanta," she replied as she put a few of her books in her locker.

"Oh yeah? So, what class are you headed to?"

"Ms. Barker's class."

"So, you're an upper classman?" I asked, giving her a sinister look of lust.

"Yeah. This is my senior year. What about you?"

"Oh, I'm only a junior," I replied, grabbing my crotch.

When I said that, Shanta gave me a funny look.

"Why are you looking at me like that?" I asked as I leaned on the lockers.

"Like what?"

"Like, why is this junior trying to holla at me."

"No, it's not like that," she replied with a smile. *Damn! This nigga must have read my mind!*

"So, what's it like?"

At a loss for words, her voice trailed off. "Well Andrew, I'm new. I'm trying to adjust to this environment, and I'm trying to find Ms. Barker's class before the bell rings."

"Well, I can get you to class, and I would be more than

happy to show you around today, if that's fine with you."

"No thank you. I'll be fine. But you can show me to Ms. Barker's class," she replied and closed her locker.

"You sure you're fine?"

"Yeah."

"Well, since you're fine, then find your own way to Ms. Barker's class!" I said, and walked off leaving her standing there dumbfounded.

I sat in my English class thinking about Shanta the whole period. I couldn't wait for my lunch break. I wondered if she would even talk to me now, being as though I didn't show her to class. But she acted as if she had a thing against juniors, and I couldn't let an out of town bitch shine on me, whether she was fine or not. As soon as the bell rang for lunch, I stepped into the hallway and spotted a couple of my teammates. "What's up fellas!" I yelled as I approached them.

"Ain't shit," replied B.B. "Yo, you seen the new girl?" he asked.

"Yeah, I seen her," I replied, giving them an evil look. "Yo, I'm out!" I said, and headed to the lunchroom.

"Hold up!" B.B. and Rocky said simultaneously as they followed in my footsteps.

When we walked into the lunchroom, all eyes were on us. I was looking for Shanta, but the lunchroom was so packed that I didn't spot her until after I got my tray. I then spotted her sitting with my cousin, Kim. "So, did you find your way to class?" I asked Shanta as I sat down with them.

"Why? You didn't show me!" she replied as she rolled her eyes at me.

"I take it that you two done met already," Kim said as she interrupted us.

"Yeah, we met earlier."

"Uhmm. By the way, this is my cousin," Kim said to Shanta as she continued to eat her sandwich.

"So, you coming to the game tomorrow night?" I asked, feeling imperturbable.

"I don't' know. Kim just invited me to her cousin Amir's

birthday party."

"That's me! I'm Amir!" I said, smiling a devilish grin.

"I thought you said your name was Andrew."

"That's my government name, and actually my birthday is today. But the party's gon' be tomorrow after the game. So why don't you come through and we'll hook up later at the party?"

"I don't know about hooking up, but I might come on the strength of Kim," she replied, giving me a cheesy smirk.

"That's what's up!" I said, knowing that she would be there. I then chatted with the girls for a brief moment before excusing myself.

"Girl, what's up with him?" Shanta asked as she watched me dump my tray and exit the lunchroom.

"Nothing. Why you ask that?"

"Because, that nigga wouldn't even show me to class earlier, and now he's got the audacity to come over here and talk to me."

"Girl, don't pay that boy no mind. He's just playing mind games with you."

"Well, I ain't the one to be playing mind games with, especially with no junior," she said in her most convincing voice.

"Girl, I feel you. But he's just big headed 'cause he's the star of the football team, and the dressingest nigga in the school. But everybody knows that Jarius buys his clothes for him."

"Who's Jarius?"

"Amir and Jarius are best friends. They're like brothers."

"How old is he?" she asked, curious about Jarius.

"Who?" Kim asked, a little confused.

"Jarius."

"Oh, eighteen, I think."

"He goes to school here too?"

"Nah, his ass got kicked out when he was fifteen. But he's cool and fine as hell too, girl."

"Didn't you say that Amir was the star of the football team?"

"Yeah."

"The varsity football team?"

"Yeah. He's the only junior on the team, and he got High School Player of the Week last week. Girl, Channel 5 was here and everything. They say he's the first junior to ever get that award, so you know his head is about this big!" she said, spreading her hands apart. "But I tell you one thing."

"What's that?"

"He must really like you."

"Why you say that?" Shanta asked, blushing from ear to ear.

"'Cause all these chicken heads be sweating his ass, and I'm talking about freshmen, sophomores, juniors as well as the seniors. Plus, he never eats lunch with any girls. He's always with them boyz over there," Kim stated, pointing in the direction of my little crew.

"So that explained all the eyes."

"Girl, don't pay them no mind. They're just jealous."

Well, he is fine, and maybe I will go to the game and party tomorrow, Shanta thought to herself. "What time does the game start?" she asked as they got up from the table.

"About seven, so you can pick me up about six."

• • • • • • •

I had been thinking about Shanta the entire day. I couldn't figure out why she stayed on my mind. I was used to girls submitting to me, but with Shanta it was a challenge. I had seen her earlier in the hallway with Kim, but I just spoke and kept it moving. I didn't want her to think that I was sweating her. Plus, I was in a rush. I was late for my team meeting. We were playing our county rivalry, Triple S, which stands for Smithfield Selma Senior High School, and this was a big game for us. This game determined who would win in our division, because both teams were undefeated.

• • • • • • •

Shanta and Kim made their way through the crowd looking like two divas. Shanta could feel the envy in the air. She knew a lot of the girls didn't like her already. They had already judged her without getting to know her. It wasn't her fault that God blessed her with beauty and the body of a goddess.

"Girl, who is that? Shanta asked Kim as they continued to move through the crowd.

"Who?" Kim asked her, trying to figure out who she was talking about.

"Him over there by the concession stand with all them niggas around him."

"Oh, girl, that's Jarius," Kim replied, realizing who she was talking about.

Jarius stood out amongst the group of young men around him. He was wearing a red Polo sweater, baggy black Polo jeans and butter Timberland boots. He was 6'2" and 215 pounds. His skin tone was black, and he kind of favored the actor Tyreese.

"Amir's friend?" she asked caught up in his fineness.

"Yep!"

"Girl, he is fine!" she said as they found a spot by the fence to watch the game.

"I told you that, but with him it's a whole lot of drama. The Dominican girl he lives with is crazy," Kim replied as she skimmed through the crowd. "Plus, if Amir told him anything about you, he wouldn't give you the time of day."

"No, I wouldn't do that. But Amir isn't my boyfriend."

"I know. I was just saying if he even knows Amir likes you, he wouldn't holla."

"Girl, here he comes anyway."

"Y'all talking about me?" Jarius asked as he approached them.

"Boy, ain't nobody even thinking about you, more or less talking about you," Kim replied, giving him her full attention. "What are you, a lip reader?"

"Whatever!" he said, knowing that they were talking about him. "I take it you must be Amir's girlfriend," he stated, admiring Shanta's beauty.

"I know he didn't tell you that!" she responded, wondering whether he was serious.

"Yes, he did."

"No, he didn't!"

"Yes, he did!"

"Humph!" she said with a contemptuous grin.

"Nah, I'm just messing with you. Y'all ladies coming to the party tonight?"

"You know it!" Kim answered. After realizing that she left her money in the car, she asked, "Jarius, buy us something to eat?"

"Girl, I ain't got no money," he responded with a smile, giving the girls a clear look at his pretty white teeth.

"Boy, stop playing! You know your ass ain't broke."

It was getting ready to be halftime, so Jarius called Ron, who was one of his flunkies, and had him go stand in the long line at the concession stand to get Kim and Shanta something to eat. Jarius wanted to watch the band perform at halftime and holla at Amir when they came back out of the tunnel.

•   •   •   •   •   •

I was doing my thing as usual. I had run for a touchdown and I had eighty four yards rushing. The score was tied at fourteen, and on our way back out of the tunnel I heard Jarius call me.

"Amir!"

I looked up and was astonished to see him standing with Kim and Shanta, looking over the fence and down on the team. "What's up?" I responded in acknowledgement.

"Take your time. Let your holes develop," Jarius said, giving me his insight on the game. He was real supportive of me, and he always gave me his view of the game.

"I know!" I stated, smiling up at Shanta while putting on my helmet. "I see you made it," I said to her while admiring her beauty. She never responded, just acknowledged me with a smile. I then told Jarius to wait for me after the game as I went to join my team on the sidelines.

. . . .

Boy, he looks good in his tight football pants. I wonder if he's packing under his uniform. Damn! This nigga is built like a grown ass man. That shit probably comes from all the weight lifting and working out.

"Y'all gon' stand here, or are y'all going to watch the game?" Jarius asked breaking Shanta's thought pattern on Amir, and catching Kim off in La-La land.

"We gon' watch the game," Kim Replied.

"Well, let's find a seat.

. . . .

It was the fourth quarter, and the score was still tied with twenty seven seconds left on the clock. It was second and eight, and my team had the ball on the thirty three yard line. Everyone in the stadium knew that I was getting ready to get the ball. They have been keying on me the whole game.

The coach called a twenty five dive, and I was hit instantly at the line of scrimmage. I bounced off of a tackle and reversed field. I then broke down the sidelines. I could hear my coach screaming, "Run! Run! Run!" The crowd was roaring, and my teammates were screaming with them.

I had come to break a sixty seven yard touchdown run with thirteen seconds left on the clock. After I crossed the goal line, I did my Deon Sanders dance, and then headed to the sidelines to celebrate with my team. I took off my helmet and turned and faced the crowd. I looked in the section my mother usually sat in and was surprised to see Kim and Shanta with her. I pounded on my chest while my mother waived at me. I then winked at Shanta before the team caught me off guard with the cold Gatorade that they showered me with.

Shanta took in the whole scenery, and was amazed at how good I actually was. She thought that the game was going into overtime until she heard everybody screaming and my mother yelling, "Run, baby! Run!"

Shanta felt a little uncomfortable sitting with my mother. She couldn't believe Jarius convinced them to sit with her and then left them there with her while he went to make sure everything was set up right for my party.

My mother tried to make Shanta feel as comfortable as possible. She knew that she felt uncomfortable, being as though every young female that had a crush on me spoke to her when they walked by. She knew the 'hood rats were doing it out of spite, and Kim assured her of that.

"I don't know what's going on with you and my son, but don't let these little girls get to you," my mother said to Shanta as the game finally came to an end.

"We're just friends," she managed to say, still a little nervous.

"Honey, look around. All these little hot in the pants females are Amir's friends, but not once has Jarius or Amir brought a young lady to sit with me during one of his games. Now I know that may not mean much to you," my mother said with sincerity in her eyes, "But I know my boys, and God knows I love them. Amir must really like you, and if y'all do decide to deal with one another, just do me one favor."

Shanta was a little confused. She had no idea what his mother wanted her to do. It surprised her that a mother could know her son so well. She even liked the fact that she looked at Jarius as a son. Eager to know what she wanted her to do, she asked, "And what might that be?"

"Keep him in those books and out of those streets," she answered, as if she knew the future and could see Amir going down the wrong road. "Now, I don't agree with what Jarius does, but he takes good care of me and he stays on him about school. Just don't let my baby follow in his footsteps. Encourage him to stay on the right path."

Shanta listened to my mother, and assured her that she would do her best. She also make it clear to her that they were nothing but friends, and she had no intention on it going any further.

Chapter Five
"The Party"

The party was packed, and I was having the time of my life. Jarius and I were at the bar talking about his plans to go to New York. He wanted to make sure that I knew everyone he had to pick up money from. I pretty much knew Jarius's operation like the back of my hand, but he never let me get involved in his day to day operations even though from time to time he would let me pick up money or drop off packages, especially if he was going out of town.

I was listening to Jarius with my ears, but at the same time searching for Shanta with my eyes. I saw her earlier on the dance floor with Kim, and she had sent me a message by Rocky to save her a dance. I was hoping that she didn't leave without speaking to me.

"You looking for me?" Shanta asked as she approached me from the side.

"Actually, I was. Where was you at?" I responded with a heart melting smile, while admiring her beauty. She was by far the finest young lady at the party, and her Donna Karen jeans hugged her body just right.

"If you must know, I was in the bathroom," she said, looking up at me while starting to feel some type of attraction for me. She couldn't deny it. I had the swagger of a superstar. "So, can I get my dance?"

"I don't know. It depends," I responded with a smirk in my face, feeling myself.

"Depends on what?"

"If I'm gon' have to fuck a nigga up in here over you."

"Boy, bring your silly self on here!" she said with a smile while grabbing me by the hand and leading me to the dance floor.

I was feeling nice due to the straight shots of Hennessy Jarius had me drinking. I was on the dance floor doing my two step, while I watched Shanta move her body seductively. I knew that she could feel my dick standing at attention as she grinded her body against me.

"Let's slow this party down!" the DJ announced as he played "Come and Talk to Me" by Jodeci.

I pulled Shanta close to me and began to lay my game down. I wanted to make sure I locked the panties down. "So, did you enjoy yourself at the game tonight?" I asked, placing my hands gently around her waist.

"Yeah, I'm afraid I did."

"So, tell me about yourself."

"Well, you already know I'm from Atlanta. I have one sister, and my mother just remarried. That's why we moved up here, 'cause this is where my stepfather's from."

"Do you like it here?" I asked as she bit her bottom lip in deep thought. She was pondering if I could fuck the way that I danced. The way I moved my body would drive any woman wild, and the bulge in my pants let her know that I was packing. I read right through her.

"It's okay," she managed to say, grinning foolishly as she peered around the room, soaking up all the envy the young ladies displayed. "It's not Atlanta, but it's not too bad so far."

"Yeah, your right. But once you get to meeting people and learn your way around, you'll love it."

"I don't know about that. So, 'Mr. Win the Football Game', why don't you have a girl?"

"Girls around here are a headache. But I just moved back to Clayton myself."

"I know. Kim told me a little bit about your situation. Plus, your mother told me to keep you on the right track."

"Is that so?" I asked, surprised that my mother would tell her that.

After we finished dancing, we walked over to the bar area to finish our conversation. "So, what did you think of my mother?" I asked.

"She's cool. She cares a lot about you and your future."

"I know. She's my heart. I'm going to make her happy one of these days."

"She's happy now. Just keep doing the right thing," Shanta said with sincerity in her eyes.

Damn! This girl got me falling for her. I shook my head in disbelief. For the first time in my life, a female showed genuine concern for my future. No one had ever encouraged me to do the right thing, except for my mother and family. My friends didn't really care what I did.

"You okay?" she asked, breaking my train of thought.

"Yeah, I'm cool. So, were you cheering for me tonight?"

"Kind of. Well actually… yeah, when I saw you running and everybody yelling and screaming. Then it was funny when you did that little dance. You're pretty good I see."

"That's what they say," I said, smiling from ear to ear. "So, what do you have planned for tomorrow?" I asked, hoping she would be free.

"I don't know. Why?"

"'Cause I was wondering if we could hook up, catch a movie and something to eat."

"Are you asking me on a date?" she asked in amazement and tossing me a patronizing smirk.

"Yeah," I replied coolly. "So, we on or what?"

"It depends," Shanta stated, knowing that she had my full attention.

"Depends on what?" I asked in a firm but even tone.

"If I'm going to have to mess one of these girls up over

you."

"Girl, stop playing!" I grabbed her by the arms and pulled her close to me as if we were already a couple. "So, what do you plan to do after you graduate?" I asked, showing a little concern for her future as well.

"I plan on attending college and studying law."

"Now that's what's up!"

Time was flying, and the party was getting ready to come to an end.

Jarius had walked up on me and Shanta. "Look at y'all all cuddled up!" he said as he approached us while downing the last of his drink. "I'm getting ready to be out. You got a ride?"

"Nah, but I'm straight. I'll get Rocky or Reese to take me home."

"A'ight, but don't forget about tomorrow," he said while giving me some dap.

"I'll take you home," Shanta said to me as we both watched Jarius slide towards the side exit.

"Nah, that's a'ight. You don't know your way around here yet, and I would hate for my girl to get lost."

"Your girl?" she asked, emphasizing my words.

"Yeah, my girl!" I stated with confidence.

"Well, *your girl* has Kim riding with her, and she knows her way around."

"Where do you stay at anyway?" I asked.

"Off of Peele Road."

"Well in that case, you can take me," I said, grinning from ear to ear and showing her all thirty-two of my pretty white teeth. I stayed approximately seven miles from the road Shanta lived on.

After we left the party, I treated Kim and Shanta to the Waffle House. I was surprised to see Shanta eat as much as she did. She most definitely wasn't shy about eating in front of me.

When she pulled into the trailer park that I stayed in with my mom, it was 4:30 a.m. We exchanged numbers as well as our first kiss.

Chapter Six
"The Remainder of the School Year"

Shanta and I ended up being the perfect couple. Girls at school finally came around when Shanta had to defend herself from one of my ex-girls.

I went ahead and led my football team to the State Championship, where they lost to E.E. Smith. I set the State rushing record for a junior, and was third in the State in rushing yards for the season with fourteen hundred and thirty-nine yards.

It was now 1995, and the school year was coming to an end. Shanta was getting ready for graduation and beginning to prepare for college. She would be attending Clemson University in South Carolina, where she would be majoring in Business Law. She and I planned to spend the entire summer together because we wouldn't see each other any more until she came home for a break.

Shanta was beginning to worry about me, because ever since I started selling weed, my whole demeanor had changed. "Amir, you need to stop," she said to me as she began to get dressed for work. She stayed with me at least three to four nights out of the week.

"Stop what?" I asked, dumbfounded as if I didn't know what she was talking about.

"Hustling!"

"Don't start with me! Every time you see me bagging up, you start that dumb shit!" I barked angrily as I continued to bag up my weed.

"Who are you talking to like that?" she snapped as she approached me and pushed me in the back of my head.

"Stop playing!"

"I ain't playing! That's all you think about!" She shook her head in disbelief. She couldn't believe that I would be so selfish and risk my future all over a few dollars.

"What's wrong?" I asked as I began to give her the attention that she needed. "Baby, I'm sorry for talking to you like that. You know that I'm trying to get me a car."

"You get around fine. You know Jarius will let you use one of his cars anytime you want."

I was beginning to get frustrated. I was tired of everyone telling me what was best for me and my future, and I was tired of everyone treating me like a fucking kid. "Look. I'm tired of handouts. Jarius has been holding me down since we were kids. It's time I started taking care of myself."

"Baby, I understand what you are saying, but you have a future ahead of you. Why waste it in these streets?"

Knowing that Shanta wanted the best for me, I tried to reason with her. "Look. After I get this car, I'm through. A'ight?"

I watched her gather the rest of her things and head towards the front door.

Chapter Seven
"Summertime"

I sat in the passenger seat of Jarius's new Acura Legend, pondering whether I should get back into hustling. I knew I wanted a new car, and a used car was out of the question, especially after riding in Jarius's new car. The butter-soft leather felt so good to me, and the only way that I could get this car and stack some paper of my own was to switch over.

"What's on your mind?" Jarius asked me as we cruised down Blunt Street, heading to the park on Bragg. Reese had a crack house two houses down from the park, and because Jarius refused to be caught in a crack house, he usually met Reese at the park.

"I'm thinking about switching over," I responded, knowing where this conversation was going to go.

"Switching over to what?"

"You know. This weed shit ain't getting it."

"Hell naw!" Jarius spat as he bent the corner of Bragg Street. "Why you want to do that for?"

"I told you that I was trying to get a car."

"So, that means you got to switch over?" he asked as he pulled in front of the park.

I sat silently contemplating my next statement as he and

I exchanged stares and watched Reese and Dre play one on one. "This weed money ain't coming fast enough," I said as I watched Jarius retrieve the stash of drugs he had for Reese and Dre.

"If a car means that much to you, then you can have one of mine."

"Look, I know what's yours is mine, but it's time I get my own. It's time that I stand on my own two feet."

"Nigga, you stand on your own two feet every day. Every day you work out at that gym or are out there running. You stand on your own. Ain't nobody doing that shit but you. Ain't nobody making them good grades in school but you. Nah, I take that back." Jarius said as he watched Reese approach the car. "Them teachers might be passing your ass because of sports."

"Nigga, you're crazy! I'm smart as a motherfucker!"

"I know you are, but you're talking crazy now."

"Who's talking crazy?" Reese asked as he opened the backdoor, catching the last part of Jarius's statement.

"Your boy here," Jarius said, nodding to me as he handed Reese his package and filled him in on our conversation.

"Amir, these streets are dangerous, nigga. I don't even want to be in these streets, but what other choice do I have? I'm a high school drop out and the father of two." Reese spoke with a voice that cracked with rage and resentment. "Boy, you got a future ahead of you. Nigga, if you make it, we all make it. We can turn this street money legal."

"I know," I replied with a look of confusion. "I just want to do my own thing right now. I'm tired of y'all niggas taking care of me. Fuck a handout! I wanna get paid!"

"Taking care of you! Nigga, we a family! That's what family is supposed to do. Now what kind of car you want?"

"You'll see it when I get it," I replied, determined to get my own car. "So, what's up! You gon' give me some work or what?" I asked, hoping that Jarius would see things my way.

"Hell naw!" he and Reese answered in unison.

"So, y'all niggas gonna front on me like that? Okay! I see what it's hitting for."

"Nigga, you don't need to be out on these streets. I'll buy you a car!" Reese said with a serous stare.

"Man, fuck both of y'all niggas! I'm out!"

. . . .

Determined to get my own car, I headed over to Raleigh North in Shanta's '92 Geo Storm to holla at Barrel. Barrel was one of the few niggas in the city that had his own connection. He didn't deal with Jarius or Big Z. I knew I didn't have enough money to even holla at Big Z. Big Z wouldn't sell you nothing less than a kilo.

As I pulled into Park Glenn Apartments, I spotted Barrel getting out of his burgundy Land Rover. I parked the Geo three parking spaces down from him and followed him into the apartment.

"So, what can I do for you?" Barrel asked me with interest.

I never told him why I wanted to talk to him. I just told him that I needed to see him as soon as possible, and due to the fact that I was Jarius's main man, he figured that I would be delivering a message for Jarius. "I need an eighth," I stated while flashing a phony smile. I couldn't believe that I was here getting ready to do business with Barrel, while my main man was sitting on four or five kilos. But since them niggas want to front, I got to do what I got to do.

"An eighth?" Barrel asked, confused by my request. "Jarius ain't holding?"

"Yeah, he holding. We just ain't seeing eye to eye right now." I then gave Barrel the watered down version of my situation.

"Word is bond, dude. I respect what you're trying to do, but your man got your best interest," Barrel said in his fake ass New York accent. "But I'm going to do this for you 'cause I ain't gon' never knock a nigga for trying to do him."

Barrel had a new outlook on my relationship with Jarius. He respected me so much that he let me get the eighth of a kilo for twenty-nine hundred.

"Good looking, B!" I said, using my best New York slang while giving Barrel some dap. *Fuck those clowns! I'm about to get my own paper!*

• • • • • • •

It was Thursday, and the summer was just getting started. It was also the first of June, which meant that people would be getting their checks, and I was going uptown early. I knew that the early bird always got the first worm.

I woke Shanta up and had her drop me off at the Pantry, which was the neighborhood corner store. When I stepped on the block, the first person that I saw was pipe head Trick. "What's up!" I said to Trick as I approached him.

"You holding?" he asked while fiending for his morning blast. His eyes told a million stories.

"Yeah!"

"Let me get a fifty, and I'll run for you all day. You know how I do," Trick said with his mouth twitching from side to side. "I need to suck on the devil's dick, bad!"

"Who don't know how you do!" I replied as I hesitated before digging into my pocket and pulling out the pill bottle that contained tiny pieces of crack.

"Amir, my word is bond. I ain't going nowhere. I'm going to be with you all day. Just look out for me," he begged as he watched me put the top back on my bottle.

Everyone in town knew Trick was a natural born hustler. He just messed around and got strung out on the pipe. Trick had hustled for damn near every hustler in town at one point or another. Everyone knew him, and everyone knew that he was suspect to run off with your package. But he would never beat you until it got late night, and by that time I had planned on making a killing off of him.

As I was giving Trick his fair share, pipe head Ann and Joe walked up, wanting some credit. I had no problem giving it to them or anybody else I knew that got a check today. I gave them a hundred dollars worth of credit, knowing that they would be back for more before their checks came. I knew this because

Barrel had assured me that this was the official "Fishscale".

While I was sitting on the steps observing Trick go hand to hand and car to car, I noticed that the hustlers started to come out in great numbers, but what little did they know. Their coke would be no match for my shit, because everyone in this neighborhood had Jarius's coke. And even though Jarius had good coke, it wasn't Fishscale. *Fuck Jarius and his weak ass coke! I'm taking all his customers!*

It wasn't even two o'clock, and I had already sold half of my eighth in twenties, fifties and hundreds. The fiends were loving my coke, and the hustlers were begging to feel the affect.

"Amir, let's walk to the store," Trick said as he approached me.

"For what?" I asked, getting a funny feeling in my stomach.

"I need to talk to you."

"You can talk to me now," I said as I looked down at the corner where a few of the hustlers were standing.

"I overheard Poo Loo and them complaining about you being out here."

"Fuck Poo Loo!" I said with a contemptuous grin. I had no respect for Poo Loo, because he was a man with female traits. It was well known around town that he loved to gossip. Plus, I didn't like him because he was hating on my cousin, Man, who was doing time in the Feds.

"All I'm saying is be careful. It's the first of the month, and these niggas be depending on this money. You're making it hard for them to eat."

"Hard for them to eat! These niggas been out here eating for I don't know how long! If they're still starving, it ain't my fault!" I spat, getting a little heated that Trick was worried about Poo Loo and his little crew. "Look, you just move this work and don't worry about them."

• • • • • • •

The night was still young, and Jarius was headed down 1-40, back to Clayton form Raleigh when he thought about

Amir. He had gotten a phone call earlier form Joe, who was one of his customers, complaining that Amir was on the block doing his thing. Joe wasn't mad that Amir was on the block. He was mad because he thought that Jarius gave Amir some better coke, and the fiends were loving it.

When Jarius made it into town, he headed to Front Street. He knew Amir would be in one of two spots, and just like he figured, there stood Amir at the top of the hill by the park like he was the lieutenant of the block.

Jarius was mad deep down inside, because he knew how much talent Amir had and he didn't want to see him go down this road. But at the same time, he knew that Amir was stubborn, and once his mind was made up, there was nothing that he or anyone else could do to change it. He really wanted to whoop him for being stupid, but he knew that might be fighting a battle he couldn't win. At sixteen, Amir stood six feet and weighed 215-Ibs. He was solid due to all the working out that he did. Jarius knew that Amir could fight, not to mention he had a short temper.

"What's up?" Jarius asked me as he rolled down the window of his Acura.

"You!" I responded, still paying attention to my surroundings while keeping a close eye on Trick. "What're you doing uptown?" I asked, knowing he was checking up on me.

"I was just passing through."

"Yeah, and I'm a white man!" I said, being sarcastic.

"Look, take a ride with me. We need to talk," he said, getting agitated by my smart remarks.

I stood still for a moment, contemplating whether I should roll with him, or continue to get my money. I then figured that it might be best to see what this nigga had to say. I was still mad at him for not giving me any drugs to sell, but I was really mad because I had to put Barrel in my business. "What's up?" I asked as I closed the door and reclined the passenger seat.

"You really trying to get this money, huh?" he questioned me as he put the car in drive and cruised off to the sounds of Tupac coming out of his speakers.

"Yeah, you know what I'm trying to do."

"I feel that, but shit ain't like it used to be when we was kids. It's a dirty game out here. Niggas robbing and killing now for a pair of Jordan's. So you got to watch who you mess with, 'cause it's a lot of snakes out here. And a snake don't care who it bites. You feel me?"

"Yeah, I feel you," I said, soaking in all of what Jarius said. I knew that he was sharp far as the streets were concerned, and I knew that he would never mislead me.

"So, you need to stay strapped if you gon' be out here, and be careful," he said in an even but firm tone. "And where did you get some coke from?"

"I make moves!" I said proudly.

"Oh, now you the man 'cause you got somebody to front you some coke."

"Ain't nobody front me shit! I bought mines!" I said, getting offended by Jarius's remark.

"Where you get some coke from?"

"Why? You ain't give it to me."

"Don't play me like that. You know why I wouldn't give you no coke," he spat as he pulled in McDonalds' parking lot. "But if you want some coke that bad, I'll give it to you. But don't be out here copping from anybody, because if something happens to you, I'm going to turn this town upside down."

"You can't be watching over me like I'm a little boy. I ain't green to these streets. I know who to fuck with and who not to."

"Oh yeah? Well did you know niggas been calling me complaining about you?"

"*What?*" I said, caught off guard by Jarius's statement. I knew I'd been getting the crooked eye all day, but I had no idea that dudes were calling Jarius complaining. "What did they say?"

"Nothing serious. Just wanting to know why I gave you better coke than them. That's why I wanted to know where you got that coke from."

Damn! Barrel said this coke was going to drive the fiends crazy, I thought to myself while pondering whether I should tell Jarius where I got my coke from.

"So, you gon' tell me or what?" Jarius asked, anxious to know.

"Barrel."

"Damn! You went to Raleigh to cop!" Jarius said, realizing why everyone was complaining. "Look, I'm going to let you run uptown, but don't be putting no work from Raleigh down here."

"Why?" I asked, confused.

"Because Clayton is a small town, and everyone uptown pretty much got the same coke. I stretch my coke uptown because everyone buys from me. So when you put out that Fishscale from Barrel, the fiends wasn't use to that."

"How do you know Barrel got Fishscale?"

"I know what everybody got. I got coke that's just as good, but I only put that out in Raleigh and Smithfield because of the level of competition," he explained to me while he waited in the drive-thru at McDonalds to place his order.

I sat back and took in the whole conversation. I took this as "Game 101" that he was giving. I knew I was getting in over my head, but my ego told me I could handle it.

"But don't get it twisted. The coke I put out uptown is good. It's just stretched a little," Jarius continued.

After Jarius and I left McDonalds, we headed over to his stash house out in country.

"So, what you mean I can run uptown?" I asked, trying to make sure that he and I were on the same page.

"Just what I said. You can run uptown, but under one condition."

"What?" I asked, knowing that he had something slick up his sleeve.

"Once the summer is over, you're done. I don't care how much bread you got saved up or what you ain't got. If you ain't got your car by then, that's your fault. I'm putting you in a gold mine."

"Bet!" I said as if I was ready to take on the world. "Bet! I'm going to finish what I got first."

"How much you got left?"

"Almost two ounces!" I said proudly.

For the next two hours, I weighed and bagged up eighths of kilos of crack for Jarius. I kept a close eye on him as he turned cocaine into crack. It was amazing how hot water and baking soda could change one substance to the other. It was also amazing how just by adding hot water and baking soda to cocaine, the Federal Government could give you thirteen years minimum if you got caught with 50 grams or more. But Jarius and I weren't hip to that part of the game.

"After we're done, I'm going to drop you back off uptown. But as soon as you're finished what you got, call me and I'll lay this quarter key on you," Jarius said to me as he put the finishing touches on his last batch.

"A'ight!"

Jarius dropped me off as planned, and I headed back to the park in search of Trick.

"Boy, where you been at?" Trick asked, excited to see me.

"I had to handle some business. Why? You finished?"

"I've been finished. It's crazy out here." Trick said, handing me a bundle of cash.

I was surprised that he hadn't run off on me with my drugs and money. "Take this," I said, giving Trick another package. "I'm going to go over Willie D's house and set up shop. So if you need me, that's where I'll be." I then glanced around and caught a few frowned up faces from a few of the hustlers that were standing a few feet away. I told Trick to make sure that he comes and gets me if any of the dudes on the block gave him any trouble.

As soon as I got to Willie D's house, I paged Jarius. It took him a few minutes before he called back.

"Hello," I said as I picked up Willie D's phone as if it was my own.

"What's up?" Jarius responded, knowing that it was me that answered the phone.

"Yo, bring me some heat."

"Why? What's up? You straight!" he asked in a panicked

tone.

"Yeah, I'm cool. Niggas are just looking crazy, and I was thinking about our conversation earlier."

"Where you at?"

"Over Willie D's."

"A'ight, I'll be through there in about thirty."

I was on the porch when Jarius came through about forty five minutes later in his Suburban. "What's going on up in there?" he asked me as he gave me some dap and sat beside me on the porch.

"You know this is where all the fiends be, so I'm chilling down here. But I got Trick up top."

"So you trying to lock it down on both ends, huh?"

"Yeah. Why? What's up with you?"

"Got to make a move in Raleigh."

"Well, I ain't gon' hold you up. You bring that for me?" I asked, referring to the gun.

"Yeah," Jarius replied as he pulled out a Glock 9mm from his waist.

My conversation with him was brief due to the fact that he had to make his move. After he left, I headed back into the house. I was sitting in the back room thinking of how I was going to blow up and get my money right. My mind was already made up that I was going to pump out of Willie D's house and let Trick pump here when I was gone. Once people knew that this is where we would be, they would bum-rush the door.

I sold crack out of Willie D's house until damn near two o'clock in the morning. I then called Shanta and had her pick me up, but before we left to go to my mother's house, I had her stop by the park so that I could holla at Trick.

"Yo, Trick!" I yelled as I got out of the car and motioned for Shanta to turn off her headlights.

"Who's that?" Trick responded while trying to fix his stem.

"Amir!"

"Hold up!" he shouted, glad that I had showed up because he was out of work. "What's up?" he asked as he came from behind the building.

"I'm fin' to go in for the night. What you got left?"

"I'm done," he replied while giving me the money he owed me. "It's an extra two hundred dollars in there too."

"What's that for?" I asked, surprised that he had given me the extra money.

"That's for you. I appreciate what you done for me today. But most of all, I respect what you're trying to do, and I want to be down with you."

"What do you mean 'be down'?" I asked as I leaned against the car.

"Just what I said. I'm tired of hitting this pipe," Trick snapped coolly as he pulled out the pipe that he was just fixing. "I've been doing this shit all my life it seems like." He paused while continuing to fumble with the pipe. "And ain't no telling how much paper I done made these niggas, and I ain't got shit; not a pot to piss in nor a window to throw it out of."

Dumb and dumber! Shanta thought to herself as she sat in the car and shook her head in disbelief. She couldn't believe what she was hearing. She loved Amir dearly, but she did not respect what he was doing. She thought it was selfish and dumb, because Amir had too much talent to be wasting it in the streets. Trick wanting to get off the pipe was good, but to get off to start selling was dumb too.

"So, you're saying you're ready to start making some money?" I asked with a piercing look in my eyes. I was trying to detect if he was serious or was he acting and trying to convince me to give him some more coke. The look in his eyes said that he was serious.

"Yeah, I just need to get off this pipe."

I sat quietly for a few minutes, contemplating what I should do. "Look. Don't let me down," I stated in a stern tone as I reached in my pocket and gave Trick my last ounce.

"This an ounce!" he quickly stated, surprised that I would give him that much coke at once.

"I know what it is. You owe me fourteen, and page me as soon as you finish," I said, reaching in the car to get a pen so that I could give Trick my pager number. "I expect for you to have some money for yourself, and if things get hot out here, go over Willie D's house. I already got shit set up for you over there."

•   •   •   •   •   •   •

The following morning, I was awakened by my pager going off. I looked at the number and noticed that it had 911 behind it. I figured that it was Trick, because the number was to Willie D's house.

"Hello. Who's this?" I asked as if I didn't have a clue to whom he was calling.

"Trick. I'm ready," he responded, knowing that it was me on the other end of the phone.

"A'ight, sit tight," I replied. "I'll be through there in about an hour."

I got up and showered, and thought to myself that this was too good to be true. I couldn't believe I had sold an eighth of a kilo in break-downs in one day. I had a total of seventy-three hundred dollars now.

After I showered, I got dressed and called Jarius. I told him that I would meet him at his stash house in an hour and a half. I then grabbed Shanta's car keys and left, leaving her asleep in my bed while I went to go pick up my money from Trick and meet Jarius.

Chapter Eight
"End Of Summer"

Trick and I hustled together throughout the entire summer. Trick had eased up off the pipe while I grew in the drug game. I now had two crack houses; the one that Trick ran uptown and my new spot out in the country that my childhood friend, Mike ran.

Mike and I grew up together in the trailer park, but his mother sent him to live with his father in New Jersey. His father sent him back down to North Carolina after Mike got involved with stealing cars.

The spot in the country was located off of Highway 42. We were selling out of this fiend named Rosco's house, and he was moving a half a kilo in breakdown every nine days.

I also bought myself a '95 Acura Legend with chrome 19-inch Krystals on it.

"So, now that the summer is coming to an end, what are you going to do?" Jarius asked me as we ate dinner at Applebee's.

"What do you mean?"

"You know what I mean!" he said, looking at me like I was crazy. "The summer is over."

"I know, but the way I got things set up, I'm not at risk. I ain't never in none of them spots. I just supply the work."

Jarius continued to eat his food as he thought about his next statement. He knew that once I got hold of the fast money, I wouldn't be able to let it go. He was hoping that I wouldn't get sidetracked from football. Everyone around me had NFL dreams, but me. I wanted to hustle and get money.

"I know what we agreed to," I said in a frustrating tone. "But let me handle this. I know what I'm doing."

•   •   •   •   •   •   •

It was now time for Shanta to go off to college. Part of her wanted to stay with me, and part of her wanted to go. I had become her heart, and we were madly in love with one another. I had gone and spoiled her throughout the entire summer. She wasn't materialistic, but I had done things for her that no man has ever done. I made sure that she had all of the latest designer clothes. I also paid for her books and bought all of the little things that she needed for school — not to mention the five thousand dollars I gave her so that she wouldn't be in South Carolina broke.

She was also starting to worry about me, because it seemed as if I was more focused on the streets than playing football. The money was beginning to get to me, and she could tell by the way that I was beginning to carry myself. My money always seemed to come first.

We were supposed to be meeting over at her mother's house so that my flunky, Rocky could drive her car down to the college while she rode with me.

"Boo, where have you been?" she asked, sucking her bottom lip, which gave me a hint that she was a little pissed at me. "You haven't answered your phone, and you're forty minutes late!" she snapped, letting her anger get the best of her.

Our eyes locked in a silent battle while I emphasized my words carefully. "I had to go see Trick before we left."

"What?" Her voice increased as tears of frustration welled up in her eyes. "That's all you think about! Money, money,

money!"

"Whatever!" I countered as I walked past her and headed towards the house. "You didn't say that when I was buying you all those clothes!"

"Fuck you!" she angrily stated. "You know I don't give a damn about those clothes. That was your idea to take me shopping. I don't need designer clothes to make me look good." She paused and grabbed me from behind, which caused me to spin around. "Have you forgotten that I work? I ain't never had a nigga take care of me!"

I flashed a brilliant white smile, which made her even madder. I knew just how to push her buttons.

"What are you smiling about?" she sneered, cutting her eyes dismissively.

"Nothing. Come here," I said as I reached out and pulled her close to me. "I'm sorry! I just got caught up. Do you forgive me?" I asked in a low whisper.

"You're always sorry. And what happened to only hustling for the summer?"

"I know, baby. As soon as I finish what I got, I'm done," I replied.

"You promise?" she asked as she looked into my eyes.

For the sake of arguing, I made a promise I knew I wouldn't be able to keep, and Shanta knew it. It was at that moment she decided to let it go. She knew I was stubborn, and that I only did what was pleasing for me.

Chapter Nine
"When It's Bad, It's Bad"

School had started back, and everything was going copasetic as far as I was concerned. The money was still coming in and I still was the man on the football field. The only thing that wasn't going my way was my relationship with Shanta. I wasn't feeling the long distance relationship. I was having trouble keeping my dick in his pants.

It was Wednesday, and I had just left football practice. I headed out to Rosco's house to meet Mike. Mike had paged me while I was in school, because he was finished with the package I had given him. I figured I could kill two birds with one stone, because I was planning on going to see Regina. Regina lived two houses down from Rosco.

When I pulled up, I noticed the normal rush as usual. I parked my car in Regina's driveway and walked over to Rosco's. When I walked into the house, Rosco motioned for me to go to the back. I knew that's where Mike would be.

"What's up?" I said as I entered the room.

"Ain't shit! Trying to get this money," Mike replied, looking up and giving me some dap. He then turned his attention back to his game. He was playing the new "Madden".

"I feel that," I said as I sat on the edge of the bed. "That game any good?"

"Yeah, the graphics are amazing. You want to play?"

"Nah. You know I don't like being in this spot," I replied.

With that said, Mike handed me my money, and I told him that I was getting ready to step because I had a bad vibe, and something told me to get the hell out of there. But I never made it.

As soon as I hit the living room, the front door was kicked in. *"Boom!"*

"Lay down! Police! Don't move!" is all I heard before I darted for the back door. But to my surprise, it was kicked in also, and I was rushed and slammed to the floor.

I wasn't worried, because I knew I was clean. I also knew that Mike was dirty, and I could only imagine who else was dirty. While the officers were cuffing me up, I heard them in the bathroom wrestling with Mike. I figured that Mike was trying to flush his drugs.

"Bingo!" one of the officers yelled.

The officers searched me and took my money. They then escorted me, Mike, Rosco, Mike's boy, Thomas and a couple of fiends that had gotten caught with paraphernalia, outside and placed us in the paddy wagon.

As we were sitting in the paddy wagon, I leaned over and asked Mike what they caught him with.

"Two ounces!" he replied while trying to adjust the handcuffs on his wrists.

I then assured everyone that I would get them out on bond as long as they didn't cooperate with the police. Mike also told me that they found a Ruger 45 in the bedroom. I asked Rosco to take that charge, being as though it was his house and the gun was found in his room.

"Y'all ready to ride?" Officer Cooley asked after he opened the door to the paddy wagon.

"Ride where!" I blurted out.

"Oh, Mr. Davis. They didn't tell you that you are being charged with possession of crack cocaine?"

"Y'all ain't find shit on me!"

"We found six thousand dollars, and we figure you and your buddy here are partners," the officer said, pointing his finger at Mike. "So we'll just charge both of y'all."

"Fuck you! Y'all crackers are full of shit!" I barked angrily.

The officer read us our rights and slammed the door.

Mike leaned over and said, "That was nine grand I gave you. Them crackers must have kept three."

"Don't even trip," I replied.

When we arrived at the jail, the first thing I noticed was Ronnie Sims' truck with the "A-1 Bail Bonding" sign on it. Ronnie was Jarius's bondsman, and I had met him on a few occasions.

After everyone was fingerprinted and booked, Officer Cooley took us in front of the magistrate judge, and she set mine and Mike's bonds at seventy five thousand apiece. They charged Rosco with the gun and set his bond at ten thousand. She also gave the pipe heads one thousand dollar bonds apiece for getting caught with drug paraphernalia.

"How much is your bond?" Ronnie asked me as we exited the magistrate's office.

"Seventy five thousand."

"Jarius called and told me to get you."

"A'ight, but you got to get everybody out," I said as I explained to him how much their bonds were. I then told him that I would give him eighty eight hundred up front, and owe him eight being as though it was going to cost him sixteen thousand eight hundred dollars to get everyone out at ten percent.

Once outside the jail, I had Ronnie give me two hundred dollars so I could give it to Rosco for him and my new co-defendants to catch a cab back to Rosco's house. I then called Jarius from Ronnie's phone.

"Speak!" Jarius said, answering his phone with no manners.

"What's good?"

"You. What happened?" he asked, curious to know all of what occurred back at Rosco's house.

"I'll holla at you when I see you. Where you at anyway?"

"I'm on my way home. Have Ronnie drop you off there," he said in a forceful tone. He was beginning to get frustrated with me because he knew that something was bound to happen sooner or later, and I was beginning to get deeper and deeper in the game.

"Bet! But have nine g's ready for me so I can give it to Ronnie. I'll get you back tomorrow."

After I hung up the phone with Jarius, I told Ronnie what had transpired, and how the police took some of the money.

Ronnie told me that he wasn't surprised, because Cooley was a dirty narcotics officer, and that he would be on me from now on out. He also told me to hire Bob Lucas as my attorney, because Bob was like the white Johnny Cochran in North Carolina.

Once we reached Jarius's house, he came out and greeted us. He gave me the money to give to Ronnie. Jarius had no patience, because he asked for the business as soon as Ronnie pulled off. After I ran everything down to him, he told me not to sweat it because he had Bob's home number.

Jarius called Bob and explained to him the situation. He told Jarius to tell me that he would meet me at my first court appearance in the morning. He also told me to dress casual.

"I got to switch spots," I said after Jarius hung up the phone.

"Nah! You need to quit!" Jarius stated as our eyes locked in a silent battle "You done lost your damn mind. You're getting ready to throw away your whole career."

"I ain't gon' throw away shit! I know what the fuck I'm doing."

"Oh yeah? That's why you got locked the fuck up today, huh!" he said, getting angry at the fact that I was talking stupid again. "Let me ask you something, and this real talk. Do you think Michael Jordan is the greatest player to ever pick up a ball?"

"Hell yeah!"

"Well, you a damn fool!" he said, looking at me like I was crazy. "He might be the greatest player to ever play in the NBA, but there are niggas in the 'hood that will kill Jordan on the court. They have just been playground legends. You know why?" he asked as if I couldn't see where this was going. "Because they got caught up in the game. The same damn thing you gon' do if you don't get your shit together."

I was caught off guard with this conversation. Jarius had me sitting on the couch at a loss for words. Reality finally had hit me, and I knew that if I didn't get out now, I would probably end up trapped in the game, dead or in jail. "You're right," I said, finally agreeing with him. "I'm done!"

"Good!" he said, satisfied that I was getting out of the game.

"Now, let me get the keys to the Suburban, 'cause my car is over Regina's. I'll have her drive it to school for me on Friday. You know I got court in the morning."

Jarius dropped some more knowledge on me before giving me the keys to the truck. He wanted to make sure that my head was straight before I left.

When I pulled out of the driveway, the first person that I called was Regina.

"Hello," a female voice answered.

"What's up?" I asked, realizing it was Regina who had answered the phone.

"Where are you at?" she asked, glad to hear my voice and knowing that I was okay.

"On my way home."

"I called Jarius and told him what happened."

"I know. He told me you called. You were worried about Big Daddy, huh?"

"Nope. I just didn't want to see you go to jail."

"Whatever!" I chuckled, knowing that she was worried about me. "Get a change of clothes and meet me at the Holiday Inn on Old Garner Road."

"Okay," she said, happy that she was finally getting ready to spend some time with me. "What about your car?"

"I'ma leave it parked there. Your parents ain't gon' trip, are they?"

"No, they're cool," she assured me.

"A'ight. Well, hurry up!" I said as I pulled into the trailer park.

I ran in the house and grabbed a set of clothes before my mother came home. I didn't want to face her right now. I knew that once she found out that I got locked up, she was going to lecture me.

I contemplated on whether I should call Regina back and tell her to come over to the house, but I quickly erased that thought. I knew my mother wasn't going for Regina staying the night. The only female that could lay her head at my house would be Shanta. And speaking of her, I haven't spoken with her in a couple of days. We were growing further and further apart.

• • • • • • •

The next morning, I got up, showered and gave Regina the keys so she could drive my car to school the following day. I then set out for court.

Once I entered the courthouse, I spotted Mike talking to a Jewish guy whom I figured was his lawyer. But little did I know that Mike was talking to Jack Frulish. Jack was a well-respected and feared lawyer in the justice system.

"This is Andrew, who I was telling you about," Mike said as I approached them.

"Hi, Andrew. I'm Jack. I'm going to be representing Mike, and from my understanding, Bob is your attorney," he said with confidence and a swagger that would send a chill down any prosecutor's spine.

"Yeah, he is," I responded.

"Well, I know Bob, and from what it sounds like, you should be okay. But your buddy here getting caught flushing stuff might be a problem. Let me get with Bob, and we are going to play it by ear for now. At least until we get y'all a Motion for Discovery. Then maybe—and I mean maybe—we might beat this thing on 'Illegal Search and Seizure'."

"Now that what's I'm talking about!" Mike replied,

hoping that we would be able to beat this case.

I gave Jack a firm handshake and told Mike that I would catch up with him later. I then headed to Courtroom One where I was scheduled for my first appearance.

When I entered the courtroom, I noticed Bob talking to the District Attorney. I found a seat and watched as he worked his magic. When he was finished, he exited the courtroom and motioned for me to follow him. He then informed me that he had rescheduled my court date due to the fact that the judge was in a grouchy mood.

I gave Bob my personal number and told him to contact me as soon as he found anything out. I also let him know that Jack would be representing Mike.

Since I had gotten out of court early, I decided to go ahead and attend school. It seemed as if all eyes were on me as soon as I entered the classroom. I had no idea that the drug raid was on the news, or that I had made the front pages of the *Daily News* and *Observer*.

It was the beginning of third period, and someone must have told the coach that I come to school, because as soon as I got seated, he called me to his office.

"Boy, what the hell have you done gotten yourself into?" he asked as soon as I walked into his office.

"Coach, they didn't find anything on me," I said, trying to plead my case.

"Well that's not what this paper says," he responded while pointing at today's headline.

I glanced at the paper and was perplexed. I couldn't believe what I saw. There it read:

Clayton High Star Running Back Caught in Drug Raid!

"Coach, this bullshit!"

"Watch your mouth!"

"Well it is! The only thing that they found on me was some money."

"And speaking of money, where the hell you get six

thousand dollars from?" he asked with a look of hurt and anger. He had no idea that I was involved in the drug game. He knew about Jarius and had even spoken to him about keeping me away from the fast life.

"Coach, I was holding that money for somebody," I replied, really wanting to tell him that it was nine thousand dollars instead of six.

"Son, I was born at night, but it sure as hell wasn't last night! So I guess that's how you got that new car?"

"No. I told you that my grandfather bought it for me," I lied, thinking back to the day when Coach asked me about the car.

"Well, I hope he takes it from you too, but that's not what this is about," he said in a serious but firm voice.

"I know you're not kicking me off the team!"

"No son, but the school is suspending you from the team until you get this matter resolved."

"Come on, Coach! How are they gon' do that?" I pleaded, hoping that the coach would have some sympathy for me.

"Son, it's in the school policy, along with the Board of Education. It simply says right here…" He pulled out the policy. "…'If any student athlete gets charged with a felony, he or she is to be suspended from the team until the charges have been reduced to a misdemeanor, or either be dismissed.'"

"And what happens if they ain't?"

"Well, if there not, you can't play any sports."

Fuck! I thought to myself as a tear came trickling down my cheek.

Coach tried to console me, but I wasn't trying to hear it, until he said that he had a friend who was a District Attorney, and that he would check with him to see if he could help me out.

I was so embarrassed and ashamed that I left school early. Not being able to play the game that I loved so much had me pissed. On my way home I called my attorney's office.

"Lucas, Sanders and Carter!" the receptionist said, answering the phone.

"May I speak with Bob Lucas?"

"May I ask who's calling?"

"Andrew Davis."

"Please hold, Mr. Davis

"Yes, Andrew? How may I help you?" Bob answered.

"You seen the newspaper?"

"No, I haven't seen it today."

"Well, I need this problem resolved ASAP"

"Things like this take time, Andrew."

"Time I don't have, but money I do. I need this taken care of, or they're not going to let me play ball!" I said in a demanding voice that caught Bob by surprise. I then explained to him the situation, and he assured me that this problem would be resolved, but in time.

When I got off of the phone with my attorney, I called Jarius and explained the situation to him also.

• • • • • • •

It was Friday night, and I was so depressed that I didn't leave the house since I found out I was suspended from the team.

"Boy, what you still doing home, and why you sitting in the dark looking stupid?" my mother asked as she walked into the house and flipped the light switch on.

"I ain't looking stupid!" I replied, sitting on the couch with a sour look on my face.

"Boy, come here and talk to me," she said as she walked into the kitchen. "What you gon' do with yourself?" she asked as she began to wash her hands so she could prepare dinner.

"I don't know. What ever happened to innocent until proven guilty?" I asked as I sat down at the kitchen table.

"I want you to listen to me, and listen to me good," my mother said as she tightened her lips to control her emotions. "God knows I've been trying to keep you out of those streets since you was ten. You're a young man now, and you're pretty much gon' do what you want. But I know you gon' run them streets, 'cause you're too much like your daddy."

I didn't know too much about my father, except that he was a big time gambler and a bank robber. My mother came home from work one day and found him dead. He was shot three times in the head when I was two years old. We were living in Jacksonville, Florida at that time, but after the incident my mother packed up and moved back to North Carolina.

"Boy, the streets don't love nobody, but you damn sure love them streets. Now, I've never told you this and I never told the police either. That's one thing I did learn from your father: Never tell the police shit!" she said, giving me a blank stare. "Your father lived by the gun and he died by the gun. 'Death before dishonor' were his favorite words. Son, keep your enemies close to you, but most of all watch your friends, especially the ones that you're close to. You're probably wondering why I'm telling you this, ain't you."

"Yeah," I replied, knowing that she was getting ready to tell me something that I didn't want to hear.

"Because, your father was killed by his partner," she stated, pausing to release a long sad sigh. "They had just pulled off a job, and your father told me before he left that morning that this would be the last one. When I got home, I found my baby dead!"

I was shocked! I wasn't expecting my mother to get this deep with me. *No wonder she was so hard on me as a youngster. She didn't want to see me become a product of my environment.* I held her while wiping the tears from her eyes.

"Boy, I refuse to bury you!" she said, squeezing me as if this was going to be her last time seeing me. "Now, I'm not telling you to go out to them streets, but be careful, please! I'd rather come visit you in jail than visit your grave."

Chapter Ten
"Addicted to the Life"

Six Months Later...

It has been six months since my mother and I had our colloquy. I had replayed that conversation over in my head at least a hundred times.

A lot had changed in the past six months. I had quit school officially. My drug charge was still pending. I figured if I couldn't play ball, then school was a waste of my time. But in all actuality, I was becoming addicted. I was addicted to money and the lifestyle that the streets brought. I was back to hustling, and the money was coming in abundance. I still had Trick on my team. Trick was clean now, and the only things that were on my mind were money and pussy.

Shanta and I had split officially. I was tired of the 'do right' speeches and told her that I thought it was best if we saw other people. She threw a hissy fit when I told her that, but after I told her that I wasn't about to change and that I needed some time to myself, she understood, and we agreed to always be friends/fuck buddies.

• • • • • • •

It was Saturday, and the fellows and I were going out to Big Daddy's. Big Daddy's was the hottest nightclub in Raleigh, and everybody who was anybody was going to be there tonight.

As I pulled in the club's parking lot, I noticed Jarius's brand new Lexus G.S.300 parked beside Mike's '92 turquoise ZR1 Corvette, followed by Reese's cream 5451 BMW.

The line to the club was going around the building, but I knew I was going to play the celebrity status roll, due to the fact that my cousin, Big Boy, was working security at the door.

Once inside, I made my way to the bar. Buying alcohol wasn't a problem for me, even though I was under age. While at the bar, I was greeted by a few dudes that I knew, and some that I didn't, but saw around. You couldn't help but to acknowledge my presence. I had on cream Prada slacks and a tight, black silk Prada shirt that showed off every muscle in my upper body. I also had on black Prada shoes to complete my outfit. I was dressed to play the part of a baller.

"What's up?" Mike asked as he approached me. "Dressed to impress tonight, ain't you?"

"Nah, this is just a little something I put together for tonight," I replied after I placed my order with the bartender.

After I received my drink, Mike and I slid off to the second floor so we could hook up with Reese, Dre and Jarius. The second floor was where all the so called big boyz hung at. When we reached the second floor, I noticed Jarius talking to Big Z in the corner. As I mentioned earlier, Big Z was a big boy for real. He was a made man, no doubt.

Mike and I went and posted up beside Reese and Dre, who was playing pool at the last pool table.

Jarius came over and joined us shortly after. "What's up?" he asked as he approached me.

"What's that nigga talking about?" I responded, referring to Big Z.

"He wants me to holla at him about some work," Jarius replied as he grabbed the blunt from Dre.

"What's his prices like?" I asked, wondering if I could

beat their connect price in New York.

"Twenty-two."

"Shit, that's two extra grand!" I spat, knowing that they were getting them for twenty grand a pop in New York. "That nigga knows we're getting ten?"

"Nah, I just told him. I had to holla at you first," Jarius said as he peered around the room to make sure that no one was eavesdropping on our conversation. "But check this out. He said that whatever we buy, he'll throw us the same."

"I don't know about that shit. I'm fine working for myself," I stated in a stern tone. "But tell that nigga to let us get them for twenty, and we don't want no front... or at least I don't anyway."

"Me either, but he said this would be a two-time thing and then he's done."

I was beginning to think seriously about Big Z's proposal. I was trying to do the math in my head, but there were too many numbers for me to figure up. "Fuck it! We'll do the math tomorrow and see what we can make off of this shit," I said as I looked around the club, admiring all of the beautiful women around me. There were at least four women to every one man, so if a nigga couldn't get any pussy tonight, his game wasn't up to par.

"Jarius, there goes your girl," Reese said as he spotted Jarius's childhood girlfriend.

"Who?" he replied, eager to know who Reese was talking about.

"Kita."

"Stop playing with me!" he said as he put his fifty cents onto the pool table for the next game.

"Nigga, you ain't say that when we was little!" Reese responded as he watched everybody bust out laughing.

"Yo, who's that with them?" I asked with my eyes full of lust.

"Who?" Jarius asked.

"Behind Iris," I said, trying to remember where I saw the young lady's face before.

"Oh shit! That's Deemi!" Jarius responded.

"Little Deemi?" I asked, as I looked closer to make sure that my eyes weren't playing tricks on me. *Damn!* I thought to myself as I tried to recall the last time that I had seen Deemi. I actually haven't seen her in five years. She used to have a crush on me when we were younger, but after I got sent to the group home, her family moved to Seattle, Washington.

"Yo, they're coming over here," Dre said, breaking into my thoughts.

Deemi used to be what some people would consider anorexic, but not anymore. She was about 5'7", 140 pounds, and thick as hell. That girl had curves in all the right places. Plus, it wasn't hurting that she was wearing the shit out of that Coogi dress.

"Hey, y'all!" the girls said as they surrounded the pool table.

"What's up?" Jarius responded. "I know y'all want something to drink. That's the only reason y'all came over here."

"Shut up, boy! And you know we want something to drink!"

"Deemi, you ain't speaking?" I asked, trying to make conversation. "Girl, come give me a hug!" I said while placing my drink on the edge of the pool table. She smelled so good and felt so soft to me as I held her tender body up against my masculine frame. "Humph! Girl, you look good!" I said as I eyed her appreciatively and took a step back so that I could admire her beauty.

"Thank you. You don't look bad yourself," she grinned in a lustful manner. "And where did you get all of them muscles from?" she asked as she squeezed my biceps.

"So, I take it that you still like me."

"I see you're still crazy."

"Nah, I'm just messing with you. So, you back to visit?"

"No, we moved back."

"Word!" I said, acting as if I was surprised. "How long y'all been back?"

"About a week."

"Where y'all staying at?"

"On Wash Street."

"Where at?"

"In the yellow house down from Willie D's."

I took a sip of my drink as I tried to remember the last time that I'd been over to Willie D's. Ever since Trick has been clean, I very seldom went on that side of town. Trick was holding it down. I made a mental note to ask him why he didn't tell me that someone moved into the yellow house on the corner. "So, you don't mind if I stop by and check on you?"

"I would like that," Deemi replied in her most convincing voice. "You know I heard about your football situation."

"I see the streets are still talking about that bullshit," I stated, surprised that she brought up my football situation. "Hopefully I'll be back next year," I said, knowing that I had no intentions on going back to school. I did miss playing football, but I was enjoying the street life and the money that it was providing for me to even think about going back to school. "So, how's your family?" I asked, trying to change subject.

"They're fine. Tre is a mess. Wait until you see him."

"What's up for tomorrow?" I asked, trying to set up a date.

"I don't know. Call me."

We exchanged numbers, and Deemi went on to enjoy the rest of her night.

The club was getting ready to close within the next hour. Jarius and the fellows went outside to the parking lot.

I was coming out of the restroom when I bumped into Sarah. Sarah was an older female. She was twenty-six to be exact, and I have been trying to get at her for quite some time now. She was wifey material, and I knew that. She was a graduate from Winston-Salem State, and was now a school teacher. She wasn't only smart and beautiful, but she knew exactly what she wanted in life and in her man.

As we were holding a conversation, a female named Gianna that I knew from State Street came running up to me, telling me that Jarius was outside fighting.

Once I got outside, it was like a royal rumble. I spotted Reese and Dre fighting heads up with two dudes. I also spotted

Mike stabbing a guy, which wasn't a surprise to me, being as though he was known for stabbing people. When I finally spotted Jarius, I took off running to the car. I knew that there was nothing that I could do due to the fact that there were at least ten dudes stomping Jarius out.

I popped the trunk and grabbed my Mini-14 with the folding stock and fifty round clip. I then ran back to where Jarius was. "Get off him!" I yelled as I shot in the air three times. "Get up, nigga!" I said to Jarius.

"Y'all got me, but somebody's gon' die tonight!" Jarius yelled with a look that would let a total stranger know that he meant business.

Jarius then grabbed the gun from me and turned it on the dudes that had stomped him. They were climbing into a white Suburban. He ran and stood about fifteen feet in front of the truck and let the Mini-14 bark. All you could hear was the shots ripping into the truck and dudes screaming like bitches. The scene looked like something you would see in a movie.

Then, out of nowhere, undercover cops yelled, "Drop the gun and lay down!"

I was standing right beside Jarius when the officers drew their weapons, but instead of seeing how things were going to play out, I ran, and I was hoping that Jarius would drop the gun and run too. When I looked back, I noticed that he was doing exactly what the officers said.

Damn fool! I thought to myself as I continued to run. I ran through the parking lot in search of anyone that I knew.

"Over here!" I heard a familiar voice say.

I turned in the direction that I heard the voice, and noticed that it was Deemi with the back door to Kita's car open. "Can you drive?" I asked Deemi as I got in the car.

"Yeah, I can drive. Why?" she responded, knowing that I wanted her to do something for me.

"I need to go get my car."

"Boy, is you crazy!" she defensively stated. "They're shooting around there!"

"No they ain't. That was Jarius," I said, while trying to

catch my breath.

"So go get your own car!"

"I can't. I had to bounce from the po-po."

With that said, Deemi stuck her hands out for me to give her my keys. "Which one is it?" she asked, but before I could respond, Irish said, "I know, girl. Come on."

· · · · · ·

Kita and I were sitting in her car at Crown gas station, smoking a blunt and waiting on Deemi and Irish. "Pass the blunt," I said as I noticed Jarius's Lexus, followed by his Acura turn into the gas station. "How did you get Jarius's car?" I asked Irish as she stepped out of the Lexus as if it where her own.

"He told the police that I was his sister."

"And they let him give you the keys?"

"Yep, and he said to give it to you," she said, referring to the car. "And, to wait for his call."

I got out of the car with Kita and into the car with Deemi. I then instructed Kita and Irish to follow me, because I was going to the apartment that Jarius and I shared in North Raleigh. Neither one of us had ever stayed at the apartment except on the weekends.

Once we got to the apartment, I called the county jail to see if they were going to give Jarius a bond. I knew they wouldn't due to the violent offense, but I felt that I had to call anyway.

"Y'all staying the night here?" I asked as I emerged from the back room.

"Hell yeah! I ain't driving all the way back to Clayton," Kita said as she kicked off her shoes and lay on the couch.

"Well, make yourself at home," I said as I went and got a glass of orange juice. I told the girls that one of them could sleep in Jarius's room, and that I would be in my room if they needed anything.

On the way back to my room, I thought about telling Deemi to come with me, but my mind was more focused on Jarius and how fucked up the past few months had been.

I was lying in my bed about to doze off when I heard a sudden knock. "Who is it?" I asked as I pulled the cover from over my head.

"You alright?" Deemi asked as she peeped her head around the door.

"Yeah, I'm cool. Just tired as hell."

"You want me to leave?"

"Nah, you straight," I said as I watched her sit at the edge of his bed.

Deemi and I engaged in conversation for about twenty minutes before she decided to lie down beside me.

"Amir, where's your girl at?" she asked, catching me off guard with that question.

"Me and my girl decided to see other people, with her being away at college. Plus, I really wasn't feeling the long distance relationship."

With that said, Deemi mounted me and gave me a passionate kiss. She wasted no time, and I was caught off guard by her aggressiveness. She slid my gym shorts and boxers off in what seemed like one motion, and watched my dick reach its full potential. She grabbed my dick with her right hand and traced the head with her fingers. She then placed me inside her mouth.

"Ssst! Oh shit!" I moaned in a voice that made her panties wet as I placed my hands gently behind her head and watched as she played hide and seek with my dick. I tried to signal to her that my volcano was about to erupt, but she never moved and took every bit of my eruption in her mouth. "Shit!" I said as she sucked me dry, drinking my cum as if she was drinking warm milk.

I continued to lie in bed as I watched Deemi undress herself. Her body was flawless, and just seeing her nude body sent a chill up my spine. "Come here!" I demanded as I made room for her to get back in the bed. I kissed and licked her whole body. I traveled back to her breasts. First her right one, then her left.

She arched her back each time I licked, sucked, and nibbled.

"Oh… my… God!" she moaned, loving the feeling of my warm mouth on her nipples.

"Squeeze your nipples for me!" I said as I slid to the floor and positioned myself on my knees. I grabbed her by her thighs and pulled her to the edge of the bed. I placed my arms under her thighs and lifted her until her entrance met my face. Deemi was completely bald, and I loved it, because it gave me a clear view of her pussy. I licked her thighs deeply, and the closer I got to her entrance, the deeper I licked. I played, licked, kissed, and sucked in rotation, switching from one thigh to the other. Finally, I licked between her lips and above them. She shivered as I sucked her clit.

"Oh! Oh… Amir! I'm coming!" she cried as she hit the point of no return.

I then inserted two fingers into her vagina with my palms facing her belly button in search of her G-spot. I rubbed her vaginal walls with my fingers approximately three to four inches up until I felt the spongy flesh of her G-spot.

"Oh… my… God! That's my spot!" she screamed as I stroked her G-spot with a "come here" motion that gave her the deepest feeling orgasm that she has ever experienced.

She then guided my dick into her soaking wet pussy. "Fuck me!" she demanded as I began to beat the pussy up with short strokes.

"You like? Huh? You like this?" I asked as I continued to dick her down.

"Yes! Ooooh, yes!" she moaned in my ear.

After several minutes of missionary position, I switched over to doggy style.

"Baby, please don't cum in me," Deemi said, knowing that I was getting ready to bust at any moment.

After I nutted, she grabbed my dick and slid it in her anus. This was new to me, but I had heard Jarius and a few old heads talk about it. Not wanting to disappoint her, I went with the flow and was surprised that she could take all eight and three-quarter inches of my dick in her ass. This was an amazing moment for me, and I enjoyed every minute of it.

• • • • • • •

"Ring - Ring – Ring!"

"Hello," I mumbled, answering the phone.

"You have a collect call from the Wake County Jail. To accept, press zero. To decline, press five. Caller, please state your name."

I pressed zero, never giving Jarius the time to say his name.

"What's up!" Jarius asked, realizing that the operator had connected us.

"Sleep. What's up with you?" I asked, glad to hear his voice.

"Shit! Just got off the phone with the lawyer."

"What 's he talking about?"

"Don't know yet. He said he'll be up here first thing in the morning."

"What do they got you charged with?"

"Three attempts."

"What?" I said, surprised that he wasn't charged with murder.

"Look, I don't want to talk too much over this phone, but I need to see you."

"When is visitation?"

"Twelve to four."

"I'll be there. I got some shit to tell you anyway."

I glanced over at the clock and realized that it was 10:45 a.m. I then got up and hit the shower.

While I was getting dressed, I couldn't help but to stare at Deemi and how beautiful she looked while asleep. I started to think about the crazy sex that we had only a few hours ago, and pondered if she was a freak, or was she just giving me special treatment. Whatever it was, I made a mental note to ask her about it.

I woke her up and told her that I had some moves to make, but they could chill. I left a thousand dollars in my dresser before I left just to see if she could be trusted, or if she would rummage through my stuff.

· · · · · · ·

That Same Day...

The line for visitation was packed. I was amazed at how many people were coming out to see their loved ones. It was going on two o'clock, and I had been waiting for over an hour to see Jarius.

"Yo, Tasha!" I said, noticing her get off the elevator.

"Hey, Amir! What's up?" she replied, happy to see that I had made it.

Tasha was Jarius's main girl. She was Dominican, and was extremely beautiful with the body of a goddess.

"Ain't nothing."

"Jarius didn't think you was coming," she said while giving me a hug.

"Oh yeah? Why you leaving so early?"

"'Cause they only get thirty minutes a visitor, and two different visits."

"Oh, okay."

I then heard the officer call my name to go up to visit Jarius. "Well, that's me, but holla at me if you need anything," I told her, giving her another hug.

· · · · · · ·

Back at the apartment, Deemi was sleeping good until Kita woke her up. "Girl, get up! It's almost three o'clock!" Kita said as she tugged on the covers.

Deemi got up and got herself together while Kita and Irish straightened up the apartment. She wondered if I thought she was some type of whore. She most definitely didn't want me to have the wrong impression of her, because she was really feeling me.

"So, how was it?" Kita asked, bringing Deemi out of her deep thoughts.

"How was what?"

"Girl, don't play crazy. We heard y'all fucking like hell."

"Damn! Y'all some nosey bitches!" Deemi said, grinning foolishly as she thought about her "sexcapades" with me.

"Ain't nobody nosy. All that hollering you was doing!"

"Just know that he can hold his own," she replied as she put the finishing touches on my room.

"Damn! I sure wish I could have fucked Jarius last night," Kita said, knowing that she would never get another piece of him.

"Girl, bring your crazy ass on so we can go!"

• • • • • •

"How you doing?" I asked Jarius as I sat across from him. He was wearing an orange jumpsuit.

"I'm fine. The lawyer wants twenty grand."

"That ain't no problem."

"I know, but shit looks fucked up for your boy," he said in a tone that worried me.

"What was that shit about anyway?"

"I was outside pimping, when I spotted Rale arguing with this broad. So, I went to get her, but the bitch she was arguing with flipped on me. So I cursed the bitch out." He paused, and we shared a tense moment of silence as he replayed the situation in his head. "Then, some dude said something, and it went from there."

"So, have you hollered at Rale?" I asked, not shocked that Rale was in the center of this whole situation. She was Jarius's baby mother, and as far as I was concerned, she had some mental issues.

"Yeah, she's cool. I told her that she couldn't come today 'cause I had to see you and Tasha."

"Did the police ask about me?"

"They just asked who was that who ran, but you know I

ain't talking to them bastards."

"So, what you need me to do?" I asked, ready for the task at hand.

"First of all, I need you to get what money I got left in the streets. Reese and Dre both owe me thirty-six grand apiece. Give twenty to the lawyer and put the rest up for me."

"You want me to give it to Tasha?"

"Nah, she's straight. I got like eighty grand over there."

"What do you want me to do with the Lexus?"

"Drive it. That joint's brand new."

"Bet!" I said, knowing that my pussy rate was getting ready to go to the moon. "Yo, you know I fucked Deemi last night."

"Stop playing!"

"Yeah. I had them come over to the spot. I fucked shorty in the ass and everything!" I said with a big smirk on my face.

"Deemi's off the hook like that?"

"I don't know, but I'm going to find out the scoop on her," I halfheartedly replied, hoping that she wasn't a freak and was just giving me special treatment. "But on the real, I need to make a move up top, but I know ol' boy and them are used to us getting our usual. And with you in here, shit's gon' change," I boasted nonchalantly. "I'm just gon' have to step up and get half the order myself."

"You know you can get that eighty if you want it. Tasha's gon' be straight. She knows where some more money is at."

"Nah, I'm straight, unless you want me to flip something for you."

"Nigga, go get that eighty and do you with it. Just don't forget about your boy."

"Come on, dog! How can I do that?"

"So when you trying to handle that?" Jarius asked.

"Probably tomorrow, after I finish handling your business. But tell ol' girl I'm going to come get that tonight."

•   •   •   •   •   •   •

I was coming out of the jail thinking of all the power moves that I was getting ready to make, when my phone rang. I glanced at the caller ID and noticed the unfamiliar number, 554-3563. I pondered, trying to recall the number. *Who is this?* I thought to myself as I answered the phone.

"May I speak to Andrew?" the sexy but unknown voice asked.

This really threw me for a loop, because I only knew two females that called me by my government name: Shanta and my mother. "This me. Who's this?" I asked, curious to know who the caller was.

"Boy, this Deemi!"

"What's up with you?"

"Nothing. Just calling to let you know that I was home and that I locked your apartment up."

"Alight! Have you eaten yet?"

"Nah. Why?"

"'Cause I'm gon' come scoop you about 5:30. I know this nice little spot where we can eat and rap."

"That's cool, 'cause we do need to talk."

"About what?" I questioned, hoping that she would say last night.

"Last night."

"Yeah, I want to talk about that too. So be ready, alright?"

• • • • • • •

I was running a little late. It was almost 6:30, when I arrived at Deemi's house.

"Where are we going to eat at?" she asked me as she sat in the car and adjusted her seat.

"This new spot out on Highway 42 called Mitchell's Steak House," I responded while glancing down at her thighs. "Girl, you look good in that outfit!"

"Thank you. So, how is Jarius? What the hell happened last night?"

"Who're you working for?" I asked her, laughing as I

placed the car in drive.

"Don't play me like that!" she retorted.

Deemi and I waited in the lobby of Mitchell's to be seated. I had requested that Tonya be our waitress, because she always let me drink.

"What's up, Tonya?" I asked as she escorted us to our table.

"Hi, Amir! Would you like something to drink now, or would you like to wait until you place your order?"

"Yeah. Let me get a Hennessy straight up, and keep them coming," I insisted, knowing that she was going to do just that.

Tonya was a few years older than I was. She was originally from Nashville, Tennessee but moved to North Carolina so she could attend college at North Carolina State, in Raleigh.

"And you, ma'am?" Tonya asked Deemi.

"Water will be fine," She replied as she continued to look through the menu. "I take it you two know each other?" Deemi asked me as Tonya went to get our drinks.

"Not really. Every time we come here she's always our waitress. Plus, she be letting us get our drink on. But I think she likes me though," I said with a smile on my face as I watched Tonya return with our drinks.

"Are y'all ready to order yet?" she asked as she placed the drinks on the table.

"I am, but I don't know about the lady," I said, and took a sip of my drink.

"Well, let me guess. You want the steak and potato, with your steak cooked well done, and broiled shrimp and salad."

"Yep!"

"And you, ma'am?"

"I would like the sirloin steak and French fries."

"Ma'am you get another side order with that."

"No, that won't be necessary."

"Okay. I'll keep a check on y'all."

"Thank you," I said, and watched Tonya walk off.

"Damn! Don't break your neck!" Deemi snapped, getting offended that I would be eyeing another woman in her presence, as if she wasn't a sight to see herself.

"What, you jealous?"

"No!" she said with attitude in her voice.

"Nah. But shorty got an ass on her to be a white girl," I said, giving credit where credit was due. Tonya had more ass than the average black woman, but not only did she have a body, she was extraordinarily beautiful.

"I can't even hate on her. She is thick for a white girl." Deemi said, finally giving Tonya her props.

"So, what's up?"

"You tell me."

"Nah, you tell me. What's up with last night?"

"I knew you were getting ready to bring that up. Well, to be honest with you, I don't want you to think I'm some kind of whore or something, because I'm not. You know you were the first boy that I had a crush on, so I had to make sure that I satisfied you."

"You most definitely did that!" I admitted as I watched a slight giggle escape her sexy lips. "I'm talking about that booty shot!"

"Well, when I was in Seattle, I dated this older guy. I moved in with him for a little while. But anyway, I'm the type of person who always wants to satisfy her man. I've read books by Zane, and even read a few articles in magazines talking about anal sex. You'd be surprised at how many women like to have it. But like I was saying, my boyfriend asked me if we could try it, and for a while I said no. Then after I continued to read different books on relationships and sex, I came to find out that if a woman won't satisfy her man, then the next bitch would, and I wasn't going for that. So, we tried it, and I liked it. You and him are the only two people I've done it with."

"So, you willing to keep your man satisfied, huh?"

"By all means necessary," she replied, and took a sip of her water.

"What happened to y'all's relationship?" I asked.

"Oh, he became real abusive, so I left him and went to stay with my girlfriend, Joy for about four months before we moved back home."

"You got any goals for the future?" I asked, trying to see where her head was at.

"Actually I do. I was attending this community college back in Seattle for cosmetology, but now that I'm back home, I'm gon' try to get into Sherl's Cosmetology School here in Raleigh."

"That's what's up!" I said, glad to know that she had a goal that she was trying to achieve.

"Yeah, I would like my own beauty salon one day." She inwardly smiled as she pictured her salon in her mind. "So, what are you gon' do?" she asked me as Tonya came out of the back with our food.

We ate while I explained to Deemi my school situation, and now that football was out of the picture, I had to hold things down, especially with Jarius being locked up. I was glad to know that she was only trying to please me, but the truth be told, she had me open.

Time was winding down, and I knew I had to get to Raleigh so that I could get with Reese and Dre. I figured since I was right here by I-40, I might as well take Deemi with me. I called Reese and Dre on my way out of the restaurant and had them meet me at Blue Whale Car Wash, on New Bern Avenue.

When I pulled up at the car wash, Reese was helping Dre wash his old school baby blue '69 Cadillac. Dre had one of the cleanest old schools throughout the city.

I stood outside of the car wash and gave Reese and Dre the game. I informed them that they would be dealing with me from this day forward. I assured them that things weren't going to change even though Jarius was locked up.

I didn't stay at the car wash long. I took the seventy-two grand that I just picked up from Reese and Dre and placed it in the attic of our apartment. I switched cars so that I could put some miles on Jarius's new G.S.

"You ready to go home?" I asked Deemi as we pulled out of the apartment complex.

"Why? You ready to take me home?"

"Nah. I just asked 'cause I got a stop to make, and if you're gon' chill with me, then I can go ahead to my destination."

"Yeah, I'm with you."

"Good, 'cause I'm going to need you to help me do something," I said as I got on the Beltline and headed to Tasha and Jarius's condo in Mini City.

When I arrived at the condo, Tasha answered the door wearing nothing but a towel. "Girl, put on some clothes!" I said as I shut the door behind me.

"Boy, you ain't nobody!" she replied, putting an extra bounce in her step and giving me a clear view of her fat ass.

"You got that for me!" I asked, ignoring her comment but admiring her ravishing body as her ass jiggled from side to side.

"It's in my room."

Once inside the bedroom, Tasha's phone rang. She pointed to the duffel bag as she went to answer it.

"Is that Jarius?" I asked as I was securing the bag across my shoulder.

"No, it's Joey."

Joey was her cousin and our connect. We have been dealing with him and his partner, Tito for almost a year.

"Let me holla at him," I said, reaching out for the phone.

"What's up, *papi*?" Joey asked, knowing that this would be a business conversation.

"*Yo necesito vente.*" I said, applying the Spanish that I had learned while I was in school.

"Okay, come see me."

"*Yo vive usted en el fin de semana.*"

"Okay, *papi*. See you by the end of the week."

"Okay," I said, and handed Tasha back the phone.

With that taken care of, I headed over to my mother's house so that I could pick up the rest of the money I needed so that I could go to New York and handle my business.

When I arrived at my mother's house, I noticed a Ford Taurus parked beside her new Nissan Maxima that I had just bought for her. My mother no longer lived in the trailer park. I had put down a fifteen thousand dollar deposit on a brand new, three-bedroom, two and a half bathroom house. It also had a garage and a back porch that was custom made.

I opened the door and was startled to see my sister sitting on the couch with some dude who she must have met while she was in the military. I hadn't seen Sharon in almost three years, ever since I graduated from the group home.

"What's up, girl?" I said as she stood up to give me a hug.

"I was just getting ready to call you," she said, holding me as if this was her first time ever seeing me.

"So, what brought you home?"

"Momma didn't tell you?"

"Tell me what?" I asked, knowing that Sharon had some shit with her.

"I'm pregnant!"

"You're what?" I asked as if I didn't hear her the first time.

"I'm pregnant!"

"I know what you said," I stated with mixed emotions. I was actually happy that I was going to be an uncle. I was just hoping that the child's father wouldn't leave Sharon to raise the baby by herself. "So, who is this? Your baby's daddy?" I asked.

My sister then introduced Charles to me.

"Boy, ain't you gon' introduce your friend?"

"Ma, this is Deemi."

"Deemi who?" she asked as she grabbed her glasses off of the coffee table.

"Little Deemi. Well, she ain't little no more, but you know her parents."

"Who are her parents?" my mother asked.

But before I could respond, Deemi said, "Rose and Mack Williams."

"Oh yeah, child! I remember you used to call here late at night wanting to talk to Amir."

With them reacquainted, I went to my room and handled my business. I knew after I gave the lawyer twenty grand that I would only have a hundred and thirty thousand dollars of Jarius's money, and I needed a hundred and eighty grand so that I could purchase the ten kilos of cocaine from our connect. The money wasn't an issue, because I had almost a hundred grand of my own money. I opened my safe and took out twelve stacks. I knew that would be sixty grand, because I kept my money in five grand stacks. I placed the money in a backpack and zoomed back to the living room.

"You ready?" I asked Deemi.

"Whenever you are."

"Where are you going?" my sister asked, not wanting me to leave.

"I got something I got to take care of."

"You coming back?"

"Nah, I'm going to my apartment."

"Where at?"

"In Raleigh."

"That boy got his own apartment and don't even stay there," my mother chimed in.

"Well, I am tonight, 'cause me and Deemi are going half."

"Half on what?" my mother asked.

"A baby!"

"Boy, get your crazy ass out of my house!" my mother said, and laughed.

I sat around the house for another twenty minutes. "Sis, you straight?" I asked her as I was getting ready to leave.

"Yeah," she replied, knowing deep down that she wanted to ask me for some money. Sharon and her boyfriend were in a financial bind, but she didn't want to uncloak their situation.

"So, you got some money?"

"A little," she replied blandly.

Getting the funny feeling that my sister didn't have too much money, I dug into my pockets and gave her fifteen hundred. "Spend that how you want," I said to my sister while giving her baby's daddy a look of pure hatred. "If that nigga don't take care of that baby, I will, so don't be saving that money!" I shouted, and slammed the door behind me to let everyone in the house know that I meant business.

. . . .

For the next two and a half hours, Deemi fed the money machine while I separated and prepared it so that I could stash it in the Suburban. Jarius had an electrical stash box in the Suburban that would hold up to twenty-five kilos or a lot of cash.

Kita had informed Deemi that Jarius and I were getting money, but she had no idea that we were getting this much money. She couldn't believe that she had just counted over one hundred and eighty thousand dollars.

After I secured the money, I called Karen, only to find out that she couldn't make the trip. She was going out of town with her family. Karen was the woman that usually trafficked our drugs and money.

"Shit!" I squalled in a frustrating tone.

"What's wrong?"

"I need this girl to go with me out of town tomorrow, but she can't go," I said, contemplating my next move.

"I'll go with you," Deemi replied, catching me off guard with her response.

I then told her what type of trip this would be, and was shocked when she told me she was down for whatever for me.

Chapter Eleven
"Can't Win For Losing"

1997

It's been over a year now that Deemi and I been fucking. We were living in the apartment that I once shared with Jarius. Deemi had proven her loyalty to me by putting her life on the line by trafficking cocaine for me.

I had taken the game to another level in the past year. Everyone in my entourage was making more money than they had ever made under Jarius.

Jarius had taken a plea for nine years, and if he keeps his nose clean and stays out of trouble he can be out in seven. Mike also had taken a plea. His was for six years. My charge had been dismissed due to the fact that Mike was caught with the drugs in his possession.

Everything was running smooth for me except for the cocaine drought. My connect hasn't had any cocaine in over two months. I would stumble over a couple of kilos once every few weeks but, I would break those down for my loyal customers.

. . . .

It was Tuesday, and I was on my way to the Waffle House on Capital Boulevard to meet Brenda, a correctional officer who worked at the prison that Jarius was being housed at. I was sending Jarius a quarter pound of marijuana through her. As I was turning into the Waffle House, my phone rang. "Hello."

"What's up, *papi*?" The familiar voice on the other end said.

"What's up!" I replied, knowing that it was my connect, Joey.

"I just called to let you know that I was in DC, dancing," he said, letting me know that he had finally got some coke.

"When can I see you?"

"Whenever."

We shared a little small talk, and I was relieved to know that I didn't have to make the nine hour trip to New York. Raleigh was only a four hour drive to DC.

As I was hanging up the phone with Joey, Brenda was pulling up beside me. "What's up, boy?" she asked as she got in the car with me.

"You! What's up with my boy?" I asked, referring to Jarius.

"He's cool. Always in every damn thing."

"Tell that nigga I'm going to come check him next week," I said, passing her the sandwich bag full of weed.

"Boy, when are you going to give me some of that dick?" she asked, confident that I would break her off sooner or later.

"What you say, girl?"

"You heard me!"

"If I wasn't in a rush I'd give it to you now!" I replied while rubbing my crotch as my soldier stood at full attention ready to salute. "Look at what you did talking crazy!"

Brenda looked down and noticed the bulge in my pants. "Don't worry about it. I'll take care of him," she said as she leaned over and unbuttoned my pants.

I leaned the seat back on the GS and watched her commence to sucking. Brenda sucked me until I exploded in her mouth. She took every bullet that my soldier shot at her. "Damn girl! I most definitely got to see you again!" I said as she looked at me with a beautiful smile.

• • • • • • •

Once in DC, Deemi and I checked into the Holiday Inn off of New York Avenue. I then paged Joey and punched in twenty-five, the code stood for how many kilos of cocaine that I wanted to purchase.

Two hours later, Joey and Tito arrived at the hotel with two medium sized bags. "This some Fishscale, *papi*," Joey said as I opened one of the duffel bags and pulled out two of the kilos.

"I see you stepped it up!" Tito chimed in, referring to the twenty-five kilos I was getting. They were used to me only getting twenty.

"With this drought going on, ain't no telling when I'm gon' be able to get any more," I replied as I put the two kilos back in the bag.

"Nah, we good. Our people said we're straight for a minute."

"That's what's up!" I said, glad to know that I wouldn't be running out of coke for a while.

"We don't mean to rush, but we got some more drops to make," Joey stated as he grabbed the bag off the bed that contained the money. "How long you gon' stay in the city?"

"Until tomorrow," I responded, knowing that I was getting ready to leave as soon as I secured the coke.

"Well, I'ma hit you later so that we can go out tonight."

"A'ight. But y'all ain't gon' count that money?"

"Nah, you straight. I'm going to count it later on. We know your money ain't never funny."

I was glad I had earned their trust, because I was beginning to trust them also. We gave each other pounds as they departed.

I waited about fifteen minutes or so after they left before I went and stashed the kilos in the Suburban. It was still early, and I figured that we could hit the highway and be back in Raleigh before 11:30 p.m., but Deemi wasn't feeling it. She said she had a bad vibe and wanted to wait until the morning so we could leave with the traffic. Even though I wanted to get back to Raleigh tonight, I knew I couldn't because we always agreed not to go against each other's vibe.

· · · · · · ·

We got back on the highway the following morning about 7:30 a.m. I checked my cell phone and noticed that Tito and Joey didn't call me last night. I was glad, because now I didn't have to explain to them why my cell phone was off.

I went ahead and called Reese and Dre, being as though I was expecting to be back in the Raleigh area within the next hour. I told them to meet me at the McDonald's in Knightdale. I usually fronted them three kilos apiece, but since I stepped my game up, I figured I would step them up as well. They were more than my childhood friends; they were my best customers and they were loyal.

When we pulled up at McDonald's, I noticed Reese and Dre sitting in Dre's wife's Ford Explorer. As I rode through the parking lot, I motioned for them to follow me across the street to the car wash.

After we handled our business, Deemi and I headed to the stash house, which was in Knightdale. It was a three bedroom house I rented in my Aunt Carol's name. Once we made it to the stash house, I grabbed the remaining fifteen kilos out of the stash, and headed into the house. I then told Deemi that she could take the GS and leave if she wanted to, because I was going to be ripping and running throughout the day. I always kept a spare car at the stash house.

I spent the whole day at the stash house cooking and packaging kilos of coke. I called a few of my customers and informed them that I was back in action. I also called Rocky and Trick and told them to sit tight because I would be headed their way shortly.

I decided to go see Trick first, being that he was the closest. When I pulled up in Trick's driveway, he was outside messing with his dogs. He had become accustomed to fighting pit bulls. He had about thirty dogs around his house, and wouldn't fight any of those animals for less than twenty-five hundred.

"What's up?" Trick asked as he got in my truck.

"Shit, what's up with you?"

"Trying to get these dogs together for the fight next week."

"Damn! It's been eight weeks already!" I said as I thought how quickly time is moving.

Trick was fighting two of his dogs the following week against these dudes that he met from New York. I gave him a kilo and told him that if he needed me, to just call me on my cell.

As soon as the word "cell" came out of my mouth, my cellular phone started beeping, letting me know that the battery was low. As I went to plug my phone into the charger, I realized that Deemi had taken the charger with her. I quickly called Deemi before the phone went dead and told her that I would meet her at her mother's house so that I could pick up the charger. I then called Rocky and told him to sit tight, because I was headed in his direction.

When I pulled up at Rocky's house thirty minutes later, he was on his porch talking to some girl. I pulled up and noticed a fine female in the passenger seat of this unfamiliar car. I rolled down my window and motioned for her to do the same.

"What's your name?" I asked her.

"Angel," she replied.

Angel was a junior at Shaw University, in Raleigh. She had heard of me and knew I was major in the streets. She had even seen me on a few different occasions, but had never had the opportunity to talk with me personally. We exchanged numbers, and I agreed that we would hook up before the week was out.

My next stop was Deemi's mother's house so that I could retrieve my phone charger. When I arrived there, I spotted Trick's M.P.V. mini-van parked in front of Willie D's house. I never got a chance to get out of the truck before Deemi came out with the charger in her hand, followed by her little brother, Tre.

"Have you seen Trick?" she asked in a low tone of voice.

"Nah. Why?"

"'Cause he said not to go nowhere. Something about it being important," Deemi said as she handed me the charger.

I wondered what could have been so important that Trick couldn't have told me when I saw him an hour and a half ago. I sat back in the truck and placed the phone on the charger.

"Bro, give me some money!" Tre asked me.

"Boy, I ain't got no money."

"Yes you do," he said as he reached and patted my pockets.

Tre was a piece of work for his age. He was smarter than the average adult and was only nine years old. He remind me of myself when I was that age.

"What're you doing, putting the press on me?"

"Nope. I just know you got some money," Tre said, flashing a big Kool-Aid smile.

"How you know I got some money?"

"'Cause I do!"

As I was giving Tre ten dollars, Trick approached me with a look of confusion. "What's wrong?" I asked him.

"This shit is fucked up! You give me some fucked up shit, nigga!"

"What?" I said as my voice increased.

"They say this shit ain't no coke!" Trick said as he pulled a bag of crack out of his pocket.

"Nigga, you tripping! I cooked that myself!" I snapped. "You know I wouldn't even play with you like this."

I knew this to be true. I had gained a great deal of respect and trust for Trick, but I had no earthly idea as to what he was talking about. "Come on!" I said as I got out of the truck and headed to Willie D's house.

"Willie, I need you to check this out for me," I said as I barged into the back room.

"Is that the same stuff?" Willie asked me as he looked up at Trick.

"Yeah."

"Boy, I ain't smoking that shit! That stuff's gon' kill somebody!"

When Willie said that, I knew something was wrong.

"Come on!" I said to Trick, and we headed back to my truck. I grabbed my phone off the charger and noticed that I had four messages. Reese and Dre both had left two messages apiece. They said that it was urgent and for me to call back ASAP.

I was muddled when I talked with Reese and Dre. I couldn't believe their packages were messed up too. "Meet me back at the car wash!" I said, and slammed my phone closed.

I then called my Aunt Carol and told her to meet me at the stash house. I wanted her to sample Reese and Dre's product. I also called Rocky and told him to check his package as well.

We rode all the way to Knightdale in silence. I couldn't believe what was going on. I was skeptical about calling Tito and Joey, but decided to wait until I checked the rest of the product. I thought that this had to be some kind of mistake. I felt that we had been doing business too long together for them to pull a stunt like this on me. I rode through the car wash and motioned for Reese and Dre to follow me out to my stash house.

"Whose crib is this?" Dre asked me as we entered the house.

"This is my stash spot," I replied while going to get the rest of the product out of my safe. "What the fuck is this shit?" I questioned myself while they unwrapped the rest of the kilos.

While we were unwrapping, my aunt came in the house. I had never been so happy to see her. I knew she was going to let me know exactly what it was that we were working with.

"Boy, what the hell is this?" she shouted as she exited the bathroom.

"I don't know."

"What the fuck you trying to do, kill me?"

"I told you that I needed you to test it," I said as I glanced over the kilos, knowing that each and everyone of them were fake. I pulled out my phone and dialed Joey's number immediately.

"The PCS customer you have called can not be reached at this time…"

I hung up and called right back. This time the answering machine picked up. "Yo, this Amir! Call me back ASAP!" I shouted, trembling with rage. I wanted to kill a muthafucker!

"How many of these joints you get?" Dre asked me as he played with one of the kilos.

"Twenty-five."

"Man, them Dominican niggas ain't gon' call back. They know what the fuck they done," Dre said, placing the kilo back on the table. "Twenty-five of the same joints. What the fuck is this shit anyway?"

"Fuck if I know! I know this shit looks like, smells like, and even comes back like coke. *Fuck!*" I screamed.

"You know where them niggas live at don't you?" asked Reese.

"Not really. I usually meet them at a condo in Harlem, but I met them in DC this trip. Matter of fact, come on!" I said as I grabbed my truck keys. I had forgotten all about Tasha. I knew that she would be the only source for me to get in contact with Joey and Tito, being as she was Joey's cousin.

I was highly disappointed when we arrived at Tasha's house. Her next door neighbor told me that he hasn't seen her in several days. He told me that the last time that he saw Tasha, she was putting suitcases in her new Benz S.L.55.

• • • • • • •

It had been two days now, and I still hadn't heard from Joey, Tito or Tasha. I called the correctional officer, Brenda, because I desperately needed to talk with Jarius and I couldn't wait another nine days for him to use the phone again. Jarius was only able to use the phone twice a month, which usually was on the first and the fifteenth. Brenda informed me that she had just gotten off of work, but said that I could come over.

I reached Brenda's house in record breaking time. As soon as I hit the door, she started hugging and kissing all over me, but I wasn't in the mood for that. She had no idea what I was going through. "Hold up, ma!" I said as I took a step back from her.

"What's wrong?"

"Nothing. It's just a lot going on right now," I replied,

grabbing her hand leading her into the living room. "I need a favor," I said as we sat on the couch.

"What?"

"Can you get Jarius a cell phone?"

"I don't know about that. We have to walk through metal detectors. Why?" she asked with a raised eyebrow.

"'Cause I need you to get him this phone. It's urgent."

"Can't I just tell him?"

Knowing that I couldn't tell her my business, I told her that I was willing to pay whatever. Seeing the desperation in my eyes, she told me to give her three hundred dollars so that she could grease some palms to get it in.

Jarius called the next day about 7:30, and I didn't waste any time. I got right down to business. "When is the last time you talked to Tasha?"

"Last time I used the phone. Why?"

"Man, you need to try and find shorty."

"Why? What's up?" Jarius asked, knowing that something was up.

"I'm trying to get up with her cousin, feel me?"

"Yeah, I feel you, but that's the emergency?"

"Hell yeah, nigga! Shit's fucked up! I've been by her crib, and I've called her and them!" I declared angrily. "I just can't get up with nobody!"

"What you mean?" Jarius asked as he peeped out of the laundry room door to make sure that no officer was coming his way.

I thought carefully, because I didn't trust these phones. I knew I had to talk in a code so Jarius could understand. "You know her cousin be selling clothes, right?"

"And?"

"How about I bought twenty-five Hilfiger shirts from that nigga, and got home only to find out the joints are artificial!"

"What?"

"Yeah, and now I can't get a hold of him nor her."

"You bullshitting!"

"I wish I was."

"Yo, let me make some phone calls. I'll hit you back in a few."

Forty minutes passed before Jarius called back. He was unable to get in contact with Tasha or any of her extended family. I spoke to him briefly before I told him that I would be there first thing Saturday morning.

• • • • • • •

Saturday came, and Jarius came out to visitation in his State-issued uniform, and wearing brand new Air Force Ones with his Christian Dior glasses on. "What's up?" he asked as I stood to give him a hug.

"Ain't shit. You still haven't talked to Tasha?"

"Hell nah!" Jarius replied as we took a seat. "So, tell me what happened again."

I broke everything down for him step by step. Jarius seemed to be more messed up about the situation than I was.

"I need you to do something for me," Jarius asked.

"What?"

"Go by my mom's house. She's already expecting you. She's gon' give you the key to my storage on U.S. #1. It's right before you get in Wake Forest. You can't miss it. It's right beside the Kroger."

"I know where it's at."

"Now, my code is 9-11-97, and my storage number is thirteen. It should be a little more than four hundred grand in my safe."

• • • • • • •

When I left from visiting Jarius, I went directly to his mother's house and straight to the storage building. When I walked into the storage room, I wasn't surprised. I knew what time it was when I saw that the safe was opened. I rode back home furiously. I couldn't believe that Jarius and I had just been got for almost a million dollars.

Mentally, I was unstable, because I was broke. I wasn't

dead broke, but I went from counting six hundred thousand plus to one hundred and thirty thousand. I was so upset while I was waiting on Jarius to call that I got intoxicated. It was nine o'clock before he finally called. "Hello?" I answered with a slur in my voice.

"What's up?"

"Shit's gone!"

"Fuck!" Jarius screamed into the phone. "I'ma kill that bitch!"

"Dog, this shit crazy!" I blurted out, looking at the empty bottle of liquor. "What am I supposed to do now?"

"Just lay low for a minute."

"Lay low!" I quoted Jarius, wondering how I could lay low after we had just been ripped off.

"Yeah. I got to make some phone calls and I'll hit you tomorrow, 'cause shorty's got to bring me another battery."

Chapter Twelve
"Ante Up"

It's been over seven months, and I still haven't heard from Joey, Tito or Tasha. I had begun working on my money situation by dealing with some dudes that I met through Trick and his dog fighting operation. I was nowhere near back to the six hundred thousand mark, but I was trying like hell to get back there.

It was New Year's Eve, and the crew and I were bringing in 1998 at Plum Crazy. Plum Crazy was the newest, hottest spot in the city, and every female from every local college would be there tonight. Raleigh was surrounded with colleges. They had two historically black colleges right in the city. They also had North Carolina State, UNC Chapel Hill, and North Carolina Central, which was another black college all within a forty-mile radius.

I was feeling like the million bucks that I had just lost. I had on a navy-blue suit by Salvatore Ferragamo, with the shoes to match. We were walking through the club on our way to the VIP section when I spotted Big Z motioning for me to come over. Big Z was surrounded by a passel of women.

"What's up?" I said as I approached them, catching the eye of every single female in the group.

"I see you looking good," Big Z replied as we slid off to the side so we could talk in private.

"I try to stay that way. So, what's up? You ready to holla at me?"

"I told you I'm retired, but you know Mack."

"And?"

"Well, he owes me a favor."

"And?"

"Holler at him, and I'm gon' tell him to look out for you with a good number."

"What's a good number?" I asked, hoping that I would finally get some justice.

"Fifteen."

"Shh! I already get them for that."

"Well, just holler at him, and I'ma see what he can do for you. Now, he probably won't throw you nothing, but I'm going to try to get you a better number than what you're getting them for."

"That's what's up!" I said as we exchanged pounds. I then headed over to the bar so that I could catch up with Reese and Dre.

"What's that nigga talking about?" Dre asked me, knowing that our talk had to be about business.

"He told me to holler at Mack."

"About what?"

"Some work."

"What you got to holler at Mack for? That nigga fucks with you like that?" Reese asked as he thought back to the night that Jarius went to jail and Big Z was trying to do business with them.

"That nigga don't fuck with me. He says he retired."

"What?" Reese stated. "I know he didn't tell you that!"

"Yeah, he did."

"Man, that nigga's faking!"

"Why do you say that?"

"'Cause that nigga gives Mack his work."

"How do you know?" I asked.

"'Cause we cop from Mack!" Dre replied while taking a glance over his shoulder.

I wasn't surprised that Reese and Dre was purchasing their drugs from Mack. I knew that I couldn't afford to supply them, but I had no idea who they were copping from.

"Yeah, dude be giving him a rack of joints."

"How you know?" I questioned, trying to get as much information as I could from them.

"For one, he told me. And for two, that nigga ain't have no work like that until he started fucking with his niece."

I sat at the bar taking in all of the information that I was getting.

"You know I don't be talking out of the side of my neck," Dre stated, letting me know that he was dead serious.

"I know. Dude's playing with my intelligence," I said, getting the feeling that Big Z was enjoying seeing me struggle to get back to the top.

I was snapped out of my thoughts by someone tapping on my shoulder. I turned around and noticed that it was Angel, the female that I met at Rocky's house. Angel and I indulged in a brief conversation, while Reese and Dre entertained her three friends. I was trying to give her the attention that she wanted from me, but I couldn't because my mind kept drifting back to Big Z.

I turned around to look for Reese and Dre and was surprised when I noticed them at the picture booth flicking it up. When they returned, it seemed as if they had planned for everyone to go out to eat at I-Hop after the club.

After I-Hop, Angel and I headed over to the Marriott Downtown, where I sexed her all night until sunrise.

The following day, I convinced myself that I was going to rob Big Z. I just had to find the right person to help me do it, because I knew Reese and Dre weren't down for any robbery. They played by the rules, and actually I did too, until I realized that there was no rulebook in the drug game. Dudes got money by any means necessary, and charge it to the game was their favorite slogan. I learned that lesson through my experience with Tito and Joey. I made a pledge to myself that I would never cross my peoples unless they crossed me first, and if that was to ever happen, the punishment would be death.

I thought carefully about who I could get to help me pull off my first heist. I knew all of the stickup kids, but I trusted none of them. The only one I felt I could trust was Lil' Clyde. I called Clyde and told him to meet me at Miami Sub, on Wake Forest Road.

Clyde made it to Miami Sub in record breaking time. He knew it was business oriented if I was contacting him. "What's good?" he asked me as we headed to a secluded area in the back of the restaurant.

"You still making moves?" I asked, already knowing the answer.

"You know how I do."

I smiled, thinking back to the time when Clyde robbed one of my workers. He robbed the dude out of spite, not knowing that he worked for me. "I got a move, but we gon' need one more person."

"This ain't even your line of work," Clyde stated, knowing that I was out of character.

"I know, but it's a power move. Plus, this nigga's been playing games with me."

"Who is it?"

"Does it matter?" I asked, knowing that every stickup kid in the city wanted a piece of Big Z, but none had the stones to try him.

"Nope!"

"So don't worry about it. You'll find out when the time is right. So, you in or what?'

"Hell yeah!"

"You got another man?"

"Yeah, but when are you talking about doing this?"

"In about a week or so. Just have your peoples ready," I said, bringing the conversation to a close.

For the next two weeks, I placed Big Z up under close surveillance. I watched his every move, and had even observed him meet with Mack on two separate occasions. I also noticed that Big Z's wife didn't usually get home until 5:30 p.m. with their little girl, who couldn't have been any more than ten months old.

After putting the final touches on my plan, I called Clyde and informed him that everything would go down the next day, and that I would be coming by to get him and his partner by noon.

The following morning, I was up bright and early. The first thing I did was purchase an '86 Astro van. The van was something I was using in case things didn't turn out in my favor, and it wouldn't be traced back to me.

I sat in the Astro van and watched Clyde and his partner come out of Clyde's apartment, wearing all black.

"Yo, this is Chuck," Clyde said, introducing Chuck to me.

As Chuck and I were shaking hands, I told Clyde to go put on something casual.

"For what? We gonna to do this, right?" he asked, hoping that I hadn't changed my mind.

"Do you trust me or not?" I barked, giving him my serious look.

Clyde knew things were about to get real, because he had never seen me so serious. He knew I was all about my business, so he headed into the house to change clothes.

While Clyde was changing clothes, I explained to Chuck my assignment. He was to drive off in the van and go check into the hotel about twenty minutes away from Big Z's house, and wait until we called him to come back. Clyde and I were going to secure the house and hold Big Z's wife hostage until he came home. When Clyde came back, I ran the plan down to him.

I was going to go to the door, acting as if I was some type of sales person. I had also brought a briefcase to make my appearance look official. But the only thing that it contained was four sets of handcuffs and duct tape. Once I forced myself into the house, Clyde was to exit the van calmly, drawing no unwanted attention from their neighbors. Chuck was to leave, because I didn't want any suspicious vehicles in the driveway when Big Z came home.

. . . .

I pulled into Big Z's driveway and grabbed my briefcase while Chuck lay down in the back seat. I got out of the van as if I had just won "Salesman of the Year" award. When I reached the door, I knocked on it gently and waited.

"Yes, may I help you?" Big Z's wife asked as she peered through the peephole.

"My name is Cory Williams, and I work for State Farm Insurance. We were wondering if you would be interested in purchasing any home, life or medical insurance."

Being satisfied that it was only a State Farm Agent, she opened the door and replied, "No thank you. We're already insured with y'all."

I glanced around to make sure that none of her neighbors were outside or looking out of their windows being nosy. When I saw that everything was clear, I pushed Big Z's wife inside and pulled out my gun.

"Please! Please don't kill me!" she howled, realizing that she had made a big mistake by opening the door. "I have a little girl in here!"

"Shut the fuck up and sit your ass down!" I demanded as I peered around the house.

"What do you want?" she cried, knowing that she and her child's lives were in danger.

"Bitch, you know what I want!" I said as Clyde entered the house carrying two duffel bags. "Where the baby at?"

"Please don't hurt my baby!" she said as I motioned for Clyde to check the house.

When Clyde came back, I had the lady handcuffed and seated at the kitchen table.

"Everything's cool. The baby's in the bed sleep," Clyde stated as he placed his pistol on the kitchen counter. "Yo, this Big Z's crib?"

"I know whose crib this is," I replied, knowing that I

intentionally never told Clyde who we were robbing.

"Ahh shit!" he shouted, blushing from ear to ear, knowing that he was finally getting ready to get some real money. "Where's the money at?" he asked the lady in a tone that let her know he meant business.

"It's in a safe in the closet!" she replied with no hesitation.

Clyde escorted the woman to the safe while I double-checked the house. I wanted to make sure that Clyde didn't overlook anything or anybody. After I examined the house thoroughly, I went in the bedroom so that I could scrutinize Clyde.

"You want me to call ol' boy?" Clyde asked me, referring to Chuck.

"Nah."

"Why not? We got what we came for."

"That ain't what I came for!" I spat as I watched Clyde look at me with a look of confusion. Robbery was Clyde's MO. "Where's the rest of the money at?" I asked Big Z's wife.

"I don't know. That's all he keeps here."

"But there is some more money, ain't it?" I asked as the woman began to sob. "Ain't it!" I yelled as I placed my gun against her temple and watched her as she gladly nodded her head yes.

"So, where is it at?"

"I told you I don't know! I swear that's all he keeps here!"

I knew that the woman was probably telling the truth, because most dudes of Big Z's caliber would leave two or three hundred thousand dollars around the house just in case someone tried to rob them, hoping that they would be satisfied with the money in the house. I was smarter than that. My plan was to retire off of Big Z.

We waited for Big Z to get home for almost two hours. "Car pulling up!" said Clyde.

I motioned for him to hide behind the door.

"Boo, where you at?" Z asked, stunned that his wife did not greet him at the door.

"She's right here!" I said as I guided her out of the kitchen.

Before Big Z could respond, Clyde pistol-whipped him, dropping him to one knee.

"Amir! What's going on?"

"Nigga, what the fuck you think is going on? Don't ask me no dumb ass questions!" I stated harshly while Clyde began to cuff him. "Where's the rest of the money at?"

Glancing over at the duffel bag in the corner, Z said, "Looks like you got it all."

"Nigga, don't play with me!"

"Dog, I thought we was better than this."

"Me too, but you want to play games."

"I told you I gave the game up."

"Shut the fuck up! You're lying!" I shouted as I simultaneously smacked him with the pistol. "You don't think I know about you and Mack!" I said, watching his eyes widen at that statement. "Now, where's the money at?"

"That's all I got here. The rest is in the bank."

Knowing that he was lying, I slapped him with the pistol again. This time blood got on his wife.

"Just tell them where the money at so they can leave!" his wife screamed.

"Shut the fuck up! They gon' kill us anyway!"

"Not if you tell me where the money's at."

"Dog, do I look like I'm fucking crazy? You came into my house with no mask!"

"Oh, nigga, you gon' tell me where that money's at!" I said, and began rummaging through their kitchen in search of some Crisco oil. When I found the oil, I poured some in a pan and let it come to a sizzle.

"Dog, what you getting ready to do with that?" Big Z asked, already knowing the answer.

"What you think!"

"Amir, you ain't even got to do this."

"Where's the money at then?"

"I ain't telling you shit!" he said, ready to endure the pain that the hot grease was about to cause. "Ahh shit!" he screamed as the grease pulled the skin off of his body.

Clyde was astonished at the sight of seeing Big Z being tortured. He never would have thought in a million years that I had a perfidious side to me.

"So, what's it going to be?"

"Fuck you!" Big Z said with rage in his voice.

Getting the feeling that this was going to be a long night, I told Clyde to call Chuck so that he could come join us.

"Please, just tell them where the money's at!" Big Z's wife screamed as I approached her with the hot pan of grease.

"So this how it's going to be?" I asked Big Z as I heard the baby begin to cry. "Yo, watch these motherfuckas," I told Clyde as I went and grabbed the baby. I placed her into her walker and pushed her into the kitchen.

I had no intentions on hurting the baby. I figured that I could use her for leverage. I just hoped that Big Z cooperated, because I was willing to go to the extreme.

"So, what's it going to be?" I asked as I grabbed the pan off of the stove.

"Please don't hurt my baby!" Z's wife wept in a manner that touched Clyde's heart.

Clyde was far from soft. He just didn't know whether I was putting on a front or if was I serious. Not wanting to see how things were going to play out, he went to open the door for Chuck.

"Okay! Okay, I'll tell you! Just leave my baby alone!" Big Z said, finally giving into my demands.

"Where's it at?"

"At a stash house in Gary."

I thought back, because during the whole time that I followed Big Z, I never saw him go out to Gary. "Yo, Z, if you're playing games with me, I swear I'm going to kill this baby!"

I reached in Big Z's pockets and tossed Chuck the keys to Z's Range Rover. I instructed him to follow closely behind the van. We then escorted Big Z and his family out to the van.

When we approached Williams Street in Gary, Big Z directed us to a brick house near the end of the block. A white Nissan Pathfinder was sitting in the driveway. I had seen Big

Z in this truck on several different occasions. "Whose house is this?" I asked him.

"Mine."

"Who's in there?"

"Nobody."

With that said, we exited the van.

Clyde ran around the house to clip the alarm. I didn't want Big Z running us into no trap.

As we entered the house, Clyde and Chuck began their search.

"Where's it at?" I asked as Big Z led us to the master bedroom and told us to move the bed. Once we moved the bed, I could see the slit in the carpet. The average person would have missed it, but I knew what time it was. I rolled the carpet back only to witness the biggest safe that my eyes have ever seen. "What's the code?"

"Five, four, three, seven, six, four, two."

I pushed in the code and the spring doors automatically opened.

"Damn! How much is that?" Clyde asked.

Big Z didn't even reply, so I asked him with the gun pointed at the baby. "It's a little over seven and a half," he quickly replied.

I couldn't believe it. Here I was, face to face with seven and a half million dollars. My first robbery was enough for me to retire.

"Yo, it's another safe in the middle room!" Chuck said as he entered the room with a handful of trash bags.

After we emptied the safe, we proceeded to the middle room. "What's in the safe?" I asked, hoping that it was more money.

"Open it and see."

"What's the code?"

Knowing that his life was about to end, Big Z focused his attention on his daughter's future. "Amir, I'ma give you this code. Just see to it that my daughter is straight. That's the least you can do."

"I'll honor that," I replied.

Big Z gave me the combination to the safe.

Clyde entered in the code, and there sat at least thirty kilos. "Out of the game, huh?" I said as I gave Big Z a look of pure hatred. *If you had only just helped me out, we wouldn't be going through this,* I thought to myself.

I told Clyde to put the dope in a bag while I escorted Big Z back to the master bedroom where his wife was lying on the floor. I screwed on my silencer and put two shots in both of their heads. "Get those bags. We're out of here," I said, closing the master bedroom door behind me.

"What about the baby?" Clyde asked.

"Put the baby in the Rover."

"And leave her!"

"Yeah... and no."

"What do you mean?" Clyde asked with a puzzled look on his face.

"When we leave, I want you to park their truck in front of their neighbor's driveway. Make sure you block them in, and leave the windows cracked and the heat on so the baby can breathe. That way, in the morning their neighbor will notice that they're blocked in, and when they do, they will look inside the truck and spot the baby."

"Bet!" Clyde said as he began to put the plan into effect.

Seeing that Clyde implemented the plan perfectly, I then instructed Chuck to drive out to Knightdale. I had the Suburban parked out by Lafayette Palace. My plan was to destroy the van. I wanted to make sure that the van couldn't be traced back to us. When we reached Lafayette Palace, I had Clyde follow behind me and Chuck in the truck.

"Dog, we came up!" Chuck said as he cruised down the back road at a safe speed.

"I know, but you got to lay low for a minute. You can't go out splurging and drawing tips with this money."

"Nah, I ain't crazy, but I got to cop me a new whip off top."

"Yo, what part of 'lay low' don't you understand?" I

snapped, cutting my eyes at Chuck in a hateful manner.

"Man, I got to have something to show for this lick!" he responded, trying to rationalize why he needed to spend some money.

"A'ight! But when the heat comes down, don't bring me down!"

"Come on, yo. I don't even rock like that."

"Humph! That's what they all say! You get that gas like I told you."

"You don't smell it?" Chuck replied as we pulled into a wooded area. There was nothing back there but a pond and an old wooden house.

I was bothered by the way Chuck was talking in the van. I knew that loose lips sank ships, and I'll be damned if I was going down for two counts of murder and probably armed robbery because of a nigga I didn't even know.

When we exited the vehicles, Clyde and I began to drench the van in gasoline.

Chuck was on the far side of the truck taking a piss. I excused myself, slid up beside him and put two slugs in his chest and one in his head.

I then returned to the far side of the truck and watched as Clyde set the van on fire. "Let's go!" I said as I wiped off the gun and threw it into the burning van.

"Where's Chuck at?" Clyde asked as I climbed into the driver's side of the Suburban.

"You'll see him when you back up."

As Clyde backed up, he noticed Chuck's body off to the right. "Yo, what the fuck!" he asked as I reached in the glove compartment and pulled out the .38 I kept there. "Amir, what's up?" he asked, hoping I wasn't about to doublecross him.

"Nigga I ain't gon' do nothing to you as long as you ain't talking crazy like that nigga."

"What the fuck you talking about?"

"I'll tell you. Let's just get the fuck out of here."

As we rode to my house, I explained to Clyde why I had to kill Chuck.

"Dog, I feel you. I ain't trying to go down for this shit either, but dude didn't swing like that," Clyde said, letting me know that Chuck was a stand up dude.

"Well, I ain't trust him, and now I know he ain't gon' swing like that," I replied, not feeling a bit of sorrow.

"Yo, you know I don't do the coke thing, so just give me two mill and I'm straight," he said, knowing that I deserved the majority of the money because it was my plan. Plus, I was the one with the three bodies. Clyde was just happy that I called upon him to assist me with this move. He had never robbed anyone for more than seventy thousand, and even then he had to split it three ways. So, he was more than happy to have two million of his own money.

I wasn't worried about Clyde laying low. He knew the rules to the game. I also knew that he wouldn't talk to the police because he hated them, and he had a few bodies himself out in Kansas.

Chapter Thirteen
"Break Bread"

It's been nine weeks since the robbery, and I was now a certified millionaire. I came off with five point seven million, and thirty-six kilos of cocaine for myself. I kept my money in a storage facility, and the only person who knew where it was, was my mother. I made sure that I didn't make the same mistake as Jarius did.

The time had come for me to move the kilos, and I knew exactly who I was going to give them to. I called Reese, Dre and Trick and had them meet me at the park in Chavis Heights. I was shootin' ball when Reese and Dre pulled up.

"What's up?" Dre asked as he grabbed the rebound from my missed shot.

"Ain't shit! What's up with y'all?"

"You. What's so important that you got us out here first thing this morning?"

"I'll tell you when Trick gets here."

We shot some hoops for about ten minutes before Trick pulled up in his new Cadillac.

"I know y'all are wondering why I got y'all up here, so I'm gon' get straight to it. Yo, I'm done."

"What? I know damn well you ain't get me up out of my

bed for this shit!" said Trick

"Yo, would you hold fast and listen to what the fuck I got to say? Now, like I was saying, I'm done. I'ma try and go to college."

Seeing that I was serious, Dre asked, "How you going to do that?"

"Easy. I'm going to go to Wake Tech and get my diploma. Then, I'm going to take the SAT's, and if I score high enough, I'll walk onto the football team."

"Here we go again!" Reese said jokingly.

"Nah, for real, yo. I'm dead serious. If I make the team, I'm damn near positive that I'll get a walk on a scholarship."

"Nigga, you ain't played ball in damn near three years."

"That's why I'ma run and hit the weights hard for a year. Nigga, I can still run the rock!" I said to Reese, letting him know that I still had game. "But like I was saying, y'all are my niggas, and I got to make sure y'all are straight. So, I want y'all to meet me at my mom's house tomorrow night so we can celebrate."

"Celebrate what?" Trick asked, still not understanding why I was getting out of the game.

"My retirement, and me going back to school. Plus, I got something for y'all, but y'all got to come to the house to get it."

Everyone agreed to meet at my mother's house the following night about seven. I glanced at my new Cartier watch and saw that it was 8:30 a.m. "Yo, fellows, I got to roll."

"Where you headed to?" Dre asked.

"I got to meet Porsha."

"Tell her I said what's up."

"Yeah, a'ight," I said as I took my last shot.

"She still mess with that white boy?" Reese asked.

"Yeah, they're married now, and his name ain't 'white boy', it's Karl," I replied, defending Karl. I knew that Reese was on some racial shit.

"I don't give a fuck what his name is! I still don't know how he got her fine ass! What you going to see her about anyway?"

"I got to holla at her about this club."

"You trying to get a club?"

"Yeah."

"Damn! You got club money!"

"Nigga, you act like I was completely fucked up."

"Nah, but y'all just lost damn near a mil, and I know you ain't pump back up that fast. Plus, you talkin' about giving the game up and going back to school. Nigga, what's really good?" Reese asked, knowing that something was going on with me.

"Everything's good. Believe that. But I'ma holla at y'all tomorrow on the big end. And bring your girl, 'cause this is a family event."

I left and headed straight to Porsha's house. I knew that she was going to be mad, because I had her cook me breakfast and I was late. I pulled up in her yard with the music on blast. I was listening to "Coming of Age Part Two" by Jay Z.

"...I done came up put my life on the line,
Sewed the game up, now it's my time to shine.
I done came up, no more second in line,
Nine nine, these streets is mine..."

"Boy, turn that damn music down!" Porsha screamed from her front porch.

I was greeted at the door by Porsha's daughter, Gabriel. Porsha and her family waited for me before they ate.

While we ate, while I informed Porsha and her husband that I was through with the game. I told her I wanted to open up a club in her name, and wanted her to run it. We would split all the profits fifty-fifty.

Porsha and her husband were skeptical until I told them that they would make a profit of at least a hundred grand apiece a year. I knew that it would be way more than that, because I had big plans for this club. Porsha and her husband agreed. All I needed now was the perfect location.

• • • • • • •

The get-together was lovely. Deemi invited some of her

family and friends. My aunts came out, along with Porsha and her family. Everyone at the house thought it was a cookout. Only Reese, Dre, Trick, Porsha, Karl and my mother knew what we were really celebrating.

Deemi's cousin, Flat-Top cooked all of the food. He grilled barbecue chicken, steaks, hamburgers and hotdogs. He also deep-fried some fish and chicken.

My mother did all the side dishes. She made potato salad, baked beans, and macaroni and cheese. She also made a banana pudding and baked a red velvet cake.

I made sure that there was plenty of alcohol. I had a gallon each of Hennessy, Courvoisier, Remy, and Seagram's Gin. I also purchased a case of Dom P. '82 for myself and the fellows.

Everyone was sitting on the patio playing Spades when the stretch Navigator pulled into the yard. I had arranged for the limo, because I knew that everyone would be a little tipsy and there was no way that I was letting them get back on the highway dirty.

"Who's that in the limo?" asked Reese.

"Nobody. That's y'all's ride."

"Ride where?"

"Home, nigga! Or wherever the fuck y'all are going!" I said. "I told y'all that I had a surprise for you."

I then had Dre grab four bottles of champagne while the rest of the team headed to the Suburban.

"Yo, I done told y'all about my plan. Well, it's official! Me and cuz are gonna do the club thing. But what I'm getting ready to give y'all, I need the money because, I'ma open Deemi her own salon with that money."

I had everyone's undivided attention. "Now, before I give y'all this, y'all got to promise me that y'all gon' stack your paper." I reached in the back and retrieved three small duffel bags. I then gave each one of them a bag and made them promise that they would never look back. "Look. It's ten joints in each one of those bags. Y'all owe me fifty grand apiece," I said as everybody looked at me like I was crazy.

"Yo, that's five grand a joint! What's this, some bullshit?"

Reese asked

"Hell nah! This is some raw. Y'all should make at least two hundred grand or better."

They sat silently for a moment until I held my bottle up and said, "To never looking back!" We toasted and drank to never looking back.

"Yo, Amir!" Reese paused as I turned around to face him." You did Big Z, didn't you?"

"Does it matter?"

"Hell nah!" they all said simultaneously.

"Well, don't ever ask me a question like that again!" I said in a stern and serious tone. "Just be glad that I'm a real nigga and want to see my peoples eat too."

Once everyone had gone, I went into my mother's room, reached under her bed and grabbed a hundred grand that I had stashed in one of her old carry bags. It was from the six kilos that I sold to Reese's cousin, Fresh for twenty grand a pop. It was a hundred and twenty grand, but I gave my cousin, Porsha twenty grand for her family.

"Here, this for you and Sharon," I told my mother.

"Boy, how much money is this?" she asked, taking a glance inside the bag.

"A hundred thousand. Just give Sharon ten stacks and you keep ten stacks. It's five grand in each stack. Tell her that's for her and the baby."

My sister had given birth to a little boy. I had only seen him on three different occasions, being as though she was still in the Army.

"I'll give it to her, but I still don't need all of this money."

"Well, just keep it. That way you ain't got to keep asking me for money."

My mother didn't approve of my lifestyle, but she accepted it due to the fact that she knew I wasn't going to change. Hustling was in my blood.

• • • • • • •

Sunday came, and I made a surprise visit to see Jarius. "Surprised to see me?" I asked him as I stood to embrace him.

"Yeah. I thought you was Rale."

"She coming up here?"

"Yeah," he replied as we both took a seat.

Over the last few days, I thought long and hard whether I should fill Jarius in on the events that took place in my life over the past two months. I felt that it was only right that I broke bread with him. I knew that if I couldn't trust anybody, that I could trust him. ''I got a million dollars for you,'' I told him.

"What?" he asked, not sure if he heard me correctly.

"You heard me. I got a mil for you."

I then explained to him detail by detail about the robbery and the murders. He had no idea that I was capable of pulling off the robbery of the year. I also informed him about my plans on going back to school. I told him about the club and how I broke bread with all of the fellows.

Jarius thought that I played fair with everyone. He just didn't like the fact that I was buying Deemi her own salon. He lost trust for all women, especially after Tasha took him for everything that he had. He made a pact within himself that he would never trust another woman outside of his mother.

Chapter Fourteen
"Why"

It's been over a year since the robbery, and things couldn't have been going any better for me. I had attained my GED through Wake Tech, and I was now studying for the SAT's. I also had been working my ass off in the gym. I weighed two hundred and twenty seven pounds, and was running a 4.3 forty. For the first time in several years I could honestly say that I've worked hard.

Porsha and I located the perfect spot for our club. It was in the process of being remodeled. The club was going to have three VIP areas, three full bars, three half bars in VIP, valet parking, two floors, pool tables and video games. I was also having state of the art audio/video systems installed. I had well over seven hundred thousand invested in this project. This definitely was going to be the hottest club on the eastern part of North Carolina.

· · · · · · ·

I strolled to the bar feeling and looking like a working, intelligent black man. I was wearing a single-breasted tailor-made suit by Hugo Boss. I was sure to catch plenty of attention tonight.

"Amir, is that you?" the bartender asked.

I squinted my eyes trying to recall the face.

"It's me, Tom," he said.

Several seconds went by before I recognized Tom. I haven't seen him since high school. Tom had put on several pounds which made him unrecognizable.

"How's it been?" Tom asked me as he brought me a shot of Hennessy on the house.

"It's been good, Tom. How about you?"

"I can't complain. Just living the married life."

"Don't tell me you and Kelly got married!"

"Yep. How did you know?"

"As in love as y'all two was, who wouldn't have thought?"

"Yeah, that's my baby. She gave me a little junior too!" he said, reaching in his wallet to show me a picture of his wife and son.

I couldn't help but to laugh to myself as I viewed the picture. Tom's son had the same blond hair and blue eyes as his father. Not to mention the oversized head the youngster was carrying. "So, how long have you been working here?"

"About two years. It ain't the best job, but it pays the bills."

"At least you got a job. So, you the head man here?"

"Hell nah! I just control the bar. I let them know what I need and they keep it stocked for me."

Tom and I chatted for about twenty minutes before he decided to make his rounds through the club.

The environment was trendy, and there were plenty of ladies out tonight. I couldn't wait until we had our grand opening. I planned on having it the first weekend in May. As I headed to the VIP section, I realized that I could use Tom on my team. I stopped dead in my tracks and headed back to the bar.

"That was quick," Tom said as I approached the bar.

"Nah. I just had to came back and run something past you."

"I'm listening."

"You know the whole time we've been talking you never

asked me what it was that I was doing for a living."

"Hell, I figured if you didn't volunteer it, then it was none of my business," he replied, letting me know that he knew how to stay in his place and mind his own fucking business.

"What if I told you I owned a club?"

"I'd say good for you."

"No, Tom. What if I told you that I owned a club that had two floors, three full bars, three half bars, three VIP areas, pool tables, video games, plus a state of the art audio/video system."

"I'd say you're bullshitting, because I haven't heard of any club like that around here. Plus, the only place you're going to find a club like that is in a big city."

I just shook my head, because Tom had no idea what Raleigh had coming. "Tom, I got one more question for you," I said before downing the shot of Hennessy that he had just passed to me. "How much you make here?"

"About nineteen a year, plus tips. But I only work part-time and four days a week."

I thought carefully, because I knew that I had to make him an offer that he couldn't refuse. "What if I offered you thirty thousand a year, plus a ten grand signing bonus to run my three bars at my fantasy club?"

"I'd tell Mr. Hill to kiss my ass!"

Got him! I thought to myself as Tom excused himself to go tend to a customer. When he came back, he slid me another triple shot of Hennessy.

"You're not going to get me drunk tonight, Tom."

"This one's not free. It's from the lady over there."

I looked in the direction that Tom pointed in, and noticed Sarah. I hadn't seen her since the night that Jarius got locked up. I excused myself and headed towards her.

"Boy, you done got all muscular on me. What's it been, three... four years?" she said, standing up to give me a hug.

"Something like that. I see you still looking good."

"You too, and thank you."

"So, you still teaching."

"Yep. What about you?" she asked.

I gave Sarah a summary of my plans. She was impressed and was glad that I finally got my life together. "So, you got plans when you leave here?" I asked out of the blue, catching her off guard.

"Sure do. I'm going home and get in my bed. Why, you trying to come tuck me in?"

"Girl, you know I'm trying to tuck you in!" I grinned slyly, letting her know that I was down for whatever.

Sarah wrote down her address and handed it to me. I glanced at the paper then placed it in my pocket.

"Do you know where that's at?" she asked.

"Nah, but I have On Star."

"Well excuse me! I guess I'll meet you at my house in about an hour." She gave me a kiss on the cheek and disappeared into the crowd. I then headed back over to the bar.

"You know her?" Tom asked.

"Yeah, but I haven't seen her in a while."

"Man, she's beautiful!" he said, offering me another drink.

"Nah, I'm good," I stated, turning down the drink. "But I need you to do me a favor."

"And what might that be?"

I reached in my pocket and pulled out three crispy hundred dollar bills.

"What's this for?"

"For you to call me in the morning."

"Three hundred just for me to call you in the morning?"

"Yep."

"You got to be kidding!"

"No, I'm serious."

"Shhhiit! For three hundred I'll call your ass all day!" Tom said as he placed the money in his pocket.

I gave him my number before I departed. Once outside, I thought about all of the things that I was getting ready to do with Sarah.

I was headed to my truck when I noticed a foreign couple getting robbed. All I heard was the woman saying, "You can have the car! Just don't kill us!"

I don't know what went through my mind, but I reached under my seat and pulled out a .44 Magnum. The masked man didn't even notice me creeping up behind him, but the foreigners did. Once I was in arm's reach of the car jacker, I smacked him with my burner. He dropped to one knee and spun around with his gun pointed at me.

"Boom!" was the sound that the Magnum gave as I squeezed the trigger. The sound of the gun brought me back to reality. I couldn't believe what I had just done. "Fuck!" I mumbled.

"What the fuck have you done?" the male foreigner asked in disbelief.

"I don't know. Guess playing hero."

The foreigner smiled and said, "Get the fuck out of here before this place is surrounded with cops."

"Fuck!" I mumbled again. I heard what the foreigner had said, but at the same time my thoughts were on my future.

"Don't worry about this. I'll take care of it."

"You sure?"

"I'm positive. My friend owns this place," he said as he reached into his suit jacket and gave me a business card that read "Club Warehouse". "Ask for Frank."

"And tell him what?"

"Tell him you're a friend of..." He paused, glanced at his car and said, "DB9."

I figured that he didn't want to tell me his name, which was cool with me as long as he made this situation disappear. With that being said, I hopped in my truck and drove into the night. I was headed home when I thought that if things didn't go the way the foreigner planned, I would need a solid alibi. That's when I pulled Sarah's address out of my pocket. I knew that if push came to shove she would step to the plate for me. I pressed the On Star button and it led me directly to her house.

Sarah was at the door waiting on me when I arrived. I entered her house and was automatically led to the bedroom.

"Would you like something to drink?" she asked as she

began to light the candles on her nightstand.

"Sure!" I responded. I was glad that she had something to drink that would relax my nerves.

"You okay?" she asked, seeing that I was a little tense.

"Yeah. I'm just tipsy that's all."

"Good. Now I can do whatever I want to you!" she said, taking off her robe to reveal the sexy lingerie she was wearing.

I couldn't help but to admire Sarah's elegant body. She slowly undressed me and led me into the bathroom where she washed me and did all types of freaky things to me in the bathtub.

Back in the bedroom, I started from her neck and worked my way down to her inner thighs. I licked all over her body making my way to some of the juiciest pussy that I'd ever eaten. Her pussy was so fresh that I could have eaten her until my Heavenly Father called me home. We sucked and fucked each other until the wee hours of the morning.

The following morning, I was awakened by my cell phone.

"Hello," I said with sleep still in my voice.

"Wake up, sleepy head!"

"What time is it?" I asked, realizing that it was Tom.

"Almost two o'clock."

I glanced over to the other side of the bed and noticed that Sarah had left me a note on her nightstand:

> *I went out to the mall and will be right back. If you wake up before I return, make yourself at home. I fixed you breakfast and your plate is in the microwave. It's now 12:20, so if you have to leave before I get back, call my cell- 737-1425.*

I placed the note back on the nightstand and asked Tom why he didn't call me earlier.

"I would have, but some punk got killed last night."

With that statement, I was fully awake. I felt as if my heart had just dropped to my knees. "They find out who did it?" I asked, hoping that DB9 stayed true to his word.

"Nope."

"No witnesses?"

"Nope."

I was somewhat revealed knowing that there was no witness as far as the police were concerned. "Can you meet me somewhere?"

"Hey, you paid me to call you, not meet you anywhere."

"I know. That was the whole point of me getting you to call me."

"Buddy, we go way back, but this is my family time here."

"That's cool. You can bring them too," I said, determined to get Tom to come and meet me.

"I don't know, buddy. I got to be at the club by seven."

"Look, this is very important. It won't take thirty minutes. Now, please meet me at Applebee's on Wake Forest road at four o'clock."

"Okay, buddy, but just thirty minutes," he stressed, letting me know that was all the time he was going to give me.

I then called Porsha so that I could give her an idea of what I was trying to do with Tom. She thought it was a good idea, because he was experienced. Plus, I also felt that Tom would have our best interest.

After I hung up the phone with Porsha, I headed to the kitchen to see just what it was that Sarah had cooked. As I was opening the microwave, she came walking through the door.

"You really made yourself at home I see!" she said, surprised to see me in her kitchen butt naked.

"That's what you said," I responded, referring to the note that she had left on the nightstand.

I took my plate out of the microwave and sat at the table while Sarah went into the bedroom to get my boxers. When she came back, she had my boxers in one hand and my ringing phone in the other. I slid on my boxers and checked my caller ID. "Hello," I answered, knowing that it was Reese on the other end.

"What's up with you?"

"Shit, I was just getting ready to call you."

"Oh yeah? What's up?"

"I need to see you. Meet me at the club at four o'clock, and bring ten dollars."

"A'ight."

"And drive your truck. I'll explain when I see you."

My plan was to switch vehicles with Reese. I wanted to be certain that my truck wasn't identified in the shooting. I really didn't mind switching vehicles with him because he had just copped the new Escalade EXT with chrome 22-inch Zebras on it. I knew if my truck was identified in the shooting, it would be pulled over.

I was very impressed with Sarah. She knew exactly how to treat a man. Not only did she cook breakfast for me, but while she was out at the mall, she grabbed me an outfit to wear as well.

On my way to meet Tom, I decided to call the number on the card that the foreigner had given me.

"Hello," a male answered.

I checked the back of the card and remembered that the foreigner told me to ask for Frank. "May I speak with Frank?" I asked, cool and collective.

"This is Frank."

"I'm a friend of DB9's. He told me to call you."

"I was looking for you to call earlier, but you have nothing to worry about. All the security cameras were down, and there were no witnesses."

With that said, I was relieved and crushed at the same time. I was crushed not because I killed a man, but because I had killed one out of stupidity, trying to play hero.

"Hey, you still there?" Frank asked.

"Yeah, I'm here."

"Well, DB9 would like for you to stop by whenever you get a chance so that we can show you our appreciation."

"Tell your friend no thank you. Tell him that he showed his appreciation already by making this go away."

I got off of the phone with Frank as I was pulling into Applebee's parking lot. Tom was sitting on his all red Harley

Davidson F-150 SVT. I pulled up beside him and told him that I wanted to show him my fantasy club.

Tom was amazed when we walked inside of the club. We were greeted at the door by Porsha. I introduced them to one another, and we began to give Tom a tour of the building. I informed him that he would be in full charge of all of the bars, and that he could hire and fire as he pleased. I also let him know that Porsha would be in charge of finances, but he could stock the bar however he saw fit. I then excused myself, because I still had to go out front and meet with Reese.

"What's up?" Reese asked as I climbed into the passenger seat.

"Trying to get this club together. You bring that money?"

"Yeah, and what's so important that you had me drive my truck?"

I explained everything to him, including how DB9 had the guy Frank take care of the situation. Reese was shocked, but he understood how I felt about not wanting to drive my truck. We exchanged keys and shared a little more small talk before I grabbed the .44 out of my truck. I placed it up under the seat of the Escalade, because my next stop was to get rid of it after I finished my business with Tom.

When I returned to the club, he and Porsha had just finished the tour.

"This fuckin' place is awesome!" Tom said, full of excitement. He couldn't believe that I was getting ready to have the hottest club that Raleigh has ever seen. "Every club owner in town is going to hate you."

"I know, but they'll be alright. So, you in or what?"

"Hell yeah!"

I then tossed Tom a stack of money.

"What's this?"

"That's your ten grand signing bonus. Cuz will have a contract typed up for you later."

Chapter Fifteen
"Game Over"

It's been six weeks since the night of the shooting, and things were still going smooth for me. The club was basically complete. Tom had hired seven bartenders, while Porsha was working on the security.

I still had Reese's truck, and Deemi just found out that she was seven weeks pregnant. I also had been spending a lot of time with Sarah lately. Even though Deemi was my main girl, I had developed some real feelings for Sarah in the past few weeks.

· · · · · · ·

Today has been a long day! Reese thought to himself as he crushed down Capital Boulevard. The day had been so stressful that he just wanted to go relax and enjoy himself at a strip club. Not wanting to go to his usual hangout, he decided to go to the DollHouse, which was a white strip club located near North Raleigh. He figured that he would be able to enjoy himself without anyone bothering him because no one in the vicinity knew him.

Reese walked into the DollHouse as if he was the don

of the city. He sat at the nearest table and ordered himself a Heineken. He was mesmerized by the beauty of some of the women. The DollHouse was far from any black club that he had ever been to. It was classier, and the price of pussy would cost him an arm and a leg.

He was enjoying the show when he noticed that a security guard was pointing in his direction. He knew that he hadn't broken any rules, but at the same time he knew that something wasn't right. He locked eyes with the security guard as a chubby looking Colombian approached him.

"Sorry to bother you, but are you driving a black Benz truck?"

"Yeah. Is there a problem?" Reese asked on the defensive side.

"No, not at all. Just thought that it belonged to someone else."

"Nah. Must be some type of mistake."

"Well again, I'm sorry to bother you. But before I go, may I ask you a question?"

"Sure, go ahead."

"Did someone else have your truck a few weeks ago?"

Reese's antennas automatically went up with that question. He knew dude was talking about the shooting, and Amir did mention something about a foreigner. So, there was a good chance that this Colombian could be the dude that Amir saved, but he wasn't going to let him know that he knew Amir. Far as Reese was concerned, this guy could be a cop. "Nah, ain't nobody have my truck. Why?" Reese asked, trying to get to the bottom of this.

"Just curious," The Colombian responded while getting up.

Reese thought that he was about to leave, but he sat back down and said, "Look, I'm not one to beat around the bush, so I'ma spit it out. I have this feeling that you know who I'm looking for. I don't know his name, but I owe him big time. So, if your memory ever comes back to you and you find your friend, tell him thanks again, and DB9 has a gift for him."

With him saying "DB9", Reese knew this was the guy that Amir had saved. "And who is DB9?" he asked as if he didn't already know.

"I take it that you know who I'm looking for."

"I never said that," Reese replied, and took a sip of his Heineken. "But I just might bump into him one day. So, what do you want me to tell him if I do? 'Cause dude might not like surprises," he said with a grin that let the Colombian know that he knew who he was looking for.

"Well, if you do, I'll give you twenty-five grand for bumping into him and telling him that I've got three hundred for him."

Reese knew that he was in over his head. Any man that could just give three hundred and twenty-five thousand away had to be powerful. He wrapped up his conversation with DB9 and headed outside to the truck. He waited to see if DB9 was going to have anybody try and follow him. Once he saw that everything was cool, he decided to go ahead and call Amir.

"Hello," I answered.

"You sleep early, ain't you boy?"

"Nah, I'm just laid back watching 'Blow'. Why? What's up?"

"You remember your friend, DB9?"

"Yeah."

"I bumped into him tonight."

"How did you know it was him?"

"You said he was a foreigner, right?"

"Yeah."

"Well, he's a Colombian."

Reese explained everything to me, detail for detail. Neither one of us felt as if DB9 was the police. We knew that he was somebody important and with a lot of pull.

"You see his car?" I asked

Reese glanced around the parking lot and said, "No, but I see a red DB7 parked right beside a cream Porsha Carrera."

"Oh yeah?"

"Yeah."

"You strapped?" I asked.

"No question. Why? What's up?"

"Go back in there and do you. I'm on my way. I want to see what's up with this cat."

"A'ight. You want me to let him know that you're on the way?"

"Nah, just chill. I'll see you in thirty."

Those thirty minutes seemed like an hour to Reese.

Finally, I came stepping through the door. I joined Reese, and shortly after I was seated, the waitress brought us a bottle of Dom P. '82. "This one is on the house," she said as she placed the bottle on the table.

Reese popped the cork as he watched me focus in on my surroundings.

Twenty minutes had passed before the waitress returned. "Excuse me, sir," she said, referring to me.

"Yes?" I replied.

"Someone in the big house wants to see y'all," she said, nodding her head towards a flight of stairs that must lead to an office upstairs that was behind the tinted glass window.

I leaned over and told Reese to wait, because there wasn't any need for both of us to run into a trap. I also told him to call my cell phone every twenty minutes, and if for some reason I didn't answer, he was to come get me or start shooting innocent bystanders.

I stepped into the office and was greeted by three men. I immediately noticed DB9 sitting behind a desk, puffing on a cigar. DB9 greeted me with a firm handshake and hug. He then introduced me to his colleagues, Tony, Bobby and Frank. I figured Frank was the guy I had talked to when the shooting first took place.

"So, what's your name?" DB9 asked, wondering whether I was going to tell him the truth.

"G-500," I replied as I watched DB9 crack a smile. I figured that if DB9 wanted to use his car as his alias, then I would use my truck as mine.

"Let's start this over. My name is Rodriguez, and your name is Andrew, a.k.a. Admir."

When he mentioned my government name, I began to feel uncomfortable, and Rodriguez felt it.

"Whoa! Be easy and here me out. I only know your name because your truck is in your mother's name. Remember I told you my friend Frank here owned the club? Well, before we destroyed the tape, I had him get your tag number, and my nephew, Bobby here is a DEA Agent. But don't worry, he's on my team,," Rodriguez said, pausing to take a puff on his cigar.

He then continued. "But like I was saying, I had him run your tag number, and it came back registered to an Yvette Davis. So he ran a check on her, and all he found out was that she had two kids. So, he ran a check on you, and that's how we found out all of our info. But to be honest with you, I made this trip back to Carolina to personally put this money in your hands myself. But lucky me, when I got here and noticed your truck, I figured today couldn't have been a better day. So, I had security show me who was driving the truck, because I didn't see you. That's when he told me that your buddy there was driving it." He pointed through the tinted glass window at Reese.

Before Rodriguez could go any further, my phone rang. Rodriguez told me not to answer it, but I let him know that if I didn't, Reese would start shooting innocent bystanders. He looked down and saw Reese looking up at the tinted window as if he could see through it. He then nodded his head in approval for me to answer the phone. I answered and assured Reese that I was cool. Rodriguez then informed me that he had three hundred thousand dollars for me in the briefcase that was leaning on the corner of the desk.

I stood quietly by the tinted window in deep contemplation. I knew that I was dealing with some major people. Rodriguez having a nephew that was a DEA Agent confirmed that. I figured that Rodriguez was either part of the Mafia, or he was a Colombian drug lord. I didn't know what it was that he was into, and I was curious to know.

I was still thinking to myself, when I noticed a very familiar face on stage. I knew that I didn't know a lot of white women, but I knew that I knew this girl form somewhere. I just couldn't place a name or where I knew her from, but the white girl was out of this world. It didn't make any sense how this white girl's body was shaped. She had to be a 34-27-45, and could move like a sister. I couldn't believe the way that she worked the pole, and when she got on all fours and made her ass thunderclap, I became aroused immediately. I was deep in thought until Rodriguez and Tony came and stood beside me.

"You like that?" Tony asked, seeing that I was gawking at one of his dancers.

"Yeah, but I know her. I just can't think where from."

"Who, Tasty?"

"If that's what y'all call her, but I know her by something else."

Tony went over to his desk and pulled out a piece of paper that contained each one of his dancer's real names and stage names. "Tonya," he said, placing the paper back in his desk.

"Yeah, that's her!"

"So, you do know her?" Rodriguez asked.

"Yeah, I know her. She used to work at this restaurant that I used to eat at, but I haven't seen her in a while."

We all stood there and admired Tasty performing her set on stage, when Reese called my phone all of the sudden. Rodriguez and I both looked down at Reese. I was glad that he had called, because my mind had drifted off of the situation.

"Mr. Rodriguez—"

"Please, just call me Rodriguez."

"Okay, well, I do appreciate the money. It will come in handy with my club, but I feel it's only right that I know something about you since you know all about me."

"What's it that you want to know?" Rodriguez asked, already knowing the answer to his question.

"I want to know what it is that you do for a living."

"Son, you did save me from the car-jacker, and maybe he would have shot and killed me, or maybe he wouldn't have. I don't know. But if I tell you my business, then you're going to want to be involved." Rodriguez paused and took a good look at everyone in the room. "And, if I decide to involve you in my business, it's only right that I let you know what I believe in."

"I'm listening," I stated.

"Now, I do believe in consequences for rats. I'll have your mother killed or someone really close to you if you try to hide in protective custody. I have too much to lose over a fuckin' rat. So, if any of my folks get caught up in a jam, we try like hell to get them out by any means necessary. And if we can't get you out of it, then there is a good chance that you could spend the rest of your life in some federal prison, but your family will never want for anything. Do you think that you want to be a part of that?"

I knew that Rodriguez meant every word that he had just said. I knew that he was involved in some serious stuff, but yet I still didn't know what it was that he was involved in. I wondered if he wanted me to be a hit man. And even though I had four bodies, I still didn't consider myself a killer. Determined to find out what it was that he was actually involved in, I nodded my head, yes.

"How much do you pay for a kilo?" Rodriguez asked.

"About eighteen," I responded, knowing that I hadn't dealt with coke in over a year.

"Well, I'll give you a decision to make. You can take this money and forget that we ever had this conversation, or I can keep my money and arrange for you to get your product for fifteen apiece. But you have to at least be able to buy twenty."

Twenty kilos at fifteen apiece was three hundred thousand. I figured that I could give those twenty kilos to my people for twenty a pop, and make a quick hundred thousand profit. I knew my people were capable of moving twenty within ten days. "What if I brought you $1.5 million? What would you do for me then?" I said as I watched everyone in the room look at each other in disbelief.

Things were quiet for a second, until Rodriguez said, "If you bring me $1.5 mil, I'll let you get them for thirteen a pop. So, you do the math." He then threw a calculator to me.

I was astonished. I couldn't believe that I was sitting here face to face with a Colombian drug lord. I felt as if I was getting the deal of the century; a hundred and twenty kilos for $1.5 million. How could I go wrong? I knew that I would profit six hundred thousand easy, even if I gave them to my people at eighteen apiece. I felt that I was in a win-win situation. I told Rodriguez that he could keep his money, because I wanted the hundred and twenty kilos for the $1.5 million.

I also told him that I would always deal with him, but I informed him that I had two other loyal friends that I dealt with. I was referring to Dre and Jarius.

Rodriguez told me that he didn't ever want to meet any of my friends. He also told me that he would like it if my friends didn't know about him. He said he didn't mind Reese, because he somewhat took a liking to him, and he felt that he was loyal because of the way that he carried their conversation earlier.

"So, when can you have the money together?" Rodriguez asked.

"Whenever. When can you have the product?"

"Whenever."

"No, I'm serious," I stated, letting him know that I was ready to get down to business.

"No disrespect, Amir, but may I have a word with my colleagues for a second?" Tony said, cutting in on our conversation.

I looked at Rodriguez and he nodded his head in approval. I left and went to join Reese, and informed him of everything that was about to jump off.

• • • • • • •

"So, what do y'all think?" asked Rodriguez.

"I like him," said Frank and Bobby.

"And I do too," Tony said as he watched the expression on each one of their faces. "But, I have a few small problems of concern. I mean, let's face it, Rodriguez. If he turns out to be a rat, you're not going to be the one doing the time. Me or Frank are, and I know he knows the consequences, but let's face reality. Some people will tell on their mothers. I'm not saying he's that type, but they will and you know it. Plus, what if he is that type? Do you think he gives a fuck if we kill his mother?"

"Maybe, maybe not, but I don't think he's that type. You didn't see the look in his eyes when he killed that fuck back at Frank's place. And I'm not just saying this because he helped me out. I really think the kid is special, and I want to give him a shot. Hell, I owe him that much!'"

Everyone agreed with Rodriguez—even Tony, but he still had a few more suggestions to make. "To be honest with you, I like the kid. I think he has the heart of a lion, but I say we have him go get the money tonight."

"Why is that?" asked Frank.

"Look at it like this; we all suspected that he was getting a little money. Now he's talking about $1.5 million, and this kid isn't even twenty-one. I mean, if he got four or five of his buddies to put up three hundred apiece, they could easily come up with $1.5. And I just don't think we should take some street dealers and turn them into moguls."

"He's got a point," said Bobby.

"So, what are you suggesting?"

"I say one of us goes with him right now and have him get the money. I mean, he has to trust us around his little money, and you're talking about letting him in on a multi-million dollar operation."

"I agree," Frank said

"Me too," said Bobby.

•   •   •   •   •   •   •

I sat in the booth and filled Reese in on everything, except for the price that I was getting them for. Reese was skeptical at first, because he knew that we were dealing with some major players. He also was concerned about my future. He asked me about the plans that I had on going to college and playing ball. I told him that the two or three years that I would spend in college trying to get an education and earning a spot on the team, we all could be mini-millionaires. With that said, he was all for it.

After we finished our discussion, I motioned for the waitress to come over. I gave her a hundred dollar bill and told her to find Tasty and tell her that she had a special guest waiting to see her ASAP.

It wasn't even five minutes before Tasty came strutting in our direction. When she recognized me, she was in total shock. "Amir! What are you doing here?" she asked, blushing from ear to ear.

"The same reason every other man is here. But the question should be, what are *you* doing here?"

"Boy, that waitress thing just wasn't working. Plus, I'm back in school now so I have to do what I have to do."

"I feel that! How long have you working here?"

"About nine months, but it won't be much longer 'cause I'm quitting next semester."

Tasty and I indulged in a semi-deep conversation when the waitress came and told me that I was needed upstairs. I excused myself, but before I left I had Tasty give her number to Reese.

"I see you and Tasty got reacquainted," Tony said as I entered his office.

"Yeah, she's cool, but we can talk about her later? I'm trying to find out what's up," I said, letting them know that I was ready to get down to business.

"Well, I already told you that I don't beat around the bush. Now, we all like you, and I don't just mean *like* you. We all see potential in you and admire your heart. But my colleagues seem to feel that if you want to be involved in our business, then you're going to have to prove your worth."

Rodriguez paused to make sure that he had my undivided attention. "Not saying that you can't come up with the money, but each one of these men can put their hands on a couple of million in cash right now. Each one has it in Swiss bank accounts, all except for Bobby, who's the DEA Agent. He has a couple of million in U.S. bank accounts. So as you can see, we're all pretty wealthy, and if you get involved in our circle, then one day you will be too. But, the bottom line is that we want you to get the money tonight."

"Tonight!"

"Yeah, tonight. You did say whenever. So, if you can't make that happen, then take the briefcase and forget we ever had this conversation."

I was far from the smartest man in the world, but I knew that they didn't believe I had the money. I couldn't fault them because not too many people my age have that type of money. I was glad that my mother told me not to keep all of my money in one place. I had take two million out of my safe and put it in a customized safe that I had installed at my office in the club.

"That's no problem. Y'all ready?" I asked.

"You only have to take one of us, and your buddy can stay here with me," Rodriguez said while looking down at Reese.

"Nah, that won't be necessary. I want to show y'all something anyway. We're only going over to Wake Forest Road."

They all looked at each other for approval. After they agreed to come, I called Reese and told him to meet us outside.

Me and my new connect exited out the back door and down the fire escape. Reese was already sitting in the truck. I went and joined him as I watched Frank and Rodriguez get into the DB7, while Bobby and Tony got in the Porsche. I also peeped two of Rodriguez's bodyguards get into a black Navigator.

When we arrived at the club, I knew they would be surprised. I had just gotten the sign done at the top that read, "Club Comfort Zone".

When they exited their vehicles, Frank was the first to speak. "Whose club is this?" he asked, still amazed at the big bright red sign.

"Mine, so be prepared to loose a few customers!"

Once inside, I had Reese show everyone around while Rodriguez and I headed to my office.

"I like this place. You own it by yourself?" asked Rodriguez after we entered my office.

"Yeah, but my cousin's gon' run it for me."

I removed a painting from the wall of slaves back in slavery days to reveal my safe. I knew there was two million even in the safe. It contained five shelves, and on four of them lay five hundred thousand dollars apiece. I grabbed two duffel bags and emptied three shelves. I sat down at my desk with my money machine and asked Rodriguez if he would like to count it.

"Yeah, but not tonight. You do trust me to count it alone, don't you?"

"Sure! Why not?"

We sat around the office, chatting as if we had been friends forever. It wasn't long before Reese and Rodriguez's guys came storming in. Tony and Bobby were laughing up a storm.

"What's so funny?" asked Rodriguez.

"I think we got ourselves a young mogul, but that's not what's funny," said Bobby.

"Well, what's funny?"

"Looks like Amir here is going to run Frank out of business!"

"No disrespect, Amir. I really like this place, and maybe one day you can help me upscale mine," said Frank.

"I told you stop being so fucking cheap!" Tony said, still laughing.

"Shut up, Tony! Now, like I was saying, I really like this place, but did you have to steal my employees?" Frank heatedly asked me.

"What are you talking about?" asked Rodriguez.

"It's nothing personal, it's the business. Just last week my head bartender gave me a two week's notice. He said that he found a better job at the Comfort Zone. At the time he told me I was kind of busy, so we didn't get into it. But now that I'm here, this is the place!"

I knew exactly what Frank as talking about. I apologized and told him how far Tom and I went back. There were no hard feelings, and Rodriguez made sure that I kept a certain section in VIP reserved for them and anyone else that they referred.

We sat around for another hour or so, laughing and getting to know one another. I found these guys hilarious. We exchanged numbers, and Rodriguez assured me that someone would contact me within the next forty-eight hours for the drop.

Chapter Sixteen
"Blow"

"Ring-Ring!"

"Hello."

"Is this Amir?" a male voice asked.

"Who's this?"

"Come on now. You have to start learning to recognize voices."

"Oh, okay. You ready?" I asked, realizing that it was Tony.

"Yeah, come on by."

When I arrived at the DollHouse, I noticed a stretch Hummer in the parking lot. I entered the club and headed straight to Tony's office as if it was my own.

"What's up, buddy?" Tony asked me as I walked into the office.

"Ain't much. Where is everyone?" I asked as I took a seat in front of Tony's desk.

"Frank and Bobby are at work, and Rodriguez is back in Miami."

"So, he said the money was straight?"

"On the nose."

Tony explained to me that my product was in the limo in three duffel bags. He also told me that this was probably the best cocaine that I ever had. He then demanded I leave my truck so that Ricky could chauffeur me around in the limo.

I really wasn't feeling that until Tony told me that Ricky was family, and that he's been the family's driver for more than fifteen years. He also told me that Rodriguez was having a Ford Excursion delivered to his car lot in Mini City. He said that the Excursion would stash up to fifty kilos. I then requested that he have three of them delivered.

As we exited through the rear and down the fire escape, I called Reese and Dre and told them to both meet me at Dre's house.

• • • • • • •

Reese and Dre both were outside on Dre's porch waiting on my arrival. "There he goes.'" Reese said as he spotted the stretch Hummer coming down the street.

They got in and sat in the back of the limo and shared a few drinks while I gave them the business. They already knew 'death before dishonor', but I still stressed it, because I knew my connect meant business. I gave them fifty kilos apiece for eighteen a pop, which came to a total of them owing me nine hundred thousand dollars each.

I then had Ricky swing over to Trick's house. I pretty much gave Trick the same speech and hit him off with the remaining twenty kilos at eighteen apiece also, which left Trick owing me three hundred and thirty thousand dollars.

The day was still young. It was barley three o'clock. I figured I would swing by the salon and take Deemi out to dinner, being as though I had access to the limo for the day. I had been feeling a little guilty because she and I hadn't been spending a lot of time together lately. I was spending most of my time with Sarah. Things were on the way to another level between us. I was staying with her at least four nights out of the week.

I had Ricky swing by the flower shop and my jeweler so that I could pick up a seven-karat diamond and platinum XO necklace. I had ordered it over a month ago and figured that today was the perfect day to give it to her. I knew she was well deserving of it. Deemi never bitched about anything. She never complained when I didn't come home at night. She knew a dog would find his way home if she let him roam a little bit.

I instructed Ricky to park in front of the salon. I stepped out of the limousine, carrying a dozen of roses.

"Where's Deemi at?" I asked Kelly, who was one of Deemi's top stylists.

"She's in her office," Kelly replied while continuing to do her client's hair.

Deemi barely did hair herself even though she could. I made sure that she didn't, at lease not until she had the baby. All eyes were on me as I strolled to the back.

"Hey, Pooh!" Deemi said to me as I entered her office.

"What's up, baby?"

"Work!" she replied as she stood to greet me. "Why are your hands behind your back?"

I then pulled my hands from behind my back, revealing the dozen roses. I also gave her the box that contained her necklace.

"This is for me, Pooh?" she asked as she ripped open the box as if she was a child on Christmas day. "Awww, this is beautiful, baby!" Deemi said, giving me a hug while I placed the necklace around her neck. She then walked out of her office so that she could show everyone in the shop. I could hear some of the women saying different things:

"No he didn't!"

"You go, girl!"

One even said something about the diamonds.

"Whose limo's out front?" Deemi asked.

"Your fine ass man's!" one of the girls replied.

Wanting to know why I was in a limo, Deemi headed back to her office. "Pooh, why are you in a limo?"

"I came to take you out to dinner, so tell Kelly to hold the shop down while you're gone."

Deemi and I walked out of the shop hand in hand. We ate at the Angus Barn out by Raleigh-Durham International Airport. Dinner was great. We reminisced and talked about our future, the baby, and the fact that I was postponing school.

We both agreed that if I postponed school for too long that I would enroll at NC State or UNC Chapel Hill. But school was the furthest thing from my mind right now.

After dinner, I noticed that time had sneaked past us. It was a now quarter 'til eight, and I had to get Deemi back to the shop so that she could close.

Before she got out of the limousine, she made me promise her that I would come home tonight. I told her that it might be late when I got home, but I promised her that I would be there.

As soon as she exited the limo my phone rang. I looked at the caller ID and noticed that it was Tony. "Hello."

"What's up, buddy?"

"I can't call it. What's up?"

"Are you busy?"

"Nah. Why?"

"'Cause Tasty has been buggin' me for the past two hours. She said something about you were supposed to call but didn't."

"I know you're not calling me for a female!"

"Under normal circumstances I never would, but I owe her a favor, and she told me that I could repay her by contacting you."

"Is she there with you now?"

"No, but she's outside my office."

"Put her on the phone," I said.

Tony placed me on hold for about forty seconds.

"Hello," Tasty said in a voice drenched with desire.

"What's up, ma?"

"You! I've been waiting for you to call for two days. I thought you may have lost my number."

"Nah, I just been busy, but you have been on my mind though."

"Humph! I bet I have!" she said, knowing that I was thinking something nasty.

"You working tonight?"

"Yeah, but I don't check in until eleven."

"Tell Tony I said to give you the night off, 'cause I'm on my way over there."

Once I made it to the club, I gave Ricky a thousand dollars

for his pockets, and just like before, I walked directly to Tony's office. Once inside the office I saw Tasty—or Tonya as I knew her—standing at the tinted window watching everything in the club. Boy did she look good to me in those jeans! This white girl had a body that would put Serena Williams to shame, and a face that would give Carmen Electra a run for her money.

"What's wrong with you?" I asked her, seeing that she was upset about something.

"Nothing. Tony won't give me the night off," she replied, giving Tony an evil look.

I looked at Tony, who was kicked back at his desk, smoking a cigar and laughing.

"What's funny?" she asked.

"You!" Tony replied. "Amir don't run this club. He owns Comfort Zone and I own DollHouse."

Soon as Tony said "Comfort Zone", my phone rang. I peeped at the caller ID and saw that it was my cousin, Porsha. I already knew what she wanted. I had forgotten that I was supposed to meet her at the club by nine. I had to give her the money to go to New York so that she could pay Karren Biggs the up-front money, because we had the entire Roc-A-Fella family performing at the club for our grand opening.

"Everything cool?" Tony asked as I got off of the phone.

"Yeah. I got to go meet Porsha at the club so I can give her the money to pay the entertainers for the grand opening."

I looked at Tasty, who was looking at Tony. He smiled and told her to get out.

When we arrived at the club, I noticed a brand new silver Mercedes Benz E320 with fresh thirty-day tags.

Porsha was surprised to see me with a white girl. The first thing that came out of her mouth was, "I ain't the only one with jungle fever!"

I smiled while looking at Tasty, who looked confused. I then told her not to pay my cousin any attention because she was married to a white guy. Porsha's husband, Karl then emerged from the back. Karl was the coolest white dude I had ever met. I

then remembered the Benz. "Whose car?" I asked Porsha.
"Mine," she replied.
"I told her you weren't going to like it," said Karl.
"Nah, it's straight. I just figured that you were going to do the damn thing."
"I tried to get her to get the Range Rover or that convertible hard top Lexus S.C. 430."
'The S.C. 430 is more like it," I said, agreeing with Karl.
I introduced them to Tonya, and had Karl show her around while I handled my business with Porsha.
After Porsha and her husband left, Tonya and I sat in my office sharing drinks and catching up on the past.
Before I knew it, she had me on the couch, giving me my own personal private show. Every time that I would try to touch her, she would remove my hands, letting me know that she was in full control. But when she stood in front of me and made her ass thunder clap, I couldn't resist it any longer. I jumped up and pinned her against the wall. This time she didn't resist.
I took her breast in my mouth and sucked it gently as I caressed her other breast. Tonya was very aggressive. She spun me around and took full control. I stood against the wall restlessly as she undressed me and placed my manhood in her mouth. She sucked on me until my knees got weak. I pulled her up and placed her on top of my desk. I then placed her feet on my shoulders and pulled her to the edge of the desk and buried my face between her legs.
I was experimenting, because I had never been with a white girl, more or less performed oral sex on one, but I couldn't tell the difference. Tonya had the right stage name because she sure was 'tasty' to me.
After she climaxed I tried to slide in her without a condom, but she wasn't going for that. She got off of the desk and retrieved a condom from her pocketbook. I slid on the condom and went to work. We fucked all over the club: in my office, on top of the main bar, we even fucked in the middle of the dance floor.

Chapter Seventeen
"Grand Opening"

Tonight was the grand opening of club Comfort Zone. Porsha had arranged for three stretch limo's and two, fifteen passenger vans to pick up Jay-Z and the entire Roc-A-Fella Family. I was running around trying to make sure that I had all of my women in place.

I had just left from visiting Sarah, being that she wasn't going to be attending the grand opening. I knew Deemi and Tasty both would be in attendance tonight, and if Sarah had come, there would have been nothing but trouble for me. Sarah had no idea that I was living a double life. She didn't know about Deemi or the baby we were expecting. She thought she was wifey. I was confused myself, because Sarah was all any man could ask for, but yet, I still couldn't give her my all.

Then there was Tasty, who just recently came into my life. Tasty was cool, real down to earth and was willing to play her position. That's why I have been messing with her so tough. I loved the fact that she knew about Deemi and Sarah. Tasty was going to be all over the club because she and Deemi both had the same Platinum VIP cards that gave them access to every VIP section and back stage. I told Tasty that she would know Deemi on sight because she would be the only pregnant female running around the club as if she owned the place. I informed her that if Deemi was to question her, that she would simply say that she was with Tom, my assistant manager.

. . . .

The club was packed. We reached the fire code capacity, and the line was still wrapped around the building.

Rodriguez flew in to show his support. Frank, Tony, Rodriguez and I sat in my office observing the scenery. Freeway and Beanie Siegel were on stage performing. Frank was impressed, and had asked me to help him upgrade his club.

Rodriguez asked me about Reese, and I informed him that he probably wouldn't be seeing Reese due to the fact that he was keeping Dre company. I let Rodriguez know that I didn't want to leave Dre alone as if he wasn't part of my family. Rodriguez understood and agreed to meet Dre in due time, which was cool with me.

The night turned out lovely. Everyone from the Roc performed, and before they closed, I announced that ladies drink for free and got in for free up until twelve o'clock the following night. Everyone knows that wherever the ladies are, the ballers would come, and anybody trying to be somebody would follow. We were now officially open.

Chapter Eighteen
"Small World"

2002

I have been dealing with Rodriguez for a little over two years now, and I could actually say that I was rich. I was worth twenty million easily. Rodriguez had taken me to another level. Not only was I rich, my whole team could count a few million apiece, all except for Trick.

Now, Trick was far from broke and could count two million at will, but Reese and Dre could double that, if not triple it. Trick was a hustler, but he couldn't move coke as fast as Reese and Dre. By the time Trick would finish twenty kilos, Reese and Dre would have done flipped a hundred or so.

Jarius was due home in less than twenty months, and Mike had just been released.

I was still seeing Sarah, and had even helped her buy a house worth three hundred thousand. I was also still seeing Tasty. She had quit dancing and was now in medical school at Duke. I had also helped her get a condo in Durham. Deemi and I were still together. She had given me a beautiful daughter named Arnisha, and I gave her everything that a child her age could possibly dream of.

Club Comfort Zone turned out to be the hottest spot in the city. We profited nine hundred thousand the first year, and $1.5 million the next. I had also helped Frank turn his club around. They changed the name from The DollHouse to 30 Plus, and Frank catered to the older crowd. Tony and I also went in on a black strip club called Platinum's.

I had finally convinced Reese and Dre to do something legal with their money. They owned R&D Hauling, and had about twelve brand new dump trucks. They were on with a major contractor called S.T. Taylor, who built highways for the government.

Deemi and I had just moved into our mansion out in Creedmore Hills. The $3.7 million estate was equipped with ten bedrooms, twelve full bathrooms, an indoor pool, sauna, basketball court outside, and an indoor gym. It also had a small movie theater and a game room.

Rodriguez told me that there was no need to have money if you couldn't enjoy the fruits of life. He owned a couple of mansions and luxury houses in and out of the U.S. He also owned clubs and hotels in Miami, along with two Hertz car rental companies. His money makes mines look like chump change.

My whole team had upgraded their car game. Reese had a silver Bentley Arnage, a pearl yellow Lamborghini Gallardo, and a burgundy Hummer H2. Dre had a red Porsche Carrera GT, a white Rolls Royce Corniche convertible, and a 1965 racing Roadster. But his every day vehicle was a blue Range Rover. Trick was more laid back, but he did have the Ferrari Spider, and everything else was Cadillac. He had a black Escalade E.S.V., a platinum Escalade EXT, a black Deville, and he also had a '67 that would give Dre's '69 a run for its money.

Out at my five-car garage mansion, I had a platinum Bentley Continental GT, an Ameriteck McLaren F1, an Aston Martin Vanquish, a 745i BMW, and a Range Rover that I drove almost every day. I also bought Deemi a red convertible Lexus S.C. 430, and a BMW X5 sport SUV. She also had the keys to every vehicle in the garage, except for the McLaren F1. That car was too fast for any woman to be behind the wheel.

· · · · · · ·

It was early May, and Reese and the crew wanted to take Mike to Atlanta for a couple of days to do some shopping. Mike was yet to experience the out of town stunting. We always attended the big events: All Star Weekend, Memorial Weekend in Miami, Mardi Gras in New Orleans, BET Awards, and if there was a big fight somewhere, we were there. I really didn't feel like going to Atlanta, but I let the fellows talk me into going.

Once in Atlanta, we headed straight to Magic City. Reese had reserved five suites for us at the Hilton. We got our drink on and made it rain as usual. None of us were worried about getting laid. We could buy any pussy in the club if we wanted to.

I was coming from the restroom when I spotted a sexy Puerto Rican chick standing by the bar. "Excuse me, what's your name?" I asked her.

She smiled and said, "Scarlet."

Scarlet had a smile that would drive any man wild. I told her that I didn't want her stage name, but preferred her birth name, but she wasn't trying to hear that. Being the player that I am, after a few drinks and small conversation, I finally convinced her to give me her real name, which was Chanel.

Chanel was a model/stripper. She was also a video girl and the proud owner of a website that provided brothers locked down an opportunity to meet people on the Internet. She also sold pictures of herself to inmates, and pictures of hundreds of other girls. The photos came in different packages: Nude, semi-nude, swimsuits, G-strings, back shots, front shots, and some with sexy facial expressions.

I was digging Chanel because she was about the paper. With Jarius being locked down and Mike just coming home, I knew exactly how it felt for a brother on lock down.

Chanel and I talked for a while longer, and she made it plain and clear to me that she made all of her money in the club. With that said, I was ready to end the conversation. We exchanged numbers, but before we departed she told me that if she saw me leave the club with another woman, I might as well lose her number. That was cool with me, because even though she was a dime, she couldn't have been anything more than a fuck. I already had three females that I had feelings for and was taking care of.

The following day, we began our shopping spree at Lennox Mall. I was inside of a jewelry store looking at a platinum XO ankle bracelet that would go perfectly with Deemi's platinum XO necklace. I was talking to the salesperson, when Trick approached me with Binky. Binky was one of the strippers that we had taken back to the hotel.

"Guess who I just saw?" Trick asked.

"Who?"

"Your girl!"

"Who?" I asked again. I was curious to know who Trick was referring to.

"What's shorty's name that you used to talk to back in the day?"

"What shorty back in the day?"

"Shorty with the Geo Storm."

"Shanta!"

"Yeah, that's her. I just saw her."

"Nigga, you ain't see no Shanta."

"Shi-i-i-t, nigga! I don't forget no faces, especially not her fine ass!" Trick replied as he watched me smile at his statement.

"Where you see her at?" I asked, hoping he didn't say that she was with a nigga.

"She works in Footlocker."

"Get the fuck outta here!"

"I ain't bullshitting.

We headed to Footlocker. I didn't even have to get a clear view of Shanta. I knew it was her from the side. She was my first love, and if it weren't for this dope game, we would probably still be together. After I got my thoughts together, I entered the store.

Shanta was helping a customer and never saw me coming, but her customer did. I held my index finger over my lips to tell the customer to be quiet. I got right behind Shanta and said, "Excuse me! Where are my fuckin' shoes?"

"Excuse me!" Shanta said as she turned around. When she realized that it was me, she jumped for the joy and hugged me as if she hadn't seen me in ten years. Even though it was only five years since we last spoke, feelings for her came back instantly. "What are you doing here?" she asked.

"I came to find you."

"Boy, stop lying! Now, what are you doing here?"

I explained to her my reason for being in Atlanta. She was surprised to see Trick. She looked over at him, and he was obviously buying some shoes, which was an usual sight for me to see. Trick had a soft spot for women. He had a bad habit of spending money on women that he just met.

"Is that crack head Trick?"

"Yeah, that's him, but he don't get high no more."

Shanta was surprised and happy for Trick at that same time. The last time she had seen him, he was smoking like a freight train.

We made small talk, and I wanted to give her my number, but she wasn't trying to hear that. She told me that she wasn't letting me get out of her sight. She was the store manager, so it was no problem for her to have her assistant cover for her.

I just shook my head, because Shanta was still the same; once her mind was made up, there was no changing it. It felt a little strange to me being around her after all of these years, but at the same time, it felt right.

Shanta, Trick, Binky and I headed over to the food court to meet up with Reese, Dre and Mike. Mike noticed Shanta instantly. After we all got reacquainted, I informed the fellows that I was going to roll with Shanta, and that I would catch up with them later.

Once in the parking garage, I was shocked to see that Shanta still had the same Geo Storm. This was her first car, and obviously it was her only car. I made a mental note to at least help her get a new one.

We both were hungry, so we headed over to the Sun Down. This was a restaurant that gave you a view of the entire city.

While we reminisced, Shanta informed me that she had a son named Lonnie who was three years old. She told me that she had to drop out of school because of Lonnie. She said that her mother wanted her to have an abortion and finish school, but she didn't believe in abortion, and neither did I. That's why Shanta had to move back to Atlanta, so that her grandmother could help her raise her son while she finished school at Clark University.

When I asked about Lonnie's father, she let it be known that his father was a deadbeat, and that he denied him up until two months before his death. That's when I found out that Lonnie's father was killed in a car accident six months after he was born.

Shanta filled me in on her status, and I felt that it was only right that I filled her in on mine. I told her about Deemi and my daughter, Arnisha, which she already knew about through my cousin, Kim. I told her that I really wasn't happy, but stayed with my baby momma for the sake of my daughter, which was a lie.

Shanta understood, because she was overprotective of her son, who she hadn't had around a man in over eight months. Her son had only seen her with one man outside of his father, who he didn't remember, but he somewhat remembered her friend, Kevin.

When I asked about Kevin, she informed me that he was a local dude that she met at school. She also told me that she hadn't dealt with him in eight months. I also found out that was the last time that she had been sexually active, which meant that she was past due for some dick, and I had every intention on catching her up.

I also told her about the club, the fleet of cars, and Jarius's status. I told her everything, except about Rodriguez and his crew, and about Sarah and Tasty. Even though I was rich, I felt comfortable talking to Shanta about my accomplishments. She was my first love, and was with me when Jarius was taking care of me, so I knew she wasn't a gold digger.

Shanta was proud of me and all of my accomplishments. She was cool with everything except for Deemi living in the mansion. When I asked her why she was jealous, she said, "I'm not jealous. That's supposed to be *me* living there, and I should be Arnisha's mother, and you should be Lonnie's father." She went on to reminisce about the nights we shared at my mother's house, about how I would tell her my dreams of going to the NFL, buying a mansion, and us having kids and being a family.

I was surprised that she still remembered those nights. I told her that I wanted to meet her son. She was hesitant at first, but once she realized who she was talking to, everything was all good.

When we arrived at Shanta's grandmother's house, Lonnie was on the porch playing with Shanta's grandmother. He was happier than R. Kelly at a Girl Scout meeting to see his mother. He favored her in so many ways. I took a liking to the little fellow right away. He had the look of a little thug, and I could tell that he was bad and probably spoiled. He looked real handsome in his Sean John outfit and black Airforce Ones. He had cornrows, and a little gold chain that read "Momma's Boy".

Shanta introduced me to her grandmother, who surprised me when she said that she already knew who I was. This threw me for a loop, because I had never met her. Curious to know how she knew me, I asked her. She then told me that I would find out once I walked into the house.

When we walked into the house, I couldn't help but notice the picture of me and Shanta at her senior prom. I have the same picture up at my mother's house.

Lonnie must have taken a liking to me, because he gave me a tour of their house. He also had me in his room, playing with Lego's.

After I played with Lonnie, we headed to his mother's room so that I could talk with her. I told Shanta that I wanted her to go out with me tonight, but she wasn't feeling that because she hadn't been out in over a year. I wasn't hearing that. I was determined she was going to go out with me.

I then called Reese and asked him his whereabouts. He told me that they were at the ESPN Zone with Binky and some of their friends. I then gave Reese Shanta's grandmother's address and told him to come and pick me up as soon as they left. Even though none of us were from Atlanta, getting around wasn't a problem because all of our vehicles were equipped with On Star.

Shanta and I were sitting on the porch when Trick and Reese pulled up. She fell in love with Trick's Escalade. She also liked Reese's Hummer, but how could you not? It was in a class of its own.

I gave Shanta my room key and told her to meet me at the room once she got dressed. She acted as if she didn't want the key and told me that just because she was going out with me didn't mean that I was getting any pussy tonight. But I let that statement go in one ear and out the other.

When we left Shanta's grandmother's house, I called my man, Rome, who owned Club 112, in Atlanta. I had met Rome in Los Angeles at a club owner's convention. I informed him that I was in Atlanta and would be stopping by.

I then called David Thompson, who owned A Cut Above Limousines. David had all types of exotic limousines, from stretch Hummers to Escalades and Bentleys. I had arranged for him to have someone pick us up in his new stretch Phantom that sat fourteen people comfortably.

When Shanta arrived at the room, it was almost eleven o'clock. We were both dressed to impress. I was wearing A/X Armani gear, while Shanta rocked an outfit by Gucci. I loved the way her outfit hugged her body. I pulled her close to me and we began to tongue kiss. When she felt my dick stand at attention, she pushed me away. There was no way she was letting me get some pussy before the club.

Since we were going to be stunting for the night, Trick and Reese wanted to go pick up Binky and her crew. I thought it was a good idea, because Shanta was the only female with us.

After we picked Binky and her girls up, we cruised the

streets of Atlanta, smoking and drinking. We had the Phantom smoked out. When we pulled up at 112, all eyes were on the Phantom. Binky and her girls felt like some true divas stepping out of the Phantom with some real ballers.

Once inside the club, we were led to VIP, where we popped bottle after bottle as if it was water. Finally, we bought out the bar, making our presence known, and repping North Carolina to the fullest.

Finally, Shanta and I hit the dance floor. When we came back, Rome came over to check on me and to make sure that I was enjoying myself. It was going on 3:30 a.m., and even though 112 didn't close until the break of dawn, I was ready to go. I was tired and hungry, not to mention drunk.

When we got outside the club, the parking lot was jam-packed. Mike had never experienced anything like this before. He had the time of his life, and enjoyed every minute of it.

Once Shanta and I made it back to the room, I wasted no time. We kissed as we undressed one another. I laid her on the bed and licked her from head to toe. I ate her out for what seemed like an eternity, and I made her cum repeatedly. When I went to enter her, she made me stop. She then reached for her bag and passed me a pack of condoms.

"For somebody who ain't giving me no pussy, you sho' come prepared!" I said as I took the pack of condoms from her.

She then instructed me to lie down. She grabbed my dick and placed it in her mouth. I could tell that she was a little rusty, but I coached her back into perfection. I knew that she was trying to please me as she did when we were younger. I worked my way in her nice and slow, and before I knew it, we were fucking all over the place.

Chapter Nineteen
"Keeping it Gangsta"

It's been a little over a month since we left Atlanta, and even though I talked with Shanta every day, I missed her dearly. I honestly thought about leaving Deemi. Even though I had feelings for Tasty and Sarah, none of them added up to the love that I still harbored for Shanta. I thought that I was over her, but in all actuality, I had just fallen in love with the streets.

I knew that I could always kick it with Tasty because we had that understanding. But Sarah was another story. She was starting to press me more about moving in full time, but I wasn't ready for a move like that. Sarah was still in the blind. I still hadn't told her about Deemi or my daughter. I kept all of my women in the blind. I wasn't worried about any of them crossing paths, because they all lived totally different lives. Plus, none of them knew each other personally.

. . . .

I had finally convinced Shanta to come to North Carolina for the weekend. I was dying to see her. I'd just been so busy that I hadn't had a chance to get back to Atlanta. I had gone the extra mile to help her. I knew that even if we would never be together again as a couple, I would want the best for her and her son.

I had my cousin, Porsha go on line and purchase a house in a nice subdivision in Marietta, which was right by Atlanta. She purchased it in the company's name, but had the deed put in Shanta's name. I also bought her a brand new Lincoln Navigator. Porsha thought that I was going overboard, being that Shanta had just come back into my life, but I explained my feelings for Shanta and how I used to share my dreams of putting her in a house when I went to the NFL. I told Porsha that even though I didn't go pro, I still turned out pretty wealthy, and doing this for Shanta wasn't going to make me or break me. After Porsha and I talked, she understood how I felt, and said that the world needed more men like me who were always willing to help an individual out.

I called Trick, because he had arranged for Binky and her friends to fly in with Shanta. I knew that the girls would have a great time, because I had the Big Tymers performing at the club on Saturday. I wasn't worried about Deemi, because she was in New York at a hair show, and Sarah never came to my club. She always attended Frank's place, 30 Plus. Tasty was attending a family reunion back in Tennessee, so this was the perfect weekend for them to come down without any drama jumping off.

•   •   •   •   •   •   •

We all met at the airport and waited on the girls' arrival. We parked one behind the other, dead in front of the airport as if we were at a car show. Reese came in his Lamborghini Gallardo, Dre was in his Porsche Carrera GT, Trick was in his Ferrari Spider, and I was in my McLaren F1. I was the only one to actually go inside the airport and wait for the girls' flight to arrive. When the girls came out of the tunnel, they looked like four beauty queens that just stepped off of the set of a *Smooth* magazine shoot.

"Where's Trick?" Binky asked.

"They had something to take care of. They said that they'll get with y'all later," I replied, and gave Shanta a hug. All of the other girls looked disappointed. When I noticed that not one girl had a bag, I asked, "Where is y'all's luggage?"

"Child, please! Reese told us to come as we are!" said Ashanti.

"Oh, excuse me!"

Now, Ashanti was fine as hell. She reminded me of the rapper, Trina, but the girl had a mouth on her. She was too fine for her own good, and she knew it.

When we exited the airport, the girls were stunned to see the fellows posted up beside the fleet of luxury cars as if they owned the airport.

I was cruising down Interstate 40 at a rapid speed until Reese went past me, balling in his Lamborghini. Then came Trick in his Ferrari, followed by Dre in his Porsche. I looked over at Shanta for her approval, and she smiled, and with that smile, I shifted back to third and the F1 took off. I pulled in front of the pack with ease, but Reese wasn't going for it. He pulled up to the side of me in his Lambo and looked at me as if he was ready for war. I shifted back to third and gave him what he wanted. The F1 had a mind of its own, and the Lambo was no match for it. We raced all the way to Crabtree Valley Mall, where the girls shopped for hours.

After we left the mall, we headed over to the club to pass the time. I was debating whether or not I was going to surprise Shanta with the house. I knew when I was going to surprise her with the truck. I had it parked at Rodriguez's mansion, because that's where everyone was going to be staying, except for Trick and Binky. They were staying at Trick's house in the country. Trick was single, so he was able to take women home, unlike Reese, Dre and myself, who all had a woman living with us.

Shanta and I headed to my office, while everyone else played pool. The crew was starting to come in so that they could prepare for tonight's opening. While in my office, I pulled up a picture on the computer of the house that I had purchased for her. "Come look at this house on the Internet," I said to her as she came and sat on my lap.

"Yes, that's beautiful!" she replied, and took the mouse from me and began clicking onto other houses.

"Do you really like it?"

"Yes. Why?" she asked as I slid back to my file cabinet so that I could give her the deed.

Shanta didn't know what it was at first. "Amir, I know this ain't the deed to that house!" she said.

"Yeah. Why, don't you like it?"

"I love it, but this house costs four hundred and fifty thousand!"

"So?"

"So, I can't take it," she said, giving me back the deed.

"Well, sell it and buy you another one with the money."

"No! I don't want the money or this house!" she said, covering her face. She couldn't believe that I had bought a house for her. She had never had a man do anything for her, outside of me.

"Hear me out," I stated as I removed her hands so that she could see the sincerity in my eyes. "What we had when we were in school was special. You were my first love, and whether you believe me or not, I still love you. We had dreams of owning a house and raising a family. Now, I might not be able to give you the family part due to my situation with Deemi, but this house, I can."

"I just can't take it."

"Look, you owe me nothing. I don't want you to have to depend on a nigga for shit!" I said in a tone that let her know that I meant every word that I was saying. "This way, I'll know you and your son are straight. You don't have to worry about me trying to take the house from you. That's why I put it in your name."

"And how were you able to do that without me being present?"

"Let's just say I know people in high places."

"Thank you!" she said as tears began to flow from her

eyes.

"Don't thank me. I owe you that much."

"Why do you say that?"

"Because if I wasn't so stuck on myself hustling when you went to college, we would probably still be together. I would have at least gone to collage and got a degree, and if I didn't make it pro, I still would have been able to provide for you through my education. I still made it, just another way, and I feel that it's only right that I do this for you."

After our talk, we headed back downstairs to join everyone else. Porsha was just coming in, and Mike came in shortly after her. Mike was too busy trying to get his paper up to be fooling around with any females. Besides, he had a main squeeze that held him down his entire bid, and they were the modern day Bonnie and Clyde.

I was only giving Mike ten kilos at a time. I felt that he had to work his way back into the mix of things before I could drop a load on him. Reese, Dre and Trick blessed Mike with a CLK500, and I bought him a candy apple red Range Rover. Those were his welcome home presents from us.

Getting tired of sitting around the club, we headed out to Rodriguez's house. When we arrived at the house, I pulled right in front of the Navigator. I had gotten Shanta's Navi airbrushed on the front tag. She didn't even notice the tag because she was too caught up in the house. Reese must have realized this, because he tapped on the hood to get her attention.

"What is he pointing at?" Shanta asked me.

I then hit my headlights so that she could see what it was that Reese was pointing at. When she realized what it said, she jumped out of the car and ran directly to the driver's side.

"You like?" I asked as I got out of the car.

"I love it, but you didn't—"

"Don't even start that again!" I said as I reached into my pocket to give her the keys and the title.

I then glanced over at Ashanti and the other girl, Breonda, and could see the envy in their eyes. I knew that they were gold diggers trying to come up, but they would never get anything of this nature from Reese or Dre. The only things that they would get from them niggas would be some dick and a shopping spree every now and then. Around the way, they called them "tennis shoe hoes" or "outfit hoes" because that's all that you had to do for them. They were too stupid to milk a nigga for a house or a car.

●   ●   ●   ●   ●   ●

It was Sunday, and the girls were headed back to Atlanta. They enjoyed themselves over the weekend. They all had pictures with the Big Tymers and their whole clique.

Shanta didn't want to leave, but she knew that she had to get back to her son. I had given her a hundred grand to furnish the house, and whatever she didn't spend, I told her to put in her bank account. She thought this was a dream come true, to come to North Carolina empty handed, and go back home with a brand new truck and house. I also made her go visit my mother, because they hadn't seen each other in years.

Chapter Twenty
"You Can Run, But You Can't Hide"

It had been four months since Shanta came to visit me. I had been to visit her in Atlanta on several occasions. We were becoming close again, and she was afraid because her son was getting attached to me. She really never pressed me, but I knew she didn't like being played second to Deemi.

I was beginning to experience problems with my women. Sarah was still pressing me about moving in, and we were starting to argue a lot. I found myself spending less and less time with her, and our relationship was on its way downhill.

What's done in the dark will eventually come to light. I found that saying to be true, because Tasty just told me that she was six weeks pregnant, and because I didn't believe in abortion, there was no hiding my child. I was forced to man up and bring Tasty to the light, because I sure as hell wasn't going to let my kids grow up and not know each other, and take the chance of them dating one another when they got older. Even though I knew that the chances of that were slim to none, it still was a possibility. My kids were going to grow up knowing each other, and loving one another the way siblings are supposed to.

• • • • • • •

I rode to Atlanta with Trick to visit Shanta and Binky. Trick had done fell head over heels for Binky, and had even bought her an Infiniti G 35 sports coupe.

It was Thursday, and Shanta and I were on our way out to dinner. We were cruising down the highway when Shanta spotted a car that she liked. "Baby, I want that car!" she said, knowing that I would buy her anything that she asked me for.

"What car?"

"That hard top convertible beside us."

I leaned up so that I could look at the SC 430 that she was talking about. "Oh shit!" I said.

"What?"

"Follow that car!"

"Boy, is you crazy? I ain't following them people!"

"No, seriously! Follow that car!" I said in a tone that confused her.

"Baby, what's going on?"

"Look, just ease up and follow that car. I'll explain later."

The saying that you can run, but you can't hide was so true. I couldn't believe I was sitting here, following behind Jarius's ex-girl and punk ass Tito, who sold me those twenty five kilos of bullshit. I had to explain to Shanta that the less she knew, the better off she was. But since she insisted that she wanted to know why she was following the Lexus, I told her, but I didn't tell her what I was about to do.

She was cool about the whole situation, and said that whatever happens to them, they deserved it, especially Tasha's shady ass.

We followed them to some apartments on the outside of the city. We parked and watched them go into the first apartment on the second floor. I called Trick ASAP, because I knew that he kept a gun with him at all times. Trick asked me for the address, and neither Shanta nor I knew it, so I pressed the On Star button and asked the operator for my location. Once she gave it to me, I relayed it to Trick, who relayed it to his On Star operator.

I had to make Shanta leave when Trick arrived, but she

was determined to wait on me. She showed me a side of her that I had never seen. She was trying to help me mastermind a plan, and was even willing to play a role by knocking on the door. That way, when they heard a female voice, they wouldn't hesitate about opening the door. I had to remind her of her son, because it seemed as if she got caught up in the spur of the moment and her excitement got to her.

Trick and I sat in his Deville, going over our plan. I was going to linger around the hallway and wait for one of them to come out. Trick was going to be the lookout man at the bottom of the steps. With our plan in order, we set out on our mission.

As soon as we got to the steps, the apartment door opened. I recognized Tasha's voice, so I stepped back and stood to the side so that I could get a better view, while Trick loitered at the bottom of the steps. I wasn't worried about Tasha noticing Trick, because she didn't know him. I noticed that she was alone. She never had a chance to react, because Trick snatched her by her neck and put her in a chokehold. Her eyes got as big as grapefruits when she noticed me. I could have sworn I heard her heart actually beating.

"What's up, Tasha? We finally see each other again!"

"I didn't want to!" she managed to say. She was still shocked that she was actually looking at me.

"Who's in the house?" I asked, but she didn't answer so I flashed the pistol in her face, ready to break her jaw if she acted stupid.

"Joey, Tito and Lisa!" she mumbled.

"Who's Lisa?"

"Joey's girl."

I told Tasha that if she cooperated with me that I would spare her life. She somehow believed me and told me that Tito and Joey were strapped, but I wasn't worried about that because I had the element of surprise, and I was sure that they weren't expecting any guests.

I knocked on the door and stood behind Tasha.

"Who is it?" Lisa asked without looking through the peephole.

I nudged Tasha in her back with the pistol. "Me, girl," she responded, fearing for her life. I was ready to lay her ass down.

When the door opened, I rushed in, knocking Lisa to the floor while I used Tasha as my shield. Joey and Tito were sitting on the couch looking SOS (stuck on stupid). I didn't even give them a chance to react or explain. I just filled both of them up with hollow-points. I then turned to Lisa, who was still on the floor, and put two shots in her head. I looked at Tasha, who stood in shock. "Bitch, get your ass over here!"

"Please! You promised you would spare my life!"

"Nah, bitch, you must pay for the way you did my nigga, Jarius."

"*Que?* What? I ain't do shit to Jarius! Joey and Tito made me do it!"

"*Que* what my ass! You dirty Dominican whore! I don't know what Jarius saw in you—"

"Please! I'll do anything you want!"

"I'm not gonna tell you again. Strip!"

Tasha came out her clothes quicker than a muthafucka.

Trick was ready to cop himself some Dominican ass, but I wasn't here for that. I was here to teach Tasha a lesson.

"Now, bend over and spread that fat ass, now!"

Tasha bent over and spread her ass cheeks open. I inserted Trick's pistol into her fat pussy and squeezed the trigger twice. Then I pulled the pistol out of her and emptied the rest of the clip in her face. I looked down at her and said, "Pay back is a bitch! Now we are even!"

Chapter Twenty-One
"Code Five"

It had been five months since the incident in Atlanta, and I had only been back twice. I still was paranoid, even though I knew that I was clean.

Everything was still the same in all of my relationships. Sarah was still tripping about me moving in. The bitch had to be crazy.

Tasty was getting bigger and bigger by the day. She was now six and a half months pregnant.

Deemi was messed up when I told her I had a white girl pregnant. She told me that she wanted to meet her, and I told her she already had. When she asked when, I asked her if she remembered the first time that we went out to eat. She then knew exactly whom I was talking about. She told me that she even remembered seeing her at the club the night of the grand opening. She started threatening and telling me what she was going to do to Tasty, but I let it be known that if she fucked with Tasty while she was carrying my baby, she would be in a world of trouble with me. I had no problem breaking her stupid ass up if she fucked with Tasty.

. . . .

"Ring-Ring!"
"Hello."
"What's up?"
"Who's this?" asked Trick.
"Rodney."
"Oh. You ready?"
"Yeah. Where you want me to met you at?"
"Meet me at Wal-Mart in an hour."

When Trick pulled up to Wal-Mart, he drove through the parking lot until he spotted Rodney's blue Expedition. Rodney got out of his truck and into the Suburban with Trick. They exchanged a little small talk before Rodney gave Trick a bag of money that was supposed to contain fifty two grand, but was only thirteen thousand in small bills.

Trick had been dealing with Rodney since I put him up under me. Rodney used to be one of my lieutenants, but when I took my game to another level, I left Rodney behind. Rodney was a natural fuck-up, but I still made sure that he was able to eat.

Trick hit the stash spot that contained six kilos and a pistol. As he went to give Rodney two kilos, Rodney opened the passenger door, and in a matter of seconds, the Suburban was surrounded by Raleigh's finest and DEA. Trick looked at Rodney, who stepped out of the truck and past the agents. Trick knew exactly what time it was, but everything happened so fast that he couldn't even react or close the stash spot back up.

• • • • • • •

"Steve Johnson, a.k.a. Trick!" said Detective Knight.

Trick just sat quietly until two DEA Agents walked in. Detective Knight, who was head of narcotics for Raleigh's Police Department, introduced the agents as DEA Agent Field Officer Bobby Hill, and his boss, Greg Anthony, Field Supervisor. After the agents introduced themselves, Agent Hill started his interview. Trick had already been read his rights, so he was fully aware of what was about to go down.

"Mr. Johnson, you do know you're in deep shit, don't you?"

"Yeah."

"Well, you got one time, and one time only to help yourself. I mean, two kilos of crack and four kilos of powder; fuck the powder! The two keys of crack and the pistol are enough to bury your ass up under the jail."

"What do you want to know?" Trick asked, knowing that they wanted him to cooperate.

"I want to know everything that you know."

"Well, if I cooperate, y'all got to put me in witness protection, and y'all got to let me go. We're not dealing with no street punks. I'm talking about some straight up killers, and this shit is bigger than you think. But I only can give *him* to you, because I don't know his connect, but I do know his main two runners who he gives at least a hundred kilos apiece. My snitch game is bigger than the two kilos of crack and that pistol you found."

"Who's this *him* you're talking about?" Agent Hill asked, knowing good and well that he was talking about me.

Agent Hill knew of Trick, and he knew all about his involvement with me. Agent Hill was supposed to be off today, but when his boss called him and asked him if he was interested in a drug bust today, he said yes. Something inside of him told him to take this case, but his boss wouldn't explain the details over the phone. And when he got with him and saw the name Steve Johnson, he already knew who it was. But he didn't know that Trick was going to cooperate so easily.

Trick had no idea who Agent Hill really was, and it was too late for Agent Hill to warn me, so he had to go along with the interview and warn me the first chance he got.

"I'm not saying shit until we have a sure enough deal," Trick said.

"I need more than that to assure you a deal."

"Oh shit!"

"What?" Agent Hill responded, wondering whether Trick was hip to him. He knew that he had never met Trick, but he didn't know if I had mentioned his name. "What?" Hill asked again.

"That gun!"

"What about it?"

"It was involved in a four-way homicide!"

"A what?" asked Agent Anthony.

"A four-way homicide."

"How do I know you ain't kill four people and are trying to blame it on somebody else?"

"'Cause I didn't, but it is my gun. I've been meaning to get rid of it, but it kept slipping my mind," Trick said, placing his head down. *I can't believe that I'm actually helping the Feds!* Agent Hill and his supervisor looked at one another in shock.

Even though Agent Anthony was DEA and his main concern were narcotics, he still loved murder cases. He had spent twelve years in DC with the DC Homicide Division, and was a pretty good homicide detective. "Where did these murders take place?" asked Agent Anthony.

"I'm not saying shit until we have a deal."

"Well, when the ballistics come back to that gun and we run it through our database, we'll find out what homicide it was used in… and guess what?"

"What?"

"You're going to wear those charges, because we didn't catch your buddy with the gun."

Trick sat quietly, because he knew what the agent was saying was true. "Atlanta," he replied.

"Atlanta, huh?"

"Yeah, Atlanta. It happened about four or five months ago and I witnessed it. I saw it all. I was there."

"If you're telling the truth, we just might have a deal. I have to make a few calls first."

Agent Anthony pulled out his cell phone and was on the phone with the lead detective in Atlanta in no time. The detective confirmed that there were four homicides about five months ago. He also said that he had an eyewitness who could identify the shooter. Anthony let him know that he would be faxing him a photo of Trick, and if this wasn't his shooter, then he knew who it was. He also let the detective know that he had a gun that was possibly the murder weapon. He then gave the detective his cell phone number and told him to contact him as soon as he knew if Trick was the shooter or not.

The agents then interrogated Trick a while longer, but he wasn't telling them anything else until they agreed to his terms.

Two hours passed before Agent Anthony got a call from the detective in Atlanta, confirming that Trick was not the shooter, according to his witness. That's all Anthony need to hear before he agreed to Trick's deal. He had already talked to the head prosecutor for the federal government on the eastern coast of North Carolina, and had the green light to do whatever he felt was necessary, even if it meant letting Trick back out to work for them.

With that taken care of, Trick was satisfied. He told them everything, including my real name and address. He told them about the club, and Reese and Dre. He said that he never met or saw my connect, but knew that they were some powerful people. He also told them the reason why I killed Tito, Joey, Tasha and the girl, Lisa.

Agent Hill sat silently, but added a few questions of his own every now and then to make sure that Trick had never seen my connect. He didn't want his uncle and them caught up in this mess. He was surprised, because he knew that I had saved his uncle, but he had no idea that I was such a killer.

Hill wrote down a couple of notes on his pad while his boss closed the interview. He was glad, because he was ready to contact his uncle and me, because he most definitely didn't want me confessing to any murders on tape because Trick was sure to wear a wire.

After another thirty minutes of small talk, Trick was taken in front of a magistrate judge and was released on his own recognizance.

• • • • • • •

Agent Hill left the office shortly after his boss. He pulled up at the BP gas station and called Rodriguez from the pay phone.

"Hello," Rodriguez answered.

"It's me," said Bobby.

"What's going on, nephew?"

"We got a code-five on Amir's team."

"Does he know about it?"

"Nah, but I need for you to contact him and have him meet me at Frank's place now. I'll explain more to you later, but Amir's a real live wire. He kind of reminds me of Uncle Ben."

Rodriguez didn't know what to think when comparing me to Ben. Ben was as good as gold, but when crossed, he'd kill his own flesh and blood. If it weren't for Ben, Rodriguez wouldn't be in the position that he's in today. He loved Ben dearly. He snapped out of his thoughts and called me.

"Hello."

"Hey, buddy!"

"What's up, big guy?"

I asked, knowing that it was Rodriguez.

"You tell me. You're the one with the code-five."

"Say what?" I asked, knowing that code-five meant a rat or snitch on my team.

"You heard me. So, meet Bobby at Frank's place now. I want this taken care of."

"Don't worry about that. I'm on my way. I'll call you when it's done."

I was out eating with Sarah when the call came through on my Nokia. Needless to say, Sarah was pissed when I told her that I had an emergency, but she didn't argue because she knew it was urgent if I got a call on my Nokia cell phone.

I pulled in the back of Frank's place and noticed Bobby's black Tahoe. When I entered the club, Tony, Bobby and Frank were sitting in Frank's office. They were the only ones there. The club was only open Thursday through Saturday, and today was just Tuesday.

I couldn't believe the mess I was hearing. *This bitch ass nigga was singing like a bitch!* I thought to myself.

Bobby let me hear the whole tape of the interview. He then informed me how everything took place, starting with Rodney. I was discomposed regarding Rodney. I had no idea that he had gotten busted with eleven ounces of crack and a pistol. That's why he set Trick up. I hated the fact that two of my peoples couldn't hold hot water.

Bobby informed me that Rodney had gone to Virginia so that he could stay with his grandmother until they completed their investigation. He also informed me that Trick had gotten caught with the pistol that was used in the murders in Atlanta.

I was shocked at this news, because Trick had told me that he had gotten rid of the gun. I was even more surprised when Bobby told me they had an eyewitness, and that Trick was not identified as the shooter. Bobby said that Atlanta would end up showing their witness my picture, and if I was identified as the shooter, they would end up issuing a warrant for my arrest. He advised me that they probably wouldn't issue the warrant until Trick wore a wire to try and get me to confess to the murders. He also warned me about his boss, Agent Anthony. He told me that he was working this murder case as if he was assigned to it.

I then had to explain to them what actually took place in Atlanta. They all were pissed at me for not thinking and acting out of anger. I knew that they had people to take care of these particular situations, but I'm a firm believer in handling my own business.

Bobby finally told me that I would end up with a warrant

regardless of how things turned out, especially if the witness identifies me as the shooter. That's the one thing that puzzled me, because I didn't see anyone, and I was sure that nobody saw me. But yet, they had an eyewitness. He also informed me that due to the fact that they were out of his district, it would be hard for him to find out who this witness was. He said that when I get my Motion for Discovery, it would show the witness's name and statement, and regardless of whether he or she was in or out of jail, they would never make it to court.

It was barely eleven o'clock, and except for Bobby, we were all still sitting around Frank's office doing nothing, until my phone rang.

"What's up, boy?" Dre asked me.

"Ain't shit. What's up with you?"

"Nothing. I was just calling to see if you wanted to go with us to Platinum's."

"Who's with you?"

"Reese and Trick."

"Oh yeah?" I said, surprised that Trick would want to hang out.

"Yeah. This nigga, Trick is tripping. He's talking about moving to Atlanta with that damn girl."

"Word?"

"Yeah. The nigga's been drinking and everything. You know that nigga don't drink like that."

"I know. Yo, swing by Frank's place and call me when you get out front."

I hung up the phone and explained to them what was about to take place. Frank didn't mind, because he knew what had to be done. He just didn't want it done at his place of business, but what other choice did he have?

Trick may have a slight inkling that I knew about him getting busted earlier. *That's why he's been drinking,* I thought to myself. He knew he just bit the hand that fed him, and you never bite the hand that feeds you. I was truly hurt, because I cared deeply for him. I nurtured him from a crack head to a millionaire.

I was glad that Tony's bodyguard was with me. Big Terry stood 6'7" and weighed three hundred and fifty pounds. Frank also called his bodyguard, Ken, who stood 6'4" and weighed two hundred and eighty pounds. When Frank got off the phone, he called Bobby. We all wanted to see the look on Trick's face when he saw Bobby — or Agent Hill as he knew him.

Fifty minutes passed before Reese and them arrived. Tony, Frank and Big Terry were seated at the bar, while I went to let them in. Trick ratting me out was eating me alive. We shared a few drinks before I nodded my head to Big Terry, who then grabbed Trick from behind, knocking over the stool that he was sitting on. Trick tried to reach for his pistol, but was unsuccessful.

Reese and Dre drew their weapons instantly. "What the fuck is going on?" Reese asked.

"Put them guns away before y'all get yourselves killed," said Frank.

"Fuck that! He gon' get killed if he don't let go of Trick by the time I count to three!"

"Reese, put the gun down!" I ordered.

Dre began to lower his pistol upon seeing that I was calm and collected.

"One!"

"You're about to make a big mistake!" said Tony.

"Two!"

"Reese, just listen!"

"Three!"

As soon as Reese said "three", the rear exit door opened, and in walked Bobby and Ken. Reese hesitated, and I told him to chill and let this situation play itself out. Reese finally lowered his gun.

Trick looked dumbfounded when he saw Bobby — or Agent Hill — stand beside me and hand me the mini-recorder that recorded their interview earlier. I didn't say anything. I just pressed "play" and let Reese and Dre hear it for themselves. They didn't even get a chance to hear the whole tape before

Dre got up and sucker punched Trick. Big Terry let Trick go to avoid getting hit. Reese raised his pistol and put two in Trick's chest. Dre then drew his pistol and put four in Trick's mouth, and three in his face. He wanted to make sure that it would be a closed casket.

Chapter Twenty-two
"Locked Up"

It was three days since Reese and Dre had killed Trick. Even though it was their first murder, neither one of them felt a bit of remorse.

I still hadn't had a real talk with Rodriguez, but I knew we were going to have one.

Tony and Frank fell in love with Reese and Dre. They loved them for their loyalty to me, but at the same time they knew that they would kill their best man if he ever crossed the line. That's what they loved most about them, because things were never personal; it was always business.

It was Friday, and I was just pulling into the club parking lot when I was surrounded by undercover police and DEA. Knowing what time it was, I just stood there and assumed the position.

Once downtown, I was interrogated by Bobby and his boss, two local detectives, and the head homicide detective from Atlanta. I was being charged with four counts of murder. They said I was identified as the shooter.

The locals also questioned me regarding Trick's murder. I was shocked, because Trick was found on the side of a country road, ass naked with his dick cut off and half of his face gone. The only way they recognized him was by his tattoos. I wasn't tripping over Trick's murder. I knew I was just a suspect because they had no witness or physical evidence.

After they became convinced that I wasn't going to cooperate, I was fingerprinted and booked.

Monday morning, I waived my extradition rights and was transferred to the Fulton County Jail in Atlanta. This jail was nothing like Wake County Jail. Fulton County had four units within its seven floors. Each floor consisted of a north and south side, and each side had six blocks, numbered one hundred through six hundred, and each unit housed anywhere from eighty to a hundred and twenty inmates.

I was being held without bond, and they housed me on the sixth floor of the north side in the four hundred block. This was one of the seven blocks used to house high profile cases.

I entered the unit and found my way to my cell. My cellmate was a well-respected dude by the name of Lonz. Lonz was the head of Atlanta's biggest federal case. The government named their case "Murder Inc." because they had thirty-six bodies that ran as far back as 1989.

Lonz and I hit it off instantly. As the saying goes, real recognizes real. Lonz was just as real as I was. He had the dorm and most of the jail on lockdown. He was the man to see if you needed anything—even narcotics. I was glad to know that, because I was in need of a good blunt.

Rodriguez sent me his attorney, who hired another attorney out of DC by the name of Bernard who specialized in murder cases. I also had my personal lawyer from back home on my case as well. I had the best legal team money could buy.

•   •   •   •   •   •   •

Six Months Later...

The year was 2003, and I had been in the Fulton County

Unfaithful to the Game   175

Jail for the past six months. The government still hadn't indicted me, and I was still being held without bond. My lawyers advised me that the government had up to nine months to indict me. And, to make matters worse, I still hadn't held my newborn son by Tasty. At birth, the baby weighed seven pounds, three ounces. He was now four months old, and they named him Alex, after my grandfather.

Reese and Dre were chilling because Rodriguez thought that it was best if they laid low for a minute. He assured them that as soon as Bobby gave him the green light, that things would be back on and popping.

My visitation days were Tuesdays and Fridays, and Shanta tried to knock the doors down, but she knew she couldn't because Deemi had to bring my daughter. Plus, I had to make time for Sarah and Tasty to come as well. Shanta knew about Deemi, but she didn't know about Sarah and Tasty or the new baby, and I most definitely wasn't going to tell her now. I felt that this was the wrong time to bring a new baby into the equation.

Jarius was due home within the next five months. He knew I was locked up for murder, but he had no idea that I had four counts. My plan was to wait until he got released before I gave him the business. I knew he wouldn't have cared that I punished Tito and Joey, but I knew that he had a soft spot in his heart for Tasha. Even after she took him for everything, I knew that he still loved her. That's why I wanted to wait until he got out so that I could deal with the situation better.

It was Tuesday, and Tasty brought the baby down to visit me. We were having a good visit until I looked up and spotted Sarah coming my way. I was shocked, because she wasn't supposed to come visit me this week.

This is not how I had my day planned, Sarah thought to herself as she walked through the visiting room. She couldn't believe that she drove eight hours to surprise me with a visit, and here I was, sitting with another woman in my face, and a white woman at that. She saw in my eyes that I knew I was busted.

I knew it was only a matter of time before I got caught, and it was now time for me to come clean and man up. I definitely wasn't going to deny my child. My eyes stayed glued on Sarah until she sat down. I then told Tasty to hand her the phone.

"What's up, ma?"

"Don't what's up me! Who is this?" Sarah asked as she looked at Tasty holding our son, Alex.

"That's my baby momma."

"Baby momma! And when was I going to find out about this?"

"I was gon' tell you. I was just waiting on the right time."

"Right time, huh!" Sara said, looking at me as if she wanted to kill me. She then looked at Tasty and said, "Hi, baby momma. I'm Sarah, and me and player-player here have been together for the past three and a half years." She then paused, because she felt herself getting ready to snap. She got herself together and continued. "Honey, I'm not even mad at you, because I'm pretty sure that you didn't know about me either."

I started to get up and go back to my dorm. I just shook my head as I watched Tasty begin to cry.

"Nah, I didn't know about you. But since it's all coming out, I've been fucking with Amir about the same amount of time."

"So this is why you couldn't move in full time?" Sarah asked me.

"Part of it."

"What the fuck you mean 'part of it'?"

"What I said; part of it. And watch your tone of voice!" I snapped, letting her know that I was still the man.

"Excuse me, I don't mean to interrupt," Tasty said, mean mugging me. "But I was about tired of being second or third, or whatever the fuck I was, but neither one of us is number one!"

"What do you mean, 'number one'?" Sarah asked with an attitude.

"Just what I said. I take it that you don't know about Deemi either."

If looks could kill, Tasty would be dead. I was madder than a motherfucka. Tasty had been good to me, and she always played her position. She figured that enough was enough. She was tired of being second or third, but in all actuality, I didn't have a number for her because I loved all of my girls… just some more than others.

I got up and left them to talk alone. Sarah motioned for me to sit back down, but I just waved her off and headed back to my unit.

• • • • • • •

Sarah

I can't believe the shit I found out today! Me and the white girl sat outside the jail and talked for almost an hour. Amir was smooth. I had to at least give him that much. I can't believe I let this young ass nigga lose me. The whole time I'm thinking I'm wifey, this motherfucka got a main squeeze *and* a three-year-old daughter! Plus, he's got a newborn son! God only knows who or what else his trifling ass got going on. I was happy and hurt all at the same time. I was happy because I could breathe again, and hurt because I loved this nigga and didn't want to let him go. But I didn't go to college and become a schoolteacher to be second to the next bitch!

• • • • • • •

I was in my cell, laid back and thinking about my visit. I couldn't believe that Tasty spilled the beans on me like that. I felt that I was a player, and even though I had love for both girls, I wasn't going to let them or this situation stress me out. I was involved with too many women in the first place. Not that it's a bad thing to fuck with four or five different women, but to be seriously involved with them like I was is a bad move.

"Did you have a good visit, young nigga?" Lonz asked,

bringing me out of my zone.

"Hell nah!"

"Why not?" he asked as he sat down at the desk and began to roll us a blunt.

I gave Lonz a brief rundown on what happened during the visit. He thought it was funny. He made things easy for me to deal with, because he had that gift where he could crack a few jokes and cheer a person up. He also called himself an "old school player". He told me not to worry about Tasty, because she would heal in time. But Sarah was another case. He said that she was older and well educated and probably didn't want anything else to do with me.

We sat back, and I listened to Lonz give me what he called his "old school game."

• • • • • • •

It had been two months since I got jammed in the visiting room. I had talked with Tasty numerous times, and she told me that she didn't know how much more of my shit that she could take. She told me that I needed to give her my all, or leave her alone. She said that our only dealings would be our child.

Bobby had given Rodriguez the green light, and I sent him a message to deal only with Reese.

Reese was glad they were back in business, because his people hadn't been able to get cocaine like they wanted it. Reese and Dre both had customers coming from all over: Norfolk and Richmond, Virginia, Charlotte and Greensboro, North Carolina, and South Carolina. Each one of their customers were buying anywhere from ten to fifty kilos apiece. I also had Reese take my cousin, Porsha—my cushion—in on the deal.

I also made sure that they hit Mike off with ten kilos. Reese said he would take care of Mike, but also told me that Mike had been acting funny. He said that Mike felt like niggas were holding out on him, and that he didn't have any money like we did, and he couldn't afford to sit on his ass without any coke like we could. I told Reese to tell Mike to be easy, and that I would bless him when I got out.

"Davis, you have a visit!" the officer yelled.

I wonder who the hell this could be, I thought to myself as I got dressed. I wasn't expecting any visitors today. Shanta told me that she wasn't coming because her son was sick. I thought that maybe she took him over to her grandmother's house and came to visit me.

When I reached the visiting room, I was shocked, because there stood Jarius, Deemi, and Deemi's friend, Joy from Seattle. Joy had been staying with Deemi for the last three and a half months. Deemi said that the house was too big for her and the baby to be living in alone.

I was cool with Joy staying with Deemi. She had visited us on several different occasions before I got locked up. Plus, I knew that Joy had always been there for Deemi. She was there for her when she first got out of an abusive relationship with the old timer who turned her out with anal sex, and she was there for her when she lost her father two years ago. Joy could have been a model if she wanted to. She was 5'4" with a caramel complexion. Her hair was cut short, and she rocked it like Toni Braxton. She had nice breasts, a tiny waist, and a nice apple bottom ass. I knew Jarius was going to push up on her.

"What's up, nigga?" Jarius asked after picking up the phone.

"How the fuck you get out so early?"

"Nigga, my case manager gave me back two months good time, and that shit put me out the door."

"Word?"

"Yeah. So, how you holding up?"

"Nigga, this shit ain't nothing," I replied, letting him know that I was holding things down. "I'll be back out there in a few."

"I know, but what the fuck happened, and who they trying to say you killed?"

I thought carefully, because I didn't trust these phones.

And with this being a high profile floor, I knew that they probably had them bugged. I looked Jarius dead in his eyes and said, "They're trying to say that I killed four people."

"What? Get the fuck outta here!"

"No bullshit. They got me charged with some bogus ass shit."

"Who they say you killed?"

"They're trying to say I did these dudes named Joey and Tito, and these chicks named Lisa and Tasha," I answered while still looking Jarius dead in his eyes. I could tell he was hurt and I hated to see my man weak over a piece of pussy. It was amazing to me what the power of pussy could do to a nigga.

Jarius couldn't believe what he was hearing. He shook his head in disbelief. I then told him to holla at Reese if he wanted to know the business.

The remainder of the visit went great. They informed me that they were staying in Atlanta until Friday. They said that Jarius wanted to go shopping, and that they would be back to visit me on Friday before they left.

•   •   •   •   •   •

When they left me, they headed to Lennox Mall. Jarius had Deemi and Joy hook him up with the latest fashions—not that he couldn't do it himself, because he was hip to all of the latest gear. It's just that his mind was in another place.

He couldn't figure out why I didn't let things be. He was getting too much money to jeopardize it on something that happened over six years ago. He really didn't give a fuck about me killing Joey, Tito or Lisa, but he felt that Tasha didn't deserve to die. He felt that she deserved a good ass whooping, but not an early visit to the Creator. Even though Tasha had put shit in the game, something inside of him told him that she didn't want to rip them off, and that Joey and Tito manipulated her into doing it.

Jarius never told me how Tasha would send him cards that said "I'm sorry" or "I miss you", with no return address.

She would also send him money orders that ranged from five hundred to five thousand dollars.

* * * * * *

I went back to my unit and called Shanta to inform her that Jarius was home, and that he and Deemi were down visiting me. I also had her call Porsha on three-way because I had to get her to call Savini Foreign Auto out of Miami to speed up the order on the Phantom that I purchased for Jarius. It wasn't due to be delivered until next month, but with Jarius home early, I needed them to get it delivered ASAP.

Porsha informed me that Reese and Dre had bought Jarius the Maybach '57. She also said that Jarius came by the club the other day in a brand new Range Rover Sport. I figured that he copped it with the mil I had given him off of the Big Z robbery.

* * * * * *

Deemi and Joy went out to party while Jarius stayed back at the hotel. He wasn't in the mood for clubbing. He couldn't get Tasha off of his mind.

Jarius was asleep until he was awakened by sexual noises coming from the room next door, which just so happened to be Deemi and Joy's room. They had adjoining rooms, so it was nothing for him to walk right into their room. He thought that his mind was playing tricks on him, so he eased to the door, and sure enough, that was where the moaning was coming from. He sat back and thought for a second, because he knew that these girls weren't crazy enough to have a nigga over there. He peeped through the door and was amazed at what he saw. He couldn't believe Joy was eating Deemi out. Deemi was so caught up in getting her pussy eaten that she didn't even notice him. But Joy did. She looked up and said, "Is you gon' stand there, or is you gon' come beat this pussy from the back?"

Jarius waited for a second because he wanted to see

Deemi's reaction, but she had none. She just grabbed Joy's head and pushed it back down to her pussy. With that being done, he knew what time it was. He eased up behind Joy and went to pounding. He pounded Joy as she ate Deemi, but she couldn't eat her the way she wanted to because she couldn't take the ten inches that he had in her. She finally forced Jarius out of her and laid him down. She wanted to see how much of him that she could place inside of her mouth.

Jarius just lay back and watched as Deemi came and joined her. He knew he was putting shit in the game. *Amir would never know about this anyway,* he thought to himself. Plus, he felt that this was the perfect opportunity for him to catch up on some fucking.

He lay there as Joy sucked him and Deemi licked his balls. They then both started licking the shaft of his dick, and before he knew it, Deemi had mounted him. Joy tried to sit on his face, but he quickly stopped her. His brother always told him to never eat anything that bled for five days and didn't die, and he was a firm believer in that too.

For the remainder of the night, the girls sucked and fucked Jarius.

Chapter Twenty-Three
"Get Ready to Rumble"

It had been three weeks since Jarius visited with me, and the government only had nine more days to indict me, or they had to let me go.

I was just returning from a visit with Shanta when I heard my name called for mail. I always received mail throughout the week, and today I had four letters and a priority mail package from my attorney. I had a letter from Shanta, my mother, Sarah, and a letter that read, "Guess Who?"

Pressed to see what Sarah had to say, I opened her letter first. I hadn't spoken to her or wrote to her since that day she busted me in the visit, but I did send Reese by her house to check on her. I opened her letter, and it read:

Dear Amir;

> *I hope this letter finds you in the best of health.*
> *Well, I know that we haven't spoken since the day you got busted.J But I've never stopped thinking about you. I still love you, but we could never be unless you get your shit together, because if you go out and start playing those bullshit ass games, I swear that I'm*

going to be the one locked up for murder.

     I really ain't got much to say, because I'm still pissed, but I do wish you the best of luck with your case.

     Well Amir, I'm going to close this letter, but never my love. That's always and forever.

Yours truly,
Sarah

P.S. I forgot to tell you that you can call the house again. I took the block off.] And please don't send any more of your goons to check on me!

"She still loves me," I mumbled to myself as I set her letter next to me and opened the package from my attorney:

Legal Correspondence
Mr. Andrew Davis
Fulton County Jail
901 Rize Street
Atlanta, GA 30334

RE: State of George vs. Andrew Davis

Dear Mr. Davis:

     Inside of this envelope you will find a copy of your Indictment and Motion for Discovery. Also, your trial has been set for October 3, 2003. I will be there to see you the first part of next week.

I was happy and angry at the same time. I was happy because I knew this case was about to be over, and angry because my trial was almost three months away. I then went on to read the indictment:

On June 8, 2003, the defendant, Andrew Davis, was indicted in Atlanta, Georgia Superior Court for the following murders in the first degree:

Count One: Joey Martinez
Count Two: Adrian Gomez a.k.a. Tito
Count Three: Tasha Martinez
Count Four: Lisa Walker

Additional Notice:

It is also known that the defendant, Andrew Davis, is a prime suspect in the murder of Steve Johnson a.k.a. Trick, in North Carolina. Mr. Johnson was a key witness in the above murders, but was found dead the day after he gave authorities a statement about the murders above.

As I read through the discovery, I couldn't believe my eyes:

It is September 28, 2002, and this is the debriefing of Gwen Brooks, who claims that she was about to leave her apartment when she heard several gunshots from the apartment across the hall. She, Gwen Brooks, states that she then closed her door back and looked through her peephole. Gwen Brooks then stated that she saw a man coming out of the apartment that the deceased were found in right after she heard the gunshots.

After being shown several photos, Gwen Brooks later identified Andrew Davis as the man that she remembered seeing exiting the apartment of the deceased.

I couldn't believe it. I noticed the apartment, but had no

idea that someone was looking out of the peephole. It's sad to say, but Gwen is going to regret the day that she looked out of her peephole and made a statement against me, because now that I had her information, she was sure to meet her Creator before the trial.

I put my indictment papers back in the envelope and finished reading the rest of my mail. When I got to the "Guess Who" letter, I was fucked up mentally, because it read:

> *Dear Amir:*
>
> *I hope this postal visit reaches you in the best of health.*
>
> *I know that you're probably wondering who I am, but that's not important right now. What's important is that I let you know that Deemi is on some straight up bullshit. Plus, there is some funny stuff going on in your inner circle. I can't prove it, but I'd be willing to bet my life on it. I'm only telling you this because I know that you're a good person, and that you have looked out for a lot of motherfuckas out here, and I'm not going to sit back and watch this shady shit go on without letting you know. If I was you, I would hire a private investigator to follow her around.*
>
> *Well, I'm going to close this letter, but I wish you the best on your court situation.*
>
> *Your Secret Admirer*

I was messed up over this letter. I wondered who had written it. I thought that it was probably some jealous female, but I also wondered what types of funny things were going on in my inner circle. I knew Deemi wasn't fucking any of my peoples. I wondered if she was out there sexing another nigga and my folks weren't saying shit to me about it.

I quickly disregarded that thought, because I knew

without a shadow of a doubt that they would jerk a knot in her ass, and the nigga would probably be laid up in Wake Medical, fighting for his life.

I still made a mental note to have the situation checked out though.

. . . .

Saturday rolled around, and the correctional officer called me for a legal visit. I went to my cell so that I could get a few things for my visit. On my way to the visiting room, I wondered which attorney this could possibly be. I knew it wasn't Bob, because he said he wasn't coming to visit me until next week.

I was surprised to see it was Gloria. Gloria was the attorney Rodriguez sent me. She was a tall 5'11", with nice big perky breasts. She had blonde hair, a tiny waist, and a nice little hump in the back. *She most definitely was fuckable,* I thought to myself as I sat down.

"How are you doing, Andrew?"

"I'm fine. How about yourself?"

"I can't complain. Did Bob send you a copy of your Indictment and Discovery?"

"Yeah. Did you give Rodriguez a copy?"

"Yes," she replied.

We shared a little small talk, and I gave her my "Guess Who" letter. I told her to give it to Rodriguez, and instructed her to have him install hidden cameras in my house and in the beauty salon. I told her to tell Rodriguez that I wanted him on this like *yesterday.*

. . . .

Those three months flew by fast for me, and it was now trial time. I was in the holding cell, changing out of my orange jumpsuit and into my navy blue suit by Tom Ford. My attorneys were debriefing me on how things were going to go, when the bailiff informed us that my family had arrived. The only people who knew that my trial was about to begin were those that I had told. I had Deemi, Tasty, Sarah, Reese and Dre stay away from my trial. The only people that I wanted there were my mother, Shanta, Porsha, my aunts, my sister Sharon, and my grandfather.

When I entered the courtroom, I winked at my family. I sat down, surrounded by my three attorneys as if I was above the law.

"All rise!" the bailiff said as the judge entered the courtroom. "This is the courtroom of the Honorable Judge William R. Tyler!"

"Thank you. You may all be seated. Mr. Davis, before we get started, are you satisfied with your attorneys?" asked the judge.

"Yes, Your Honor," I responded.

"You do understand that you're being tried for the murders of Joey Martinez, Tasha Martinez, Lisa Walker and Adrian Gomez?"

"Yes, Your Honor."

"Does the State wish to proceed with this case?" the Judge asked in a calm tone.

"Yes and no, Your Honor," the prosecutor stated.

"What do you mean by yes and no?"

"The State would like to push this trial back until April twelfth of next year."

"That's 2004, and that's six more months," the Judge said.

"Excuse me, Your Honor, but it's well known that—"

"Wait your turn, Mr. Lucas." The judge cut my attorney off in mid-sentence. "So, Ms. Shea, the State would like for me to postpone this trial until April twelfth of next year?"

"Yes, Your Honor."

"Does the defense have anything to say?" he asked, looking at Bob.

"Yes, Your Honor. Like I was saying, the State is keeping my client incarcerated for no apparent reason. The government has no witnesses, because both of the witnesses that are listed in my client's Discovery are dead. And, I ask that this trial goes on today, or that the court dismiss these bogus charges against my client. Furthermore, the State has no physical evidence linking my client to these alleged charges, or even placing him at the scene of the crime."

"Yes, the State does, Your Honor. We have the murder weapon."

"The weapon was found on a deceased man in a drug raid, not on my client," Bob said with a smile.

"I would like to take a fifteen-minute recess. Would both attorneys meet me in my chambers?"

• • • • • •

"Ms. Shea, what is the State doing?" the Judge asked.

"Wasting everyone's time, Your Honor," Bob said.

"Mr. Lucas, I don't know how they do it where you're from, but here in Atlanta we show some respect!"

"I haven't disrespected anyone yet, Your Honor."

The judge looked at Bob, and if looks could kill he would be dead.

"Well, Your Honor, the State doesn't really have much. My two witnesses just so happened to have been brutally murdered."

"Ms. Shea, I ask you not to waste my time or the taxpayers' money on a trail that's going to end in an acquittal. Now, what I'm going to do is dismiss these charges, with prejudice. So, if the State gets any more solid evidence, then you may re-indict Mr. Davis."

• • • • • •

I was sitting in the holding cell when the deputy came back to get me. He then escorted me back into the courtroom. When I sat down, Gloria pinched my leg and gave me a thumbs-up.

"All rise! Court is now back in session!" the Bailiff said.

"Mr. Davis."

"Yes, Your Honor." I stood to show the judge some respect.

"I have no choice but to dismiss all charges against you, with prejudice, because the State has no solid case. I will advise you, Mr. Davis, to keep a clean nose. I now order that Mr. Davis be released from the custody of the Sate and the Fulton County Jail. You are free to go, Mr. Davis!" he said in a angry tone of voice.

"Thank you, Your Honor!"

I shook my attorneys' hands. I then was met by all of my loved ones with hugs and kisses. Some of them were crying, but it was a happy cry.

We exited the court building as my attorneys explained to me what "with prejudice" meant. I was cool with it, because I knew there wasn't anyone else that could link me to the crime scene.

We all headed over to TGI Friday's to celebrate.

Gloria then gave me a cell phone that Rodriguez had sent me, and I hadn't had it twenty minutes before it started ringing. I excused myself and stepped outside. "Holla at your boy!" I said as I answered the phone, knowing that it was Rodriguez.

"Welcome home!"

"Thanks. It's good to be home."

"Where are you at?"

"We're out eating right now."

"Gloria still with you?"

"Yeah. Everyone is still with me."

"That's good. Well, I don't want to hold you up too long, but I need to see you as soon as possible. We need to have a long talk."

"I know. I'ma be down there in a couple of days. I'm going to go ahead and chill with Shanta for a few days while I'm in Atlanta, but I'll be down there before I go back to Carolina. I'll call you and let you know when my flight will arrive."

"Alright, buddy, see you in a couple of days. And please, lay low and don't do nothing crazy!"

"I'm chilling! I'll see you in a couple of days."

"Alright."

We said our good-byes, and I headed back into the restaurant. We ate, drank, and shared a few jokes before everyone headed over to Shanta's house.

The following morning, we went out to eat breakfast at Shoney's before everyone headed back to Carolina.

I stayed with Shanta for another three days, because I had to catch up on some fucking, and we most definitely did a lot of fucking. The first day that I got out of jail, Shanta pulled out a pack of condoms.

"What's them for?" I asked as if I had an attitude.

"With you being locked up, I stopped taking the pill."

"Well, you better start back, 'cause I ain't wearing no damn condom!"

And with that said, I entered her tight warm pussy, and released all of my stress inside of her.

Chapter Twenty-Four
"Been Around the World"

It was Tuesday, and my plane landed in Miami at 4:20 p.m. When I came out of the tunnel, the first person that I spotted was Ricky, the family driver. Ricky gave me a hug, and we exited the airport and got into a Lincoln Continental.

When we arrived at Rodriguez's mansion in South Beach, he was outside tanning by the pool, and watching four beautiful naked women swimming. He stood and gave me a hug. He then instructed one of the girls to go get me a triple shot of Crown Royal.

"Glad you're home," said Rodriguez.

"Glad to be home," I responded.

"So tell me, what the fuck were you thinking back there?"

"I don't know."

"Well, this ain't the cowboy days where you can just go around killing people. What's that, seven now?"

"Seven what?"

"Bodies."

"What are you talking about?" I asked in a tone that I had never spoken to Rodriguez in before.

"Well, there's four in Atlanta, the one at Frank's place,

and Big Z and his wife."

I was shocked when I heard that because I never told Rodriguez about Big Z. I wasn't nervous, but my heart skipped a beat. I hoped that Big Z wasn't Rodriguez's prodigy, and that was his money I took. "How do you know about that?" I asked him.

"First of all, there's not much that goes on that I don't know. But to be honest with you, we put two and two together."

"What do you mean?"

"Look. I know about every major drug dealer up and down the East Coast, and for you to have that type of money and not be under investigation is slim to none. So, when you offered me the $1.5 mil, it made me suspicious. But when I saw that club, I knew you did it. Plus, what twenty-year-old do you know in the streets that's playing with millions legally? You took that money and tried to go legit. Then we met, and you saw an opportunity to make more money. Right or wrong?" he asked, knowing that he was right.

"You're right."

"I know I am."

"So, was Big Z your people?" I asked out of curiosity.

"Nah, not mine, but a friend of mine's."

I was relieved, especially when he told me that Big Z was a rat, and that his people were in the process of having him whacked anyway.

I then asked him about Deemi, and Rodriguez informed me that we would talk about that later. He said that he wasn't going to let anything spoil this moment. He then told me that we were going to Colombia.

"For what?" I asked.

"To meet Ben."

"Who's Ben?"

Rodriguez then explained to me that things were bigger than he was. He said he was the captain of the yacht, but Ben was the owner. He told me that Ben was tired of them bragging about me to him, and said that he finally wanted to meet me.

We left Rodriguez's house and boarded his private jet at Miami International. When we touched down in Colombia, we were met by five of the most beautiful women I had ever seen. I leaned over and asked Rodriguez, "What, y'all trying to make me feel like a king?"

"This is nothing. Wait until we get to the house," he replied as we entered the limousine.

When we pulled up to the gated estate, I was startled. I couldn't believe that Ben had armed security at the gate.

"This is a real Playboy Mansion," Rodriguez told me as we pulled up to the side of an eight-car garage that housed the most outlandish antique cars. Ben had a 1965 Shelby Cobra with a 427, a 1955 Jaguar XKD, a 1928 Chrysler Imperial Roadster, a 1929 Bowler Bentley, a 1930 Cord 1.29, and a 1968 Camaro.

I was so caught up in the cars; I didn't realize that Bobby, Frank and Tony had sneaked up on me until Tony threw a playful jab at me. I then took my fighting stance as Tony and I began to play-fight. Tony and I had grown extremely close over the past few years.

"Break it up!" Frank said as he approached me and gave me a hug. He then introduced me to their Uncle Ben, and his stick man, Dan. Both of the gentlemen were in their mid-seventies.

"You like them?" Ben asked me, referring to his fleet of antique cars.

"Yes sir!"

"Hey, don't 'sir' me. It makes me feel old," Ben said with a smile that showed me that he still had all of his teeth. "Which one do you like?" he asked while pointing at the cars.

"All of them."

"Which one do you like the most?"

"The '68. There are only seven of those in the world," I said, letting him know that I knew the history of the Camaro.

"Well, there's only six now, 'cause that other one is yours."

"Man, stop playing!"

"I'm too old to be playing, but come on in here so we can give you a tour of the house and show you what we got waiting for you by the pool."

I was astonished. I had actually seen the unimaginable.

I couldn't believe that Ben had a real live shark aquarium built into one of the floors of his house.

After we toured the house, we headed to the pool, where there were about twenty beauteous women in bikinis. As they lounged around the pool, I noticed that Ben had a pet chimpanzee. He was floating on a raft in the pool with six women around him as if he was a celebrity. Ben clapped his hands twice, and the chimp gave me the finger. Everyone fell out laughing, including me.

I then noticed a familiar face staring at me. As I got closer, I realized that it was Chanel, the Puerto Rican chick that I met at Magic City when Mike first came home. "What's up?" I asked her as I knelt down to talk with her.

"You!" she replied, stunned to see me with this elite group of men.

"Oh, it's *me* now?"

"It's *been* you. Why haven't you called me?"

"Been busy. You act like you're surprised to see me here."

"I am. What are you doing here?"

"That's none of your business," I said, putting her in check. "What are you doing here? And I thought that you got your money in the club."

"I do. And, I was invited."

"Good. Now go freshen up and get that 'thing' ready for me," I said, letting her know that we would be fucking. I then pinched her jaw and slid off to where Rodriguez and Ben were talking.

"You know her?" Ben asked me.

"Somewhat," I replied.

I told them how I had met Chanel. I was shocked when Ben told me that all of the women were strippers. He informed me they came from all around the world. The son of Ben's stick man, Dan, owned every Black and Gold Strip Club in the State of Florida. Every one of these girls appeared as a star dancer at one of his clubs at some point in their career. That's how they were able to get all of the girls together under one roof.

We continued to talk as we headed into the house and

into an office that looked like something that the president would hold his meetings in.

"Well, before we get started, let me ask you something," Rodriguez said, confirming that this was a serious matter. "Do you believe that people can change over a long period of time?"

"Why?"

"Just asking for now, but remember that, and we'll discuss this again at our next meeting on Sunday before we depart."

"Well, what's this meeting about?" I asked.

"This one is about you," Ben replied.

"What about me?"

"Well buddy, you've done a lot for this organization in the short time that you've been on board, but it's time for you to move on."

"Move on to where?" I asked, inquisitive about what Ben meant by that.

"Listen. The Feds are going to be on you like white on rice, and we have too much at stake to jeopardize with you still being in the game." He told me that he wanted me to move out of the States or over to the West Coast. He said that even though we had money, we weren't untouchable. He then explained to me how the Feds worked. He told me they didn't give a fuck about money, especially when they touched his long-time friend, Pablo Escobar, who was worth thirty billion dollars before he was killed in 1993.

I understood where they were coming from, and I felt that it was a good move, because it gave me a second chance to start my life over again and raise my kids.

Rodriguez assured me that I would still deal with Reese, and that I would still get a percentage of what they moved. Ben also told me that he expected me to be out of Carolina within the next ninety days. He told me that I could always visit, but it wasn't a good idea for me to be there permanently.

•   •   •   •   •   •   •

The weekend turned out lovely for me. I fucked Chanel,

and even had her freak me out with two of the other girls. I fucked until I couldn't fuck anymore, all at the expense of Ben.

It was now time for us to head back to the United States, but we still had to have our last and final meeting. We all met back in the presidential-looking office.

"You did tell me you had cameras put in your house, right?" Rodriguez asked me.

"Yeah," I replied, knowing that I was about to find out some fucked up shit.

"And you did say that people could change over time, right?"

"Yeah. Now stop beating around the bush! What's up?" I asked in a stern tone.

Rodriguez then hit a button, and down came a TV from the ceiling. He pressed "play", and my heart actually stopped beating for a second. I couldn't believe what I was seeing. There stood Jarius, fucking Deemi from the back while she was eating Joy. I didn't even tell Rodriguez to stop the video. I took it like a man and watched every bit of it.

"You alright?" Ben asked me.

"Yeah," I replied as a tear trickled down my cheek. "How could this motherfucka do me like this?" I asked out loud, but to no one in particular.

"People change," said Tony.

"No, they don't! It was always in them! They're just some unfaithful motherfuckas!" Ben snapped with a slight attitude, as if it was his man that was fucking his girl.

We talked, and Ben made me promise that I would take care of this, and that I would be out of North Carolina within ninety days.

After I assured him that I would be out of Carolina within ninety days, we headed over to Ben's privately owned airstrip. Before I exited the limo, Ben told me that once I got myself situated at my new location, he would ship me the '60 Camaro.

On the plane, I sat in silence. Rodriguez knew that I was mentally troubled at this very moment, so he didn't pressure me for conversation.

Eager to see how much longer we would be in the air, I walked to the front and asked the pilot how long it would be before we landed at Raleigh-Durham International Airport. The pilot told me that it would be another two hours and fifteen minutes.

I peeped at my watch and noticed that it was only 6:15 p.m. I picked up the jet's mobile phone and called Reese. I instructed him to have Dre and Jarius meet me at my house at nine o'clock.

Tony called his bodyguard, Big Terry, and told him to get in contact with Frank's bodyguard, Ken, and for them to pick us up at the airport. He also told them to drive two separate vehicles.

When the plane finally landed, I gave Rodriguez a hug and told him that I would catch him later. I knew he couldn't stay because he had business back in Miami to attend to. We exited the plane, and Frank and Tony sent Big Terry and Ken with me.

When we arrived at my house, I noticed that everyone was there. Reese had driven his Hummer, and Dre his 1965 Roadster, and right behind him was the Phantom that I had bought for Jarius.

When I entered the house, the first thought that came to my mind was my daughter. "Where's Arnisha at?" I asked Deemi.

"She's at your mother's house. She said that she was keeping her for the rest of the week."

I was glad to hear that. I was so angry earlier that I forgot all about my daughter, because if she were home, then I would have to postpone my plans.

I entered my entertainment room where everyone was awaiting my arrival. The first to embrace me was Joy. I felt like smacking the shit out of her, but decided against it.

The next person to embrace me was Jarius, and while we were hugging, I eased the stun gun out of my pocket and hit him with it, sending ten thousand volts through his body. He went down instantly. Ken and Big Terry snatched him off the floor and placed him in an awkward position. They strapped him to one of my pool tables.

Reese and Dre remained calm, because they had seen this episode before with Trick.

Starting to fear for her life, Joy tried to ease out of the door, but I yanked her by her neck and tossed her over to Dre.

"I know not Jarius!" Reese asked, knowing that Jarius had violated in a major way.

"Nah, he ain't no rat, but he is a snake!" I replied as I left to go get Deemi. By the time I came back with her, they had stripped Jarius to his birthday suit. Deemi took one look at him and broke down crying. She knew what this was about, but what she didn't know was how I found out. She knew that I was powerful, and playing with me was just as dangerous as playing Russian Roulette.

"What the fuck is going on?" Dre asked as I tossed Deemi to Reese.

I didn't respond. I just fixed myself a drink and walked over to one of my sixty-two inch televisions. My entertainment room was lavish. I had a full bar, two pool tables, video games, and two sixty-two inch televisions that came out of the wall. In front of the TV's were three plush Italian leather couches. I put in the DVD that Rodriguez had given me and pressed "play".

Reese and Dre shook their heads in disbelief as tears welled up in their eyes.

"How could you do this?" I asked Jarius, grabbing his head and forcing him to watch the DVD.

Jarius closed his eyes because he knew that death was just around the corner. This was the side of me he didn't know.

"So, you don't want to talk? Toss me that pool stick!" I instructed Dre as I climbed on top of the pool table. I grabbed the stick and forced it up Jarius's anus. "You like fucking my girl?" I shouted as I shoved the stick as far as it would go in his ass.

Blood covered the pool table, and I couldn't tell who was screaming louder; the girls or Jarius. "Bitch, shut the fuck up!" I said to Deemi, giving her a look that would scare a bear.

I then snapped the pool stick, leaving part of it stuck in Jarius's ass.

"Flip that nigga over!" I demanded. I then grabbed Ken's Ruger 45 and placed it in Jarius's mouth. "You throw away a brotherhood over a bitch?"

Jarius wanted to explain, but the words wouldn't come out.

"Nigga, you could have had any bitch you wanted, but you chose mine!" I said as the tears poured down my face. "I love you, nigga!" was the last thing that Jarius heard before I squeezed the trigger. "As a matter of fact, take another one nigga for what your punk ass brother did to my mother when we were shorties back in the day," I said, and squeezed the trigger one more time.

I walked over to Deemi, who was crying hysterically. All she managed to say was, "I'm sorry!" I then gave her an option between her life or Joy's, and she quickly told Joy that she wasn't about to die for something that she had been manipulated into doing.

Joy looked at me and begged me not to kill her.

"I ain't, but you will die," I said as I turned around and headed to my bar so that I could fix myself another drink. But I never made it. Before I reached the bar, I heard two shots go off. I turned around, only to see blood gushing out of the side of Joy's head.

"I ain't never like that bitch no way!" Reese said as he tucked his pistol back into his pants.

I sat at the bar, contemplating my next move. I knew what had to be done, but I just couldn't do it. I didn't want to see it done either. *How could I tell my daughter, that I had her mother killed?* I thought to myself. I knew deep down that if a person would betray you once, they would betray you twice. Plus, I knew that loose lips sink ships, and I most definitely wasn't going to let Deemi sink my ship. Not only would she drown me, but she would drown Reese and Dre as well, and I wasn't going to risk that. With my mind set, I headed to the door.

"What about me?" Deemi cried, seeing Reese and Dre following me.

I looked at Ken, and told him to make sure that these bodies were never found. I said that I was going to file a missing persons report on her and Jarius in a couple of days.

Once outside, we sat in Reese's Hummer. "I can't believe this shit!" Reese said as he reclined in his seat.

"*You* can't!" I sobbed, my eyes still filled with tears.

"So, what now?"

I then told Reese to ride around while I explained to them how things were going to go. I would have spared Deemi if she would have fucked another nigga, but Jarius was totally disrespectful. I knew that this would trouble me for the rest of my life, especially Jarius. We had shared many memories together. But, I knew killing him was my only option. Jarius knew too much of my personal business, and if he let a woman come between us, then I knew that if the Feds were to ever get a hold of him, he would roll over on me to save his own ass.

"You a'ight?" Dre asked, seeing that I had spaced out for a moment.

"Yeah," I replied, snapping out of my thoughts. I gave them the spill in everything that was to take place. I informed them about my relocation, and that Rodriguez would still be their supplier. I wasn't worried about Reese and Dre, because I knew they would hold it down. I also made sure that they looked out for Mike.

We rode around for what seemed like an eternity. I then had them drop me off at Tasty's condo. I wanted to hold my son for the first time. I was going to surprise her because she had no idea that I was out.

I stuck my key in the door and entered the house. I figured Tasty was asleep, because she didn't come down the stairs or ask who was there.

I walked into the living room and stopped dead in my tracks. I couldn't believe what I was seeing. *Today must not be my fucking day*, I thought to myself. I couldn't believe that Tasty had the audacity to have a nigga over her house and around my son. They were sitting on the couch, cuddling, and watching a movie. When I hit the lights, they looked up in shock.

"This is not what it looks like!" Tasty said, scared to death.

"Then what is it, then?" I asked calmly, trying to control my anger.

"I—I—I—"

"I—I my ass! Where's my son at?"

"Upstairs."

I went upstairs and got my son out of his crib. When I came back down, Tasty's friend was gone.

"When did you get home?"

"Does it matter?"

"Amir, it's not what you think."

"Whatever!" I said, glad to hold my son in my arms for the first time. "Look, I'ma be moving soon, and I'ma take Alex with me."

"Move where? And you're not taking my son!"

"I don't know yet."

"Why are you moving?"

"Because I'm starting my life over," I said, giving her as little information as possible.

Tasty knew that I was involved in drugs, and she knew that I dealt with Frank. She had never seen me with any drugs or heard me talk about them, but her intuition told her that I was involved.

"Look. I'm not discussing this with you. Just know that I'm not going to let my son grow up like I did. I'm going to teach him morals about self, and virtues about life." I paused and took a good look at my son. "What're you gon' do when he wants to play sports? Let your little friend teach him?"

"Amir, I swear on my life, it's not what you think!"

"All I know is that I feel that you disrespected me. That nigga probably held my son before I did."

Tasty broke down crying, because she knew that I was upset with her, and she knew that I was serious about moving.

We talked for over an hour, and after debating with me,

she finally agreed to let me take our son. I told her that she could come visit any time she wanted to, and that I would bring the baby to stay with her every summer. I also vowed to her that I would always take care of her, whether she was involved with someone else or not. I told her that as long as she never disrespected me, she would never want for anything.

·   ·   ·   ·   ·   ·

My birthday was falling on a Saturday this year. I was having the party of the century as far as I was concerned. This wasn't just an ordinary party. This was my going away and birthday party all in one.

I had to convince Shanta to come to Carolina for my party. She was disturbed about my son. She wasn't mad that I had one; she just didn't like the fact that I hid it from her.

I told her that I was taking my son, Alex and my daughter, Arnisha out to Phoenix Arizona, so that I could start my life over. I told her that she was more than welcome to come if she could accept me and my "baggage", because we were a package deal.

She told me that she would think about it, and it would be an issue that we would have to discuss in person when she came up for the party.

I went to the extreme. I even told her that I was turning in my player card, and the only things that I wanted in life was her and the kids.

Shanta knew me all too well, and she felt as if she needed to see the sincerity in my eyes before she gave me an answer. Plus, she had an issue that we needed to discuss.

·   ·   ·   ·   ·   ·

The party turned out lovely, and the club was jam-packed, which I already knew. Anything that goes on for free, Black people are going to be there.

Everyone sat in my office, enjoying themselves, because

like I stated earlier, this wasn't just any ordinary party. I was preparing to leave for Phoenix within the next four to six weeks.

Porsha made sure that all of our loved ones attended, including my mother, who hated my club due to the music that they played.

Reese stood up and gave a toast to loyalty, friendship, family, and to my birthday. He then demanded that I give a speech.

"Please! Please! No pictures!" I joked as I stood in the middle of the floor. "Seriously, first of all, I would like to thank God for giving me such a wonderful family, and such loyal friends. Without y'all, I wouldn't be where I'm at today. I'm going to miss y'all dearly, but even with all my success, my life still isn't complete."

I then turned and faced Shanta. "The only way my life is going to be complete is if you…" I paused and dropped to one knee and pulled out a ten-karat engagement ring that ran me three hundred and sixty four thousand dollars. "Ms. Shanta Taylor, would you marry me?"

Shanta covered her face, because she couldn't believe that I was asking her to marry me. "Yes! Yes, Andrew, I will marry you!" she said as she uncovered her face which was full of tears.

I placed the ring on her finger as everyone clapped and gave us hugs.

"Speech from my man's future wife!" Dre, who was half drunk, blurted out.

"Well, I'm not good with speeches, but since Dre insists that I give one, I will. First of all, everyone knows that we go way back. I remember the first time we met, Amir wouldn't even show me to class. At that point in my life, you couldn't have told me that in nine years I would be marrying this man, but I'm truly honored to be his future wife."

Shanta stopped and took a glance around the room before she continued. "Now, I know that this is something that I should discuss with my future husband, but first, since I got the stage right now, this is the perfect moment."

She stopped again, this time taking a deep breath. "I want y'all to know that I'm even more honored to be carrying his baby!"

"My *what*?" I responded, shocked, happy and excited all at the same time.

"I'm almost seven weeks. I told you that I wasn't on the pill."

I grabbed her and hugged her. "Just me, you, and the kids!" I whispered in her ear as I watched my mother cry. She was glad that I was finally settling down. Deep down in her heart, she always felt that Shanta was the one for me.

• • • • • • •

It was Monday, and I was due in Atlanta on Thursday so that I could help Shanta finish packing so that the moving company could come and get the remainder of her things.

My daughter, Arnisha was excited about living with her little brother, Alex, but she was even more excited when I told her that there would be another little boy living with us as well. Shanta and I both agreed to wait until she started showing before we told the kids about the baby we were expecting.

I had just come in from making my last drop in the game. Rodriguez had sent me six hundred kilos, and he gave every last one of them to Reese and Dre, except for twenty. I was going to give those to Mike. I had also picked up the $2.4 million from Reese and Dre that they owed me from their last package.

I sat in my living room, separating money when I had to stop to answer my phone. "Hello," I said as I put the stack of money to the side.

"Hey, Daddy!" my daughter, Arnisha said, full of joy. She was glad to hear my voice.

'What's up, baby? What are you doing?"

"Nothing. Me and Grandma are going to eat at the Mayflower. You want to go?"

"Yeah, I want to go," I said, knowing that the Mayflower

was my daughter's favorite seafood restaurant. "Let me speak to Grandma."

"What?" my mother said, answering the phone in a grouchy manner.

"What's wrong with you?"

"This damn girl's getting on my nerves!" she replied.

I fell out laughing, because I knew that Arnisha could be worrisome at times. But what child her age wasn't? "Y'all come pick me up in about an hour. I'm waiting on Mike right now, but by the time y'all get here, I'll be ready."

"Alright. Love you!"

"Tell my Daddy I love him too, Grandma!"

"You hear your daughter?"

"Yeah. Tell her I love her too."

Fifteen minutes passed before Mike arrived. I opened the door for him, and we headed back to the living room.

"I'm taking you up to twenty, but from now on, you're going to have to deal with Reese and Dre," I told him as I turned around to retrieve the duffel bag of coke. When I turned back around, I thought that my eyes were playing tricks on me, because Mike had a pistol pointed at my chest. "What the fuck is you doing?" I asked as I dropped the duffel bag next to my feet. I gave him a blank stare and waited on his response.

"What do you think?" Mike replied with a quivering voice and tears of frustration welled up in his eyes.

"What, you fin' to kill me?"

"I ain't got no other choice. I ain't fin' to keep hustling all my life, and I ain't gon' be no do-boy for Reese and Dre. I ain't got millions like y'all niggas, and I ain't got enough money to move away and live some fairytale life like you."

"So that's what this is about, huh? Is that what this is about, Mike? It's about money?" I barked angrily. I couldn't believe that he was actually standing in front of me, waving a pistol in my face. *The things some people will do for money*, I thought to myself. "If it's about money, then keep the money you owe me and take this punk ass two million and go! Leave the state or the country. I don't give a fuck what you do, just don't take my life!"

"Oh, you can take a life, but you don't want yours taken?"

"Nigga, every life I took deserved it."

"And who the fuck is you to say who lives or dies? Is you God, motherfucka? Huh? Is you God?" Mike snapped with hostility in his voice. "Did Chuck deserve to die?"

Hearing Chuck's name threw me for a loop. I hadn't thought about Chuck in years. Chuck was with me when I robbed Big Z. He was Clyde's partner. "How do you know about that?" I asked, already knowing that it had to be Clyde. *I should have known that I couldn't trust Clyde,* I thought as I watched him walk through my front door. "How the fuck did you two hook up?" I asked.

Clyde and Mike used to hang out together back in the day. That's how Clyde ended up meeting Chuck. Chuck was Mike's cousin on his father's side, but I had no knowledge of that. If I did, I might have spared him on the strength of Mike.

"Clyde, I thought we were straight," I said.

"We was, but how long did you think that money was going to last?"

Clyde had gone back out to Kansas and became addicted to the luxury lifestyle. That's how he ended up jerking off all of his money. It just so happened that when he ran across Mike, he was upset. Envy had started to set in his heart, and he found himself jealous of me, Reese and Dre. So, being the mastermind that he was, Clyde used Chuck's death to turn Mike against me.

"So what, you think y'all are going to do me like I did Big Z?" I asked, seeing that Clyde had a roll of duct tape in his hand. I knew that my life was in danger, but I wasn't worried about *my* life. I knew that my mother and daughter were on their way to my house, and I sure as hell wasn't going to let them use my mother and daughter to get to me. "You know y'all ain't going to get away with this."

"We already have."

With that said, I made an attempt to take the gun away from Mike, but failed because he shot me out of natural reflex.

"What the fuck you do that for?" Clyde barked, knowing

that they had to hurry up and get out of my house because of the gunshot.

They grabbed what they could and left, but not before they finished me off.

Chapter Twenty-Five
"The Funeral"

They all thought the death of Amir had Momma Davis tripping when she said that Mike killed her son. After a few days went by and no one could find Mike, they knew something was up. But when he didn't show up for the wake or the funeral, they knew for sure without a doubt that he had done this to Amir, and Reese vowed with his life that he would drop Mike whenever he saw him.

They laid Amir to rest like the don that he was. They put him away in a customized platinum Bentley casket, and laced him in an all white Armani suit. Reese pulled a few strings in the music business and had a surprise guest appearance by R. Kelly. He had him sing "I Wish" and "Gangsta Lean" by DRS. He also had A Cut Above Limousines out of Atlanta come and chauffeur the immediate family and friends around in luxury limousines, which included his stretch Phantom, a stretch Bentley, two stretch Escalades, and his new stretch Maybach.

The funeral was packed from wall to wall, and there were at least two hundred more people outside. I don't know who took it the hardest between Shanta, Porsha, Dre, or Amir's sister, Sharon. Amir's mother stayed strong like the strong single mother that she was.

Rodriguez came in a stretch Hummer, along with Tony, Frank, Big Terry, Ken, Ben and Dan. Bobby was hurt that he couldn't attend the funeral, but he knew that he couldn't be seen in public with this crowd.

Reese, Rodriguez, Tony, Frank, Big Terry, Ken, Dre and Dan were all dressed in black Armani suits. Ben was the only one dressed in an all white Armani suit that was identical to the one they laid Amir to rest in.

Ben ended up escorting Amir's mother inside the funeral home, while Rodriguez escorted Shanta, Frank escorted Porsha, Tony escorted Amir's sister, Sharon, and Reese escorted Tasty. Dre was escorting Sarah, which looked like she could have been escorting him. This was the first time that Tasty had seen Sarah since the day they met at the jail when she busted Amir.

After the funeral, Reese held Amir's daughter in his arms and watched as they covered her father's grave. He was glad that Arnisha was too young to understand what was going on. She thought that her father was asleep, which he was, only it was an eternal sleep. Arnisha said that her daddy was going to be mad when he woke up and saw all that dirt on him. She said that her daddy didn't like being dirty. Reese just hugged her as tears rolled down his face.

Those who attended the funeral and the burial were invited to the reception at the club, where Reese had arranged for catering to serve everyone. This wasn't just any ordinary catering service, this was Peggy Lee's Catering, and she served nothing but soul food. Frank and Tony also had their bartenders serve the drinks, being as though everyone who worked for Amir attended his funeral.

Once at the reception, Rodriguez and Ben called for a meeting that only Reese, Dre, Tony, Frank, Dan, Momma Davis, Shanta and Amir's cousin, Porsha were allowed to attend. They held the meeting in Amir's office. Rodriguez and Ben promised Momma Davis that they would catch Mike, and she told them that when they did, that she wanted to be the one to kill him. Rodriguez also told them that he knew that Amir left them pretty wealthy, but if they were ever to need for anything, he was just a phone call away.

Ben was more concerned about Amir's kids and Shanta. He asked her what she had planned. She said that she was going to sell the house out in Phoenix and move back to Atlanta, and get ready to raise two kids on her own. Ben, Rodriguez and Momma Davis all thought that was a bad idea. They said that Amir would want his kids to grow up around each other. Rodriguez said that the last few times that he spoke with Amir, that was all he talked about. He said that Amir just wanted to go out to Phoenix and raise all of his kids together with his wife.

When he said that, Shanta just broke down crying. He then told her that if she were to move back to North Carolina so that all of Amir's kids could grow up together, he would give her his house.

"What house?" Shanta asked.

Reese then cut in and told her that it was the house that they stayed in when Amir gave her the Navigator.

"You're going to give me that big house?"

Rodriguez then told her that he didn't have any kids, and that Amir was like the son he never had. He said that in the short time that he'd known him, they were extremely close and it felt as if he had known him his whole life. He then went on to say that he would trade in his success if it would bring Amir back, and that he knew loyalty was everything to Amir. He said that he would forever remain loyal to Amir and his family, and with her being his fiancée, he knew that Amir wouldn't have settled for anything but the best for her and his kids.

Shanta then asked about his son, Alex by Tasty—or Tonya as she knew her. Frank told her that he would make sure that Tonya was taken care of. He also assured her that she would have no problems out of Tonya. He would see to it that she brought Alex over on the weekends, and that he would make sure that she kept Amir's kids as well when she needed a break. He told Shanta that she and Tonya would have to get along for the sake of the kids.

Epilogue

It has been two years now since they laid Amir to rest.

Shanta went ahead and gave birth to a baby boy, and she named him Andrew Davis, Jr. She also moved back to North Carolina, and Rodriguez gave her the house just like he said he would. She and Tonya were getting along great.

Porsha still ran the club, and she took all of Amir's money out of the bank and transferred it over to his mother's account. Momma Davis took it and put $1.5 million in each of Amir's kids' savings accounts, including Shanta's son, Lonnie. She then split the remainder of it with Shanta, being as though she had proven her loyalty.

Shanta went ahead and took full custody of Arnisha from Momma Davis. Shanta said that she felt as if it was her responsibility to raise her since her mother just up and disappeared.

There were two different rumors going around about that. One was that Jarius and Deemi took off together with Amir's money, leaving Arnisha behind. The other one was that the families of the people that Amir killed in Atlanta had put a hit out on him, but being that they couldn't touch him, they got Deemi and Jarius, and they had come back and hit Amir.

Ben and Rodriguez also made Reese retire from the game. They said that he had to be the father figure to Amir and

Dre's kids. Dre died eleven months ago in a car accident. He was running his 1965 Roadster when he lost control of it and slammed into a light pole at an unidentified speed. They lay Dre to rest similarly to the way that they laid Amir. They laced him in an all white Armani suit as well, and he was buried right beside Amir. Everyone attended the funeral, except for Ben due to health reasons. They all had on black Armani suits, except for Rodriguez, who had on a white Armani suit like Dre did. Dre left behind a wife and two kids as well.

Reese took Dre's fifty percent profit every quarter from R&D's Hauling and put it in Dre's kids' savings accounts. Porsha also did the same thing with Amir's fifty percent.

Every Sunday, they had a family get-together and dinner over at Shanta's house. Everyone always attended. Dre's wife and his two kids, Porsha and her family, Tasty and Amir's son, Alex, Momma Davis, Reese and his wife and their daughter, and once in a blue moon, Tony, Frank or Rodriguez would stop over.

Reese was outside in the garage messing with Amir's McLaren F1 before they sold it. Shanta said that she had no need for the car. She said that the F1 was too fast for her, and there was no way that she was going to save the car for any of her kids. She said that she refused to let them do the same thing that Dre did. Reese felt where she was coming from, because he himself had sold his Lamborghini right after Dre's accident.

Reese was getting out of the car when he noticed Rodriguez's family Hummer pulling up. He stepped out of the garage and waited for his arrival. When the limo stopped, Frank, Tony, Rodriguez and Bobby stepped out.

"What are y'all doing here?" Reese asked as he greeted them.

"We came to visit the family. I got a surprise for y'all," Rodriguez responded as they headed towards the house.

Everyone was glad to see them, especially Arnisha. She and Rodriguez had formed a serious bond. She even called him Papa Rod, and he loved her deeply.

After they ate dinner, Rodriguez told Momma Davis, Shanta, Tonya and Porsha that he wanted to see them in the entertainment room. Once inside the room, he said, "Momma Davis, we promised you that we were going to get him, and we did."

Porsha, Shanta, Tonya and Momma Davis broke down crying when they heard that statement.

"Is he dead?" asked Momma Davis.

"Nah, I wouldn't let him off the hook that easy."

"What do you mean?" Shanta asked.

Rodriguez then told them that when Amir died, he didn't feel much pain. He said that the multiple gunshots that he took probably killed him instantly, and he wouldn't give Mike the satisfaction of dying a quick death. Rodriguez had Mike in captivity for the past eight months. He said that he wanted Mike to feel the pain that he had caused this family.

"Would you like to see him before I get rid of him?" Rodriguez asked, and observed the looks on each individual face. It seemed as if every one wanted to see him, except for Porsha. She said that she couldn't stand to see a person die, but she knew that she had to watch Mike die for the sake of her cousin.

"Well, who's going to watch the kids?" Rodriguez asked, seeing that every one wanted to pay Mike a visit.

Reese quickly told him that he would have his wife stay and watch them. With that said, they all left in the limo and headed to Raleigh-Durham International Airport.

"We getting on a plane?" Momma Davis asked.

"Yeah. Why? You don't fly?" asked Tony.

"Hell nah! But I will for this shit!"

Everyone fell out laughing, because they knew that once Momma Davis got a drink or two in her, she was subject to say anything.

They drove through the tunnel and came out on the airstrip where nothing but jets and privately owned planes took off and landed.

Once on the plane, Momma Davis noticed that there was a bar and all sorts of other luxuries on Rodriguez's personal plane. She fixed herself a drink and went and sat beside him.

"Not trying to be in your business, but how in the hell did you meet my son?" she whispered in Rodriguez's ear.

"Believe me, you don't want to know," he whispered back as he smiled to himself on the inside.

The plane took off, and they landed several hours later. No one knew exactly where they were, because Rodriguez kept their destination to himself. All they knew was that they had just landed on a privately owned airstrip. They exited the plane and boarded one of the biggest helicopters that any one of them had ever seen. The helicopter took off, and took them out to what seemed like the middle of the ocean. It then landed on a landing pad on an enormous yacht. They exited the helicopter, and the first person that greeted them was Ben.

"I told you that I was going to keep my promise, didn't I?" Ben asked as he hugged Momma Davis.

"Yes, you did."

Ben then led them down to where Mike was being held. They were all shocked when they saw him. Reese couldn't believe that they had him cemented in a barrel that came up to his waist. Reese went over and unloaded body blow after body blow for what seemed like five minutes. Then, he grabbed him by his throat and asked him, "Why?"

Mike didn't respond. He just lifted his head and was too weak to say anything.

"Why, Mike, after all that Amir had done for you?" Porsha asked, hoping that he would give her an answer.

"Because he's an ungrateful, unfaithful motherfucka!" Amir's mother said. She couldn't believe that she was actually in the same room with the man that killed her son. "Give me a gun!" she yelled as she looked at Rodriguez and Ben.

"Nah, Ms. Davis. We wouldn't give him the pleasure of going out that easy," said Ben.

I don't know where Tonya got a razor from, but she walked up to Mike and sliced him a good six times.

"That's enough!" Ben said, knowing that if he didn't stop her, she was going to eventually kill him.

That's when everyone looked at Ben with confusion.

Reese knew that they were vicious, but he had no idea what Ben had planned. He couldn't understand why he would stop Tonya from slicing Mike to death.

"Follow me!" Ben demanded as he led everyone to the upper deck and beside the rail. A few minutes later, Big Terry and Ken came past, pushing Mike in the barrel on a dolly.

Rodriguez then pulled out a long razorblade of his own and began to slice mike across his chest and back. He then explained to them that the blood would attract sharks, and that these were shark-infested waters.

Knowing that his life was getting ready to come to an end, Mike looked up and said, "You should have seen how that bitch ass nigga was begging me for his life! I should have robbed and killed all of y'all motherfuckas!"

This was the moment that Rodriguez had been waiting for.

"Killed who?" a familiar voice asked.

Everyone turned around as they watched a stranger push himself towards them in a wheelchair. "I ain't dead, muthafucka! I may be paralyzed, but I damn sure ain't dead!"

Mike felt that his mind was playing tricks on him, and so did everyone else. The voice damn sure sounded like Amir's, but it sure as hell wasn't his face.

"Nigga, I'm like a cat! I got nine lives, you bitch ass nigga!" I spat as I watched my loved ones looking at me in complete shock. "Throw that nigga's ass off!"

"See you in hell!" were Mike's last and final words before he hit the water.

"Amir, is that you?" my mother asked as she approached me.

I knew my mother was shocked, and I hated the fact that I had to send my family through so much pain. But faking my death was the only option. Ben knew that if the authorities got a whiff that I had survived the shooting, they would be all over me and that would really put our operation in jeopardy.

"Yeah, Ma, it's me," I said as my mother looked behind my ear. I had a birthmark on the left side of my ear, and she wanted to make sure that I was her son. My face had to be surgically repaired, so I had to wear a custom made mask that actually looked real. It gave me a normal look, but it just wasn't my natural face.

One of the bullets hit my C4 vertebra, and left me a paraplegic. I was paralyzed from the waist down. I hated the fact that I was paralyzed, but I'd rather be a paraplegic than a quadriplegic, because with my condition, I could still get my dick hard.

"What's going on?" my mother asked as tears rolled down her face. "I buried you! I identified your body on that table!"

"Allow me to explain," Bobby said as he emerged from the captain's deck with both of my doctors by his side.

My mother recognized all three men instantly. They were the ones who took her to identify the body.

"Ms. Davis, I know you are confused right now..." Bobby paused because Shanta, Tonya and Porsha were crying hysterically, and Reese was still in shock. He couldn't believe that they kept this from him.

I was glad I was wearing the mask, because no one had ever seen me cry, and the mask was hiding the tears that were streaming down my face.

"Do you remember me?" Bobby asked Momma Davis.

"Yes, I do," she replied as she grabbed hold of my hand. "I remember all of you."

"Good. That makes it that much easier. Now, when you saw Amir, he was anesthetized, which basically means that he was unconscious, and the doctors kept his breathing to a minimum just so that you could identify his body. So, while you thought that he was on that table dead, he was actually still alive."

"So the doctors were in on this too?"

"Actually, they weren't at first, but it's amazing what money will make someone do." When Bobby found out that Amir was going to live, he made the two doctors an offer that they couldn't refuse to help him fake Amir's death.

"So, who did we bury?" Shanta asked.

"That was a John Doe we had in the morgue for several months," one of the doctors replied.

"I can't believe you're still alive! You have no idea what I've been going through!" Shanta said, happy and angry at the same time. She was happy I was alive. I meant everything to her, and she still hadn't been with another man since, even though my mother and Reese told her that it was okay for her start dating again. They didn't expect for the girl to go on with her life without another man.

"So, what now?" I asked Shanta.

"What do you mean by 'what now'?"

"Do you still want to be my wife?"

"I'll push you out of that chair for asking me a dumb question like that! I don't care if you're in that wheelchair. Me and those kids need you!" she said.

I motioned for her to sit on my lap.

"Baby, I don't want to hurt you," she told me.

"I'm paralyzed."

With that said, she sat on my lap, and I held her in my arms for the first time in two years. It felt good to hold my future wife again. It felt so good that I began to get an hard on, and Shanta felt it. She looked at me with a confused look. "I thought you were paralyzed!" she whispered in my ear.

"I am. I can still get a hard on and make babies. You just have to do all the work; ride the dick like you know how."

She was glad to hear that. She had no problem riding me.

"Listen. This is how everything is going to go," I said as I took control of the situation. "I can't go back to the States for five more years. Because my death was faked, I have to wait seven years before I re-enter the country, but I still don't know if I'm going to go back or not. And if I do, I'm still not going back to North Carolina."

I paused, because I wanted to make sure everyone was listening. "Shanta, you're going to get the kids, and you're going to stay over here with me." I had been living with Ben ever since I faked my death. "But not until I have my surgery. The doctors will be repairing my face next week. You are all welcome to stay."

I paused again and reached out my hand for Tonya's. I then told Shanta to get up so that I could show Tonya some love. "Now you, baby girl," I said to Tonya. "The sky's the limit for you. I got your back in whatever you do, and because I've been out of our son's life for two years, it's best if you raise him. But I want to keep him every summer, and Reese will be involved in his life just as he has been."

I knew that Tonya had swallowed her pride and done right by me by letting our son be a part of the rest of the kids' lives. Rodriguez kept me updated on how my family was doing, and I was pleased to know that she was playing a major part in all of my kids' lives, and she and Shanta had become really good friends.

"Now, cuz, you keep doing everything that you've been doing. I'm proud of you, girl!" I was very pleased with Porsha. She still kept the club running, and was the anchor of the family. If anyone had a problem, they always brought it to her.

"And you, Reese. I know you're pissed, but it had to be this way. You know this organization has a lot at stake. I really hated having to take y'all through all of this pain, but we are back together now, and I'm done. I ask myself every day was it worth it. True indeed, I made a lot of money, and I opened doors for y'all to make money. I also met some wonderful people," I said, referring to Ben, Rodriguez, Frank, Bobby and Tony. "Y'all are more than my business partners, y'all are my family, and I want to thank y'all for all of the support."

"And Mom, I know this ain't what you wanted for me, but this chair ain't going to hold me down. Now, don't y'all go feeling sorry for me, because this came with the lifestyle that I chose. But know that I love each and every one of y'all unconditionally."

Ben was proud of me, and he felt my speech. He knew I was one of a kind, and he knew that another me might not come along for another hundred years, and he would be dead and gone before that happened.

My name would forever be remembered in the streets of North Carolina, because I never was Unfaithful to the Game. I never ratted a nigga out. I never crossed a nigga, and I took care of my team. Even though I'm out the game and in a wheelchair, with a different identity, I'm still that nigga most rappers rap about, because a real niggas don't die!

THE FIRM PUBLICATIONS
P R E S E N T S

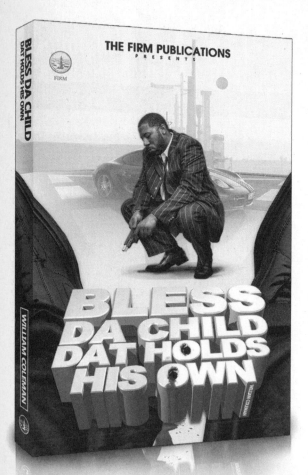

To place an order for one of these books, please send a money order or cashier's check for $15.00 Ea.. Shipping is $4.95 for 1 book and $1.50 for each additional book to the address below or call us for wholesale orders 267-254-0201 or 215-848-4385.

P.O. Box 2723 • Philadelphia, PA 19120
www.thefirmpublication.com

NEW VISION
PUBLICATION

P.O. Box 2815
Stockbridge, GA 30281

Or

P.O. Box 310367
Jamaica, NY 11431

Order Form

Name: _____

Address: _____

City: _____ **State:** _____ **Zip:** _____

Qty	Title	Price	Total
	Tit 4 Tat	$15.00	
	A Blind Shot	$15.00	
	Damaged	$15.00	
	Tit 4 Tat 2	$15.00	
	Boss Lady	$15.00	
	Shank	$15.00	
	Unfaithful To The Game	$15.00	
	-Coming Soon-		
	Tit 4 Tat 3	$15.00	
	Thicker Than Blood	$15.00	
	Still Damaged	$15.00	
		Subtotal	
	...Shipping Charges...	**Shipping**	_____
	Media Mail First Book .... $3.95 Each additional book............$1.50	**Total**	$ _____

(No Personal Checks Accepted)
Make Institutional Checks or Money Orders payable to:
New Vision Publication